PLAY

the

FOOL

PLAY
the
FOOL

  A Mystery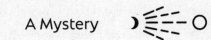

LINA CHERN

B

BANTAM
NEW YORK

A Bantam Trade Paperback Original

Published in the United States by Bantam Books, an imprint of Random House, a division of Penguin Random House LLC, New York.

Bantam Books is a registered trademark and the B colophon is a trademark of Penguin Random House LLC.

Library of Congress Cataloging-in-Publication Data
Names: Chern, Lina, author.
Title: Play the fool : a mystery / Lina Chern.
Description: New York : Bantam, [2023]
Identifiers: LCCN 2022030075 (print) | LCCN 2022030076 (ebook) |
ISBN 9780593500668 (trade paperback ; acid-free paper) |
ISBN 9780593500675 (ebook)
Subjects: LCGFT: Detective and mystery fiction. | Novels.
Classification: LCC PS3603.H479 P57 2023 (print) |
LCC PS3603.H479 (ebook) | DDC 813/.6—dc23/eng/20220623
LC record available at https://lccn.loc.gov/2022030075
LC ebook record available at https://lccn.loc.gov/2022030076

Printed in the United States of America on acid-free paper

randomhousebooks.com

2 4 6 8 9 7 5 3 1

Book design by Sara Bereta

For Tammy, who sees the future

PLAY
the
FOOL

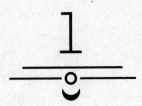

I always knew Marley would disappear. We worked across from each other at the Deerpath Shopping Center, me at the Russian knickknack place and her at the goth boutique, where she rang up anarchy T-shirts for tweens in five-hundred-dollar Nikes. She was a lot like me—smart enough to get the hell out of Lake Terrace once she grew up, but dumb enough to come back. For how long, I didn't know. She put out a chill bloom-where-you're-planted vibe but always looked like she was watching the exits, marking the days until she could peel out and leave Lake Terrace in the rearview.

When she did disappear, it didn't go down how I expected.

The guy who set the whole thing off walked into Firebird Imports on a Sunday, the deadest day of the week and consequently the only time my boss, Larissa, trusted me to run the place alone. Less for me to screw up. I was laying out a three-card tarot spread when the store's heavy glass door slammed open.

I jerked up. He was plastered against the inside of the door, breathing hard and staring out into the mall—a weight-lifter-looking guy with a bristly haircut on a blocky head, a faded Gold's Gym T-shirt, and jogger sweats. He spun toward me and I froze, hands on the cards. There was an angry red gash on the man's forehead.

A low warning throbbed in my mind. "Are you— Do you need—"

He took a stumbling step into the store and collided with a sign reading 60% OFF ALL MUSICAL SPOONS. The sign bowled over and he floundered after it, hooking it with his arm before it hit the ground. He looked like he was tangoing with a beautiful lady who had been, alas, enchanted into a piece of advertising.

A squeaky honk flew out of me, part dimwit guffaw, part concerned *oh!* The guy jiggled the sign back into place. I glanced across the mall court: was Marley watching this? At Stone Blossom, the "alternative lifestyle boutique" where Marley worked, a pale mope in a Black Flag T-shirt slouched at the counter. No Marley. I hadn't seen her all day.

"Do you need a tissue?" I pointed to my own forehead. "Or an ambulance or something?" My eyes slid to my phone. The low-charge light was blinking, as usual. I didn't have extra cash lying around for new tech toys, so I plundered my brother's castoffs. By the time they reached me, their best days were far behind them.

The guy flinched like he'd already forgotten I was there. A red splotch crawled down his temple and landed—*plop*—on his shirt. "I'm fine," he said hoarsely and disappeared in the jungle of display racks at the front of the store. I craned my neck after him. At least if he stole something, I could tell Larissa a piece of merchandise had made it out of here today. He picked up a lacquered box and stared at it with glassy eyes. "Just looking around."

Shocker. Everyone was always just looking around. Earlier, a guy came in looking for a Cubs jersey, and I had to inform him, reading off our perfectly visible sign, that we sold only "fine goods from Russia and Eastern Europe." Then a mom came in with three kids and a screaming baby, looking for a bathroom. I pointed her to the family one out in the mall, where someone had Sharpied a set of anatomically correct genitals on the dad icon.

"Suit yourself." I sat down and swept the loose cards into the deck. I pegged this guy for a Cup, but a sloppy, backassward one, awash in reversed Swords. All emotion, no control. He'd probably just gotten in a parking lot shoving match with some other muscle-head over a dinged-up Jeep. In my head, I was already telling Marley about him. We'd been hanging out every Sunday night after our shifts for the past two months, in a tiny courtyard off the emptying forty-year-old white stone hulk of the mall. We talked while she smoked her unfiltered cigarettes, lighting up the dark with tiny fireballs. She was older than me by ten years or so, a tall, lean bruiser of a woman watching me from behind a wall of crimson-streaked hair, black eyeliner, and silver jewelry. The kind of look I'd always toyed with but never had the stones to pull off. She was my best friend, if you can call someone you've known only two months your best friend. It helped not to have any other friends. We were like rare specimens of some exotic breed of loser.

"Anybody actually buy this junk?" Gym Guy's thick voice burst through my thoughts. He picked up a miniature balalaika and twanged its strings.

I did a quick mental tally of the bathroom family. "We just had six customers in here before you." This guy was breaking all of Larissa's rules: touching stuff, loitering, wearing sweats as regular clothing. Also being a dick, but that was more my rule.

Gym Guy doubled over, clutching his gut and grabbing a shelf of decorative plates for balance. The plates jingled.

"Hey." I hopped off my stool. "Are you . . . ?"

He produced a bottle of pills. "I'm fine," he huffed. "I got a nervous stomach is all."

My phone uttered the first in its series of death beeps. Larissa was too cheap to get a landline for the store, so if this guy was going to pass out, he needed to do it before my phone died or I'd be stuck carting him to the hospital in my Ford Fiesta. I watched him shoot a handful of pills into his mouth and crunch loudly. "You know," I said, "we have water if you—"

"I said I was fine," he snapped.

A sorry laugh nearly bubbled out of me at this knucklehead pretending he wasn't upset that someone had just bashed his damn head in. He'd probably been told all his life to *suck it up, grow a pair, don't be a pussy.* Whatever road rage pushy-pushy he'd just survived had obviously messed with him, but hell if he'd let anybody see that. He was already hiding the bottle of pills.

"Have it your way." I sat back down, watching him out of the corner of my eye.

He fished his phone out of his pocket, glanced at it, then stuffed it back in. He wasn't here to shop, but he wasn't leaving. He kept looking out into the mall like he was waiting for someone. Or killing time until it was safe to leave. I stacked the cards up for the Vegas dealer shuffle my aunt Rosie taught me when I was a kid. The deck went *frrrrt* into a neat dome in my hands.

Gym Guy swiveled toward me. He zeroed in on the cards. "Is that those fortune-telling cards?"

"Yeah, that's right." Interesting. I wouldn't have pegged him for a guy who put much stock in spooks and spirits. I spread the cards back out, moving in slow circles. "Want me to read them for you?"

He looked out into the mall. "You know how to do that?"

"I picked it up here and there." Aunt Rosie was a full-on grifter who hung around carnivals wearing headscarves and bilking grandmas out of their Christmas money. She'd started teaching me to read tarot cards when I was six, on one of the extended drop-ins that happened whenever she ran out of money or ditched her latest sleazebag boyfriend. My parents let her crash with us in exchange for "babysitting," which consisted mostly of me accompanying Rosie on fantastic, semi-reputable errands that I knew better than to report to my parents. I spent a lot of time in empty daytime bars sipping Cokes and eating maraschino cherries while Rosie picked up crudely wrapped packages in the back room, or racing back and forth between monitors at the OTB to help her track her bets. She wasn't super great with kids, so she just treated me like a very short adult, which I loved. *Hey*, she'd say, picking out a stranger from across the casino buffet, *what's his story?* Then she'd point out all the signs you could pick up from people when they thought no one was watching, all the details they broadcasted loud and clear without saying a word. *He's here because he hates it at home*, she would say, or *She hides the credit card bills from her husband.* "What's their story?" was my favorite babysitting game.

Eventually, Rosie moved out west by way of a short stint in lockup for trying to sell a fake Louis Vuitton handbag to an undercover cop. After that, she and my parents conveniently "grew apart." She still sent the occasional postcard, but the drop-ins stopped when I was in high school. By that time I was a pretty good reader of cards and of people, and even spent one raucous

summer working the Renaissance Faire up by the Wisconsin bor-
der doing readings and hanging with a crew of struggling theater
rats and LARPers. *Don't read the cards, read the person,* Rosie
always said, so I read worn shoes in otherwise spotless outfits,
dark eye circles underneath makeup, locks of hair twisted on fingers, over and over. Raised eyebrows, parts in stories where voices
went dry. I just sort of let my mind go blank and catch it all, like
one of those giant satellite dishes I'd seen on a science show,
standing in the desert, gathering signals from space. There was
always a pattern in the noise, a story in code. I laid it out, watching the customers' faces. Sometimes they didn't see it. Other
times it hit them like a ray of light splashing over what was in
front of them all along. *You know what?* a teary-eyed dad said during my first reading, after he decided to reconcile with his son,
who was living on a survivalist organic farm in Montana. *You're
pretty good.* I stared at him as he left. I'd never been good at anything before.

Gym Guy was scratching one foot with the other, holding a
painted gravy boat. Larissa would have tossed him out by now for
pawing at stuff, but I didn't say anything. I wanted to see what he
would do next.

"Do they work?" he said, still staring out into the mall. "The
cards, I mean."

"Well, that depends."

"On what?" He stopped fidgeting and watched my hands.

"On you." I made my voice soft and mysterious. "If you think
the cards work, then they work."

"*Pft.*" He rubbed the back of his thick neck and turned away,
then glanced at me again. "I don't believe in that crap." This guy
was tricky: he wanted the reading, but he didn't *want* to want the
reading. He was probably the kind of guy who bawled when the

dog died at the end of the movie but insisted there was something in his eye. Now I really wanted to hook him, just to see if I could.

"Hey. Come on, man." I dropped into a low, straight-talking voice. "This is a bullshit-free zone. Why don't you take a moment, huh? Something's got your pants in a twist. Maybe I can help you." I felt a jolt of excitement, slipping into the familiar rhythms of reading—*Listen, react, listen. Listen, listen.*

Gym Guy narrowed his eyes. He was about to say there was nothing wrong, nope, no head wound or gastric turmoil or obvious panic at all. I waited.

"How much?" he said, checking his phone.

Yes. "Twenty for a fifteen-minute reading." I pulled off another perfect shuffle.

He reached for his wallet. "Freaking highway robbery." He walked to the counter and tossed a crumpled twenty in front of me.

I went to the fitting rooms to find him something to sit on. Before Firebird Imports, the place was a clothing store for edgy teens, all mirrors and glass and shiny black tile like a rehabbed warehouse, urban but not *too* urban. Now the glam outer shell was stuffed wall-to-wall with shelves of fake Fabergé eggs, giant silver samovars, and glowering Grandfathers Frost. We tossed extra furniture and assorted junk into the former fitting rooms, behind cream-colored doors splashed with ghostly photographs of old New York.

By the time I came out with a chair, Gym Guy's gastric crisis had passed. I noticed his absurdly bright yellow gym shoes with winged blue RWs on the sides. The logo looked familiar.

He plunked himself down and looked around. "K. True." He was staring at my brass name tag. "What's that supposed to mean?"

"It's my name." I sat down and cleared space on the counter. "Katie True." Larissa, fresh off a management seminar, had decided all employees (me) needed to wear name tags to look more professional. "What's your name?"

He rubbed the back of his head and watched me. "I'm Nico," he said finally.

Boom. I'd gotten his name; the rest wasn't far behind. He checked his phone and set it down next to his keys. Then he glanced at my name tag again. "Is that your real name?"

"What do *you* think?" *Answer questions with more questions,* Aunt Rosie said in my mind.

He tugged on a gold chain dangling at his collar. There was a tiny medal on it with a bald monk holding a baby. "I think you're in the wrong line of work with a name like that, if you catch my drift." I hated the phrase *if you catch my drift.* Anyone who said it either was a moron or thought you were.

"Am I?" I put down the deck and stared at him. "I know something bad happened to you." I glanced at his forehead. The scratch had crusted over. "Just now."

Nico froze and looked at me like a raccoon caught digging in a trash can. I slid the deck toward him. "Cut the cards. Think about your problem. You can say it out loud, if you want."

He snorted. "What, you don't already know my problem?" Aha. Houston, we *do* have a problem. He cut the cards, pinching them by the edges. I scooped them up and laid out a Celtic Cross.

"This first card represents you." I flipped over the center card and we both leaned over it. "The Fool."

"Great." Nico gave a barking laugh. "This jackass about to walk off a cliff is supposed to be me?"

"It just means you're like everybody else," I said. "You don't have all the answers. You make mistakes."

"Yeah, like forking over twenty bucks for this bullshit." Joking now, feeling like he had the upper hand. He scratched his forehead. The gash started to bleed again and his fingers came away red. "Aw, Jesus." He glared at me. "What the hell is this?" I gave him an innocent shrug. A fresh wave of pain seemed to rock him, and he clutched at his gut. "You got a bathroom in this joint?"

"There's one in the hallway outside. You can't miss it." *Look for the huge dick.*

He scrambled off the chair and shot out the door. The situation must have been dire indeed because he left his phone, unlocked, on the counter, next to the twenty. I pocketed the cash and stared at Nico's phone. A nasty idea bloomed in my mind. I rarely needed to cheat since most of my customers were already believers, or suspended their disbelief long enough for the reading to do its job. Nico was an outlier—I'd hooked him but I hadn't landed him, and all his ham-fisted secrecy was making it tough to get a decent read. An itchy, impatient curiosity stole over me. I needed to know why this sorry meathead was staggering around the mall at closing time with his gut tied in knots and his forehead smashed in. *What's his story?* Rosie whispered in my mind.

I checked the door, then grabbed the phone before it locked up on me. His texts were open—perfect. I tapped the most recent one before I could register that something about it looked wrong.

The message flared open. There was nothing in it. No text, only a picture: a woman with long red-streaked hair sitting in a dirty corner, propped up against a brick wall next to a forest-green graffiti-covered dumpster. Ratty black clothes, dirty face, silver rings on every finger. I looked closer. The red hair . . . Marley. Her eyes were closed. I thought she was sleeping or passed-out drunk.

Until I saw the gunshot wound in her temple.

The phone slipped out of my hands. I backed up into the garbage can, and it fell over with a sharp clang. Cold slid through my chest like I had drunk a glass of ice water too fast. I poked at the phone again and Marley's face twisted toward me. Blood spattered the side of her cheek from the ragged wound. She was slumped between the brick wall and the dumpster, next to an upside-down leasing sign and a tangle of discolored pipes. I knew the place: the boarded-up Sears on the east side of the mall. The text number gaped at me like a row of bright digital teeth: UNKNOWN.

The time stamp read thirty minutes ago. She was here. This had just happened.

A dull pounding split my head, like a gong being walloped behind a brick wall. My thoughts scattered and I scrambled after them: Who was Nico? How did he know Marley? Did she give him that scratch on his forehead?

Did he kill her?

As if to punctuate the question, my own phone beeped, then performed its triumphant little shut-down tune: *Congratulations, asshole!* No way to call for help now. Out in the mall, the hairsprayed JCPenney perfume ladies were leaving. The vitamin store across the atrium was shuttered. I swiveled toward Stone Blossom, still looking, stupidly, for Marley.

A flicker at the corner of my eye. I dropped the phone just as Nico pulled open the door.

"Freakin' kids." He straddled his chair. "Did you see what they drew on that bathroom door?" He had cleaned his forehead. The dried blood had made the cut look worse than it was. When he saw he had left his phone, he snapped it up and stuffed it in his pocket, glaring at me like I'd stolen it. Marley's ruined face flashed in front of me. My head filled with slow heat, like a boiling tea-kettle. I couldn't let him know I'd seen the photo. If I cut the reading short and ran, he'd be on to me. And he knew my name.

"Well?" Nico said with a dopey grin. "Are we gonna do this?" His face was a healthy pink again and he had finger-combed his thatch of ash-blond hair.

I sat down, grabbed the rest of the deck, and shuffled. *Shhhhh.* The butterfly-wing flutter cooled my fingers. He didn't look like a killer. He looked like a dummy who was in over his head. I sat still, only my hands moving. The sharp little seeds I'd planted with my phone trick took root, snaking around me in dark, vicious vines. *Take it,* Rosie whispered. *It's yours. You owe him nothing. He's the one who owes you.*

Big time, I answered Rosie. He owed me an explanation of what happened to Marley, the only person I'd met in eight years of knocking around this recycle bin of a town who didn't judge me, didn't try to fix me, didn't point out all the ways I'd fucked up and how badly. Didn't pepper me with advice about taking night classes at CLC, or books by organization gurus, or listicles of the top ten most up-and-coming careers. She took me as I was, what-ever I was, even when I didn't know.

My hands tightened on the cards. A white-hot rage rolled through me, backed by a greedy curiosity. I could do this. I could pluck the truth from him before he even knew what hit him. I just needed to stay calm and play dumb. Let the spooks and spir-its ask the questions.

"You're goddamn right," I said, too loudly, forgetting where I was.

Nico took my weirdo outburst for enthusiasm. He scooted up closer on his rickety chair and waited. I glanced at the tangle of cards: the Fool, faceup in a swirl of blanks. *Here we go.*

"This"—I tapped the card that covered the Fool—"is what's in your way right now. Your main obstacle." I flipped over the card and choked down a bubble of nervous laughter. "Death," I croaked.

Nico blanched, staring at the leering skull surrounded by dead soldiers. It wasn't meant to be taken literally, but he didn't need to know that.

"Someone's dead." I waited for him to look at me, then closed my eyes, rubbed my temples, and made a little *mmm* pain noise.

"Are you— What's going on?" Nico peered at me. "Your head hurt or something?"

"I'm sorry. It's nothing, I'm okay." I pinched the bridge of my nose, shook my head, and giggled, like, *What a twit, huh?* I was pushing it. If I wobbled too far into crystal ball kook territory, I would lose him. Or worse, tip him off that I was toying with him. "It's just, for a second it felt like . . ."

He grabbed the bald monk medal around his neck. "Felt like what?" He was buying it. I kept going.

"This death feels . . . close." I looked around like I expected a tap on the shoulder. "Like it happened close by. Or just now. Or both."

Sweat popped out on Nico's forehead like someone had juiced him. "Do you—" His hands crept to his keys. "Is this— Do you need to stop?"

"It's okay, I can go on." I gave him a sickly through-the-pain smile. "You're a good guy. I just want to help." The photo of Marley flashed in my mind and a wave of real, oily sweat washed over me. I wiped my forehead and flipped over the third card. King of Wands. Crap. I'd have to ditch the Celtic Cross positioning and off-road it a little. "A woman."

He squinted at the card. "That's a woman?"

I gave him a *bless your heart* look and searched the card: a king on a throne, draped in a red cloak. "Red." I gave him a curious look. "Do you know any redheads?" I licked my lips. "Or maybe partial redheads?"

I watched it sink in. He twisted the medal on its chain, hard. It left a white slash on his throat. I waited, but he didn't answer.

I closed my eyes, then threw them open. "There's more." I breathed harder. *Don't overdo it*, I thought, but I couldn't stop. His eyes were wide and watery. We were there now—the point in every reading when they felt something bigger turning the wheels. That something was me.

"More red. Here." I touched my temple. "Blood." I rubbed the side of my face. "Her head. She's injured." I gestured to the card. "And the wand . . . it's a weapon. Someone hurt her."

Nico sat up. His lips clamped together, bone white. He began to wag his head like a broken toy, *no, no, no*. "She brought it on herself," he said in an odd, flat voice. "It was her own fault."

A victim-blamer. I narrowed my eyes. Murder or not, this guy was guilty of *something*. I willed the next card to be the Sun or Star, something smiley I could use to turn things around, tell Nico he was all good, and run like hell. But what would that change? Where would I run to? Home, to eat a can of cold peas over the sink? To fall asleep on the couch with the Netflix menu burning into the TV screen?

Flip. The card stared up at me, sharp and black. "Nine of Swords." A weeping woman sat in a black void, an army of glowing swords poised horizontally over her. "You did this," I whispered, unable to keep the accusing shiver out of my voice. "She died because of you."

He was panting now, like he had been when he first came in. "I didn't mean for her to die," he whispered. His head snapped up at me. His eyes were dead black. The greedy current fusing me to the cards broke and I woke up cold, like I'd been doused in ice water.

"What the hell is this?" he hissed. "Who are you?"

He jumped to his feet, knocking over the chair, and towered over me. I squeezed my eyes shut, making myself tiny, invisible. His hands slammed down on the counter. The cards scattered into the air like frightened birds.

"You stay away from me." He grabbed his phone and keys, backed into the glass door, wrestled it open, and disappeared. A cold-sweat realization struck me, like a last flash of sky before the waves pull you under. I blinked, hard, and when I opened my eyes the room was silvery and bright, like I'd passed through a veil. Marley was dead. There was no unknowing that. There was only knowing more.

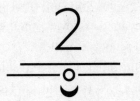

T he first time I met Marley she was smoking at the picnic
table by the side door.

It was the worst place ever to put a picnic table, a little
circle of concrete you couldn't even call a courtyard, sloped
toward the low brick barrier between the back of the mall and the
grassy hill that fell toward I-94. When you sat on the mall side of
the table you kind of pitched forward, and when you sat on the
highway side you felt like you were about to plummet backward
to your death. It was my favorite place in the mall because no
one ever went there.

Until about two months ago. Marley was sitting on the highway side facing out, one leg hiked up, elbows on the table behind
her. She was wearing jeans, a lacy black T-shirt, and sky-blue
cowboy boots. A cigarette dangled from her fingers.

I stopped short when I saw her and stuffed my red velvet bag of
tarot cards into the back pocket of my jeans.

Marley turned to me. "Shit," she said, not unpleasantly. "You busted me. I'm not supposed to be smoking." Silver flowers bloomed from her cigarette and dissolved in the sun.

"I won't tell," I said. I'd seen her around. She looked a little don't-fuck-with-me, like the rest of the Stone Blossom staff. The difference was she showed up to work on time and had stuck around longer than a week. She also smoked instead of vaping. Larissa, the septuagenarian ex-Soviet, was the only person I knew who still smoked old-school cigarettes.

She motioned to the other side of the table, and I perched on the edge, shielding my eyes. It was the kind of day that made you sneeze when you went outside. Marley had her back to the sun, and I could see her only in squinty glances, a dark shape against the midafternoon blaze. "Who am I not telling?" I said.

"Max." She rolled her eyes. "I'm going to get a lecture on keeping my body clean of corporate poisons." Max was Stone Blossom's owner, a guy in his forties who dyed his hair black and wore lace-up platform boots.

I scooted in toward the center of the bench. The velvet bag slipped out of my pocket, and I put it on the table.

"I used to go see him play with Murderbride down at the Empty Bottle when I was a kid." She ran her fingers through flame-streaked hair, exposing dark roots. "He'd harass you from the stage if you didn't tip the waitresses." Her voice was an ironic monotone, like she was always about to laugh at a good joke.

"He seems like he'd be a flaky boss."

"He's all right. He pays like we're doing cancer research." She tilted her head. "And he loves me because I'm old enough to know all those shitty old bands he's into." She turned in to the sun and I got my first good look at her. Underneath the wasted-teen hair and bangle bracelets, she was older than she looked, tall and muscular, with a face that was all angles—a wide toothy mouth and high cheekbones. Cards sprang up in my head on clicky plastic wheels, like a slot machine. I tried to match them to Marley as they flew past.

"I've seen you around," she said. "You work at that Firebird place, right?" She had ice-blue eyes that looked blind and all-seeing at the same time. "When I came around a few months ago looking for work, that's the first place I went." She took a slow drag on her cigarette. "But that Brunhilda boss of yours said she was all set for staff." She pointed her cigarette at me. "Guess that's you."

I pictured Larissa with Valkyrie horns, prancing around with Elmer Fudd. "Lucky me," I said. "She would probably let you smoke right in the store. You'd just have to listen to lectures on government overreach instead of corporate poisons. Why did you want to work there, anyway?"

Marley chuckled. "It was just this dumb idea I had." She twisted her mouth. "Firebird is an old nickname of mine." She turned sideways and lifted the sleeve of her T-shirt.

At first I didn't know what I was looking at. The tattoo wasn't round and cheesy like a muscle car logo, or gaudily detailed like the storybook firebirds crawling all over Larissa's porcelain plates and cups. Marley's firebird had no feathers or fire, only stylized streaks and curves, striking and slashing in red, gold, and black. It faced away from me, darting into an unseen sky. When I looked again it was watching me over its shoulder with dark hollows for eyes. I looked closer, and the eyes disappeared.

"Just thought it would be cool to work at a place named for me." She dropped her sleeve with an ironic shrug. "Grab your little joys wherever you can, am I right?" I understood, like a bolt of lightning, that she had grown up poor. *Firebird*. It had a heral-dic ring to it. *Dragonslayer, Giantkiller*. Nicknames that showed people how you fucking survived. When I was a kid my family called me Dumpling because I liked dumplings.

Marley pointed to the red velvet bag. "What you got there?"

"Oh." The tips of my ears went warm. "Tarot cards." I loosened the drawstrings, took out the deck, and showed her.

She glanced at them. "Those look well loved." She didn't ask what kind of an idiot carried tarot cards with her everywhere.

"I've had them since I was a kid. I used to . . ." *Read professionally,* I had almost said, but that sounded pretentious. "I just always have them around. To play with when I need to clear my head." I stacked the deck on the table. Then I picked it up again. "Or keep my hands busy."

Marley shrugged and emitted a gray cloud. "Better for you than smoking." She pointed to the cards. "Do they mean something?" she said. "Or do you make them mean something?"

"Both, I guess," I said. "Anybody can read them. You just need to know a little about people. And how to tell a story." I paused. "Or read a story. It's kind of the same thing."

I glanced behind me at the mall. I had only a few minutes before I had to get back. "So, did you say you grew up in the city?" I was hearing a slight Chicago drag on her vowels.

She blew smoke off to the side. "Moved up here when I was in high school."

"Oh yeah? Lake Terrace High?"

"Go Mustangs." She did a limp fist bump. "Was Mr. Frakes still screwing that gym teacher when you were there? Stringy bitch with the green eyeshadow?"

"Ms. McAllister. They got married."

"Shut up." She cackled. "Must have been after my time." She folded her needle-sleek hair around her ear, revealing tiny silver hoops. I liked her little side-glances, the way she watched me even when she wasn't watching me. "How about you?" she said. "You grow up around here?"

I looked at the table. "Yeah, but I lived in the city for a while. Wrigleyville." When I looked back up, she had thrown a blue boot over the bench and sat sideways, waiting for me to keep going. It threw me. Most people give you a few seconds and keep talking about themselves. "Oh. Um, okay. I lived down there with a friend for a while after, you know, after college."

She tilted her head. "College didn't work out." It was a statement, not a question.

"Not really." I wondered what I'd said to give that away. "It had a really cute brochure. Hills. Red brick buildings. Talked a lot about *doing your thing*." I shuffled the cards absently. "Guess I didn't have a *thing* yet. Or maybe not at all."

Marley ashed her cigarette, shielding it from blowing in my face. She didn't say *Oh well, you gave it a whirl*, or *College isn't for everyone*, or any of the other supportive things people say that are actually condescending. She sat there and waited.

I swept the deck facedown in a wide arc. "By the end of my first year, my grades were solidly mediocre, and my parents *strongly encouraged me to explore another path*."

Marley propped up her cheek. "What path was that?"

"Well, that was supposed to be up to me, wasn't it?" I laid out a straight five-card spread. "*We just want you to be happy*, blah, blah, blah."

"Assholes."

I flipped over the first card: Three of Cups, reversed. Party girls dancing in a drunken circle, but upside-down, canceled, interrupted: a great time that didn't turn out that way. I thought of my dad driving our Subaru wagon off campus for the last time, all my shit packed in the back. Kids shouting at each other across the sunlit quad, *See you next year!* My mom's sleek, chipper face turned back to chatter at me like she did when she was not disappointed at all, don't be silly.

"I'm screwing up their brand," I said. "My sister's this powerhouse realtor and my brother's in grad school, so I'm the dud in the product line." I picked at a knot in the wood. "They have all kinds of ideas for how I can get *back on track*, or *back in gear*, or *in the driver's seat*. They use a lot of transportation metaphors."

Marley swung both legs over the bench and faced me. A huge funky necklace perched above her neckline, a tight mass of black netting laced with tiny roses and hearts, with a fat black spade charm dangling off it like an upside-down heart. It was a bit much, like costuming from a tween-targeted show about witches. But silly and cute, like she was wearing it with a wink. It fit her perfectly. "So what were you doing in Wrigleyville?" she asked.

"Living with my friend Anne." I was pretty sure my break was over, but I didn't move. "She wanted to start her own fashion label."

Marley raised her eyebrows. "That takes no shortage of balls."

"She was always sketching dresses on napkins and stuff, even when we were kids." I flipped over the Eight of Pentacles: a guy in a tool belt hammering at a set of bright coins with an absentminded smile on his face, so deep in his work he didn't need anything else. "It was just who she was." Anne, hunched over the lopsided desk we'd rescued from a neighbor's trash, filling sheets of tracing paper with designs while car horns, techno beats, and drunken shouting floated up from Clark Street.

"Now, that's what I call having a *thing*." Marley pointed her cigarette at me. "But you didn't answer my question."

"What question?"

"You told me what Anne was doing." Marley ashed into a crack between the table's panels—a tiny, careful gesture. "What were *you* doing?"

"Oh, me?" I shrugged. "Not much. I worked at this place, Miss Lucille's." I circled my fingers on the back of the next card. "It was sort of a psychic-shop-slash-teahouse that had been there forever but was all trendy now. We were always busy. Lucille was, like, a hundred years old, and she was either an old film star or an international spy, nobody knew for sure." *Flip*: the Queen of Swords, on a throne of tiny winged faces. "She was the kind of *lady* who had a standing daily appointment at the beauty salon."

"A lady's looks are her most valuable currency," Marley said in a snooty black-and-white Hollywood voice so dead-on it made me flinch. She gave me a cheeky little grin and I felt a disorienting flash, like a sudden reflection of sunlight in glass. The wheel of cards in my head spun and spun, going nowhere.

"Did you like it?" she said. "Working there?"

"I did." I lifted the corner of the next card. "I liked it a lot." Ace of Wands, a glowing hand bursting out of a storm, holding a fat, leafy wand: the right work at the right time. "I liked figuring out why people did things." I looked up at her. "People have no idea, sometimes, why they do things. If they knew, they wouldn't get stuck doing the same things over and over."

Marley blew a smoke ring that looked like a deformed egg. "You liked helping them?"

"Maybe," I said. "Or maybe I just liked knowing something they didn't."

Marley threw back her head and laughed like I had said something really clever and profound. I couldn't tell how she was going to react to anything. "So why'd you stop?" she said.

"Anne moved away after a year. Got into some fancy design program on the East Coast." I shrugged. "I couldn't afford to stay down there on my own, with my crap job."

Marley furrowed her brow. "I thought you liked your job."

"Oh. Well, yeah, I did." *Crap job* was what my sister, Jessie, had called it. The words had slipped out before I could stop them. "I just mean it didn't pay much. So I moved back up here." My mouth went dry. "And now here I am. Eight years later."

Marley watched me. "Do you ever read anymore?"

"Not really. There aren't that many places around here to do it. And I don't even think Lucille's is open anymore."

"Too bad." Marley nodded at the cards. "You seem like you're a real pro with those things." *Pro.* It didn't sound stupid when she said it.

"I'm okay." I picked up the stack of unused cards, then put it down again. "Actually, I was the best reader at Miss Lucille's," I said. "People asked for me."

Marley gave me a slow, wide grin, big and sweet and full of dark glee. Her strange eyes flashed. "Own it," she said. She reached across the table and for a second I thought she was going to muss my hair. She flipped over the last card, studied it, then showed it to me: the High Priestess. "This bitch here knows everything, but she doesn't *know* she knows everything." She put the card down in front of me. "Just like you."

Little knots unraveled in my chest. Out of nowhere, a monarch butterfly sparked up in front of us, fire against air. I couldn't see the highway from where I was sitting, but I could hear it—a low, airy hum. The High Priestess stared at me with stony eyes. *You can know things with more than just your brain,* Rosie used to say about her.

Marley laced her arms and the firebird tattoo unfurled again, wings out, like a shimmering hallucination of hot air over asphalt. I felt like I was being offered something that, good or bad, would disappear if I didn't grab it, fade like a fever dream until I wasn't even sure I'd seen it. I wanted to say something nice to her—*I'm glad we ran into each other*, maybe, or *thank you*, although I didn't know what for.

"I . . ." I licked my lips. "I like your necklace."

"Yeah?" She looked down like she was seeing it for the first time. "It's a piece of crap. I don't know how many times I've fixed it. My boyfriend keeps trying to get me something nicer, but . . ." She ran her finger around the spade. "This one goes with everything, you know?"

She stood up, dropped her cigarette stub, and crushed it with her boot. "Hey, I should get back. Max has probably forgotten about me and hired my replacement." She stuffed her lighter and pack of cigarettes in her pocket and headed to the door.

"Wait," I called. She turned back, hand on the door. "How did you know what the card meant? The High Priestess?"

Marley blinked. "I had no clue what the card meant." She wrestled the heavy door open, then turned to me again. "I'm Marley, by the way."

"I'm Katie. Katie True."

"That's a boss name," Marley said. "Is it real?"

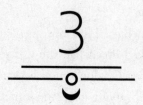

I t took me three tries to punch in the code on the back door's alarm panel after my half-assed closing of the store. My shaky fingers kept missing the buttons and the thing kept beeping at me. I hurtled out the mall side door, rounded the picnic table, and burst through the cluster of scratchy bushes that concealed a sloping shortcut to the parking lot.

The upper-level lot was empty—normal for Sunday night and pretty much for any other night. Half the stores in the mall were shuttered, and the rest were heading that way, especially with Lake Terrace Estates—*a lifestyle mall for YOUR lifestyle!*— opening up across town. My rust-bucket car hunched alone in a pale island of light next to the other end of the shortcut, where I always parked. I rushed at it, fully intending to haul ass home, plug in my phone, and call the cops.

To my right, over a rusty railing and down a wide set of concrete steps, lay the walled-in patch of empty ground at the back of the old Sears. A green dumpster crouched in the corner behind its own smaller wall. *The crime scene*, a scratchy voice-over whispered in my head. I peered over the dumpster wall but saw nothing.

I can't, I thought.

And then: *I have to.* If I ran home and called the cops, what would I say? That I saw a dead body on a guy's phone? Which, by the way, I had grabbed in order to grift him out of twenty bucks? The best I could hope for was a polite hang-up and a featured spot in their water cooler gossip the next day. The photo could have been faked, they'd say, or part of some elaborate zombie cosplay—and they'd be right. I didn't know for sure Marley was dead. I wouldn't know until I saw her body myself.

I stared at my car, then turned and started down the steps. My car disappeared from view. The lower I went, the more slowly I walked. Pressure ratcheted up my chest like I was pushing through the electromagnetic field of some dark, pounding machine.

Across a field of blistered asphalt at the bottom of the stairs, the store's back entrance was boarded up with plywood. The garage doors that led into the automotive center were chipped and cock-eyed, their glass panels staring out like tired eyes. Off in the corner, the walled-off dumpster sat under a dim pole light. Two of the three clustered bulbs were out. The third buzzed on and off.

I reached out to the dumpster wall. The rough painted bricks were cool, even in the July heat. I screwed my eyes shut and inched around the corner. This was the part in the movie where a cat—or worse—came yowling out of the shadows.

The light flickered off. I peered into the gloom, lining up the scene to Nico's picture: the dumpster piled high with broken chairs, empty paint cans, and wooden pallets. The spray of graffiti that looked like a crooked bouquet of flowers. The defunct

DEERPATH MALL leasing sign upside down against the wall like a distress flag. The cartoonish twist of plumbing like a video game where you line up the pipes to make the water flow. The corner where the dumpster met the wall . . .

. . . was empty.

My skin prickled and went numb. Was I in the right place? I cycled through the markers again—dumpster, flower graffiti, sign, pipes. All there. Nothing missing.

Except Marley.

Steel fingers squeezed my insides. Maybe she was still alive and needed help. Pressure mounted again in my chest, and I darted around the alcove, peering into corners, kicking aside flattened cardboard boxes. The dumpster was too tall to climb. I hammered on it, shouting for Marley. No answer.

My eyes went blurry, and I wobbled on the cracked concrete. The overhead light clicked on again. In the glare, something sparkled under the dumpster. I crept closer. A web of black stones lay crumpled under the edge, tossed away and forgotten. I crouched to pick it up.

Marley's necklace.

A quiet dragging noise stole out of the corner. Probably a cardboard box riding the breeze, but I didn't wait to find out. I stuffed the necklace into my pocket, turned, and pounded across the weed-strewn pavement, up the stairs, and to my car. I fumbled it open, fell inside, and slammed the door.

A violent shaking ripped through me. I tore at the crank and rolled down the window, gulping at the hot, asphalt-smelling air. I stabbed at the dome light and whipped out the necklace. It was all in one piece, but the lobster-claw fastener was broken. I wiggled the tiny lever back and forth. It worked, but not well. Did it fall off Marley's neck?

She wouldn't have left it behind, though. Not while she was alive.

I grabbed a half-empty can of Coke from the cup holder. The soda was flat and warm, but I guzzled it anyway and slumped in the seat. Marley's face swam toward me out of the dark, against the empty parking lot. I just saw her last Thursday. We ate croissants out in the courtyard. She talked about dumping her deadbeat boyfriend. And now she was dead. The idea refused to settle in, like a marble rattling around an old wooden maze toy, looking for a hole to sink into.

I crumpled the soda can and tossed it out the window. Then I felt bad, got out, and picked it up again. Down the hill and over the concrete lip of the mall lot, cars snaked by on 94 against a gold and pink sky. I never knew anyone who had died before, not anyone close to me. Were Marley and I close? Since we met in May, we'd seen each other for a total of only a few hours a week and one memorable evening on the town. And yet, those snippets of time stood out to me in full color against the gray of the past eight years, like I had dropped my Kansas farmhouse out of the sky into Oz. It didn't matter to Marley that I was late with my electric bill every month, or that I never put the August registration sticker on my car any earlier than December. That I'd never finished college or held down a job for longer than a year. All the tiny prices of admission to my own world that I could never seem to scrape together. Marley didn't care because she wasn't from our world at all—she was just passing through. She reminded me of the time my high school chemistry teacher smashed an old mercury thermometer and had to chase the silver balls all over the floor in his PVC poison-gloves. The way they scrambled away from him—wild, shimmering visitors from a place with alien physics. They didn't belong here; they were already gone.

Gone. I tossed the mangled soda can into an overflowing garbage bin. Questions popped up like frantic cartoon bubbles in my mind. Who killed her? Nico? He had seemed shocked at the photo. Maybe he was only shocked that he'd gotten caught. Was the photo a piece of blackmail, someone telling him *I know what you did*?

One question poked unpleasantly through the others, like a dead bug at the bottom of a bag of popcorn. What had possessed me to snoop on Nico's phone to begin with? *He needed help,* I thought. *I couldn't help him if he didn't believe.*

I stalked back to my car, got in, and slammed the door. *Bullshit.* Reading for Nico made me feel good at something, for the first time in years. It made me feel like a pro, like Marley said, an authority. *That* was why I lied to him—and kept lying long after it was safe or made any sense. It felt so good to unravel a story again, tease out the truth. I would have done anything to keep that feeling going, even if it meant launching into a cheap psychic act and goading a murderer in a deserted mall into a confession. *I didn't mean for her to die.*

I held the necklace out against the wan light spilling through the windshield. The stones shone at me like a smile with no face and I was flooded by a sudden wild certainty, like a crashing wave, that Marley had left the necklace for me to find.

Shivering, I folded the necklace into my hoodie pocket. Then I jammed the key into the ignition and—

Nico walked in front of my car, only a few feet away. The reflective stripes on his yellow shoes flashed white through the windshield. His face, like an out-of-control ball lost in a playground, bounced past me.

I sat bolt upright, then sank down. Nico crossed the empty lot to a black truck with tinted windows, got in, revved the engine, and peeled out. His rear lights moved down the lane to the mall exit and stopped at the light.

I watched his turn signal blink yellow, yellow, yellow in the deepening twilight. Then I started my car and went after him.

4

BEAST 25.

Nico's alpha-bro license plate glowed in front of me in a blue neon frame. We inched through the east side of town past dingy strip malls full of gold shops, tanning parlors, dollar stores, and auto body repair shops. Traffic was light, so it was easy to hang back and stay behind the black truck without looking like that's what I was doing. When we crossed the Metra tracks and the forest preserve into the west side, the strip malls got nicer, offering Starbucks and Jamba Juice, vintage boutiques, and "unique" gift shops in brand-new buildings designed to look old.

He turned onto a side street. I hung back, then crept around the corner after him. This was the old part of town, as far from my place as you could get and still be in Lake Terrace. Big multistory houses lined the streets, some showing their century-plus of age and others spruced up with new paint jobs and elaborate land-scaping. The truck stopped in front of a light blue house with a sagging second floor and dirty lace curtains in the windows. It looked like a wedding cake that someone had sat on.

I fished my phone out of my backpack. Still dead. Still no help with my original plan to call the cops, which was totally a go, I assured the jittery skeptic in my mind, just on hold until I could get some more information. *From the guy you just barely got away from?* The skeptic was wearing a sour grimace and tapping her Gucci mid-heel leather pumps. She looked remarkably like my sister, Jessie.

Nico walked up the steps to the big covered porch and glanced around. He fished something out of his pocket, jimmied the door open, and slipped inside.

I took a breath and held it. This wasn't his house.

I killed the engine and got out of the car. Lights snapped on in the house, and a dark shape darted past the front window. I tiptoed up the porch steps and peeked through the gap in the gauzy curtain. Nico was racing around the living room, pulling open cabinets, tossing emptied drawers and bins to the floor. He dropped to his knees and rooted through the fireplace with a poker. When he scrambled up, his face was twisted with panic. He dropped the poker and dashed up the wide staircase at the center of the house.

The questions started squawking again in my head, like one of those cheap baby toys with no off switch. What was he looking for? Whose house was this? I closed my eyes and shook my head savagely. *Enough.* I'd already tossed away one chance to lose him. Nico's hands slammed the counter again, in my mind as loud as a gunshot. I turned around and marched back down the steps. I was going home, finding my tangled-up charger, and calling the cops.

I got as far as the second step and stopped. By the time the cops got here, if they bothered to come, Nico would be gone. I would never have this kind of chance again to know who he was. To know what happened to Marley. My hands crept into my pocket and found the necklace. It was warm to the touch, like someone had just been wearing it.

I swallowed a lump in my throat, walked back up the steps, edged open the door, and slipped into the house.

I was in a small entryway in front of the staircase. Off to one side, a hallway led to a bright linoleum-floored kitchen. On the other side sat a living room full of stiff, dusty furniture. Tall, severe-looking chairs with curvy arms dared you to sit on them. A wheeled glass-and-gold side table displayed a rainbow of decorative glass bottles with nothing in them. A giant urn full of spiky stick plants loomed in the corner. The place looked like a nursing home lobby.

"Goddamn it, Marley," Nico growled from upstairs. "Where the hell did you put it?" Doors banged open and shut. I stared at the ceiling, tracing his footsteps. Did Marley really live in this mothball of a house?

In a ceramic key bowl, I spotted a strip of mall photo-booth shots: Nico and Marley, in all manner of wacky poses. She was making a devil face and he was holding horn fingers up behind her. They were arm-wrestling, with puffed-out fight faces. They were wrapped around each other in a digital heart frame, locked in a full-on sloppy rom-com kiss. Wow—I would not have put those two together in a million years. In the next photo he was mangling her cheek with his lips, and she was rolling her eyes in mock aggravation that I kind of hoped was real.

Nico was the deadbeat Marley was trying to get rid of? This made things more complicated. Or maybe simpler. I looked around. Nothing fit. Not the choice of guy, not the house.

Definitely not being shot in the head. A spiky chill passed through me, like a door had banged open in a winter storm.

Wheels scrambled over the gravel driveway outside. Through the glass side panels on the front door I could see a blond scarecrow of a cop with a hangdog face climbing out of a blue-and-white LTPD squad car. A fortyish matron in full Lululemon gear was crossing the street, already talking at him. Next to the squad car, an old beige Ford pulled up, the kind only plainclothes cops and old people drove. A neat-looking guy in jeans and a blazer hopped out. This guy was a cop? He looked about fifteen.

The floor upstairs let out an agonized squeak. A muffled *Fuck!* floated down. Nico had seen our visitors. I ducked through a set of slatted foldout doors into a hall closet, jamming myself into a wall of dark clothing. Nico pounded down the stairs leaving a *fuck, fuck, fuck* trail. His footsteps retreated down the hall. The back door slammed.

I took a gulp of stuffy closet air and waited to make sure he didn't come back. This was the first place so far that looked like Marley had been anywhere near it. Black lacy clothes hung in sheets all around me. Marley's blue cowboy boots topped a pile of upended shoeboxes. Belts, scarves, books, and CDs with spiky gothic text littered the floor. There were a surprising number of pandas—plushies, jewelry with panda charms, plastic toys. She had probably made some joke about pandas, and then someone gave her one, and then someone else, and then it became a thing.

There was a tiny click. I looked up sharply. Through the slats, I could see the front door creep open. The young cop moved in slowly, gun drawn. He was older than he'd looked outside— skinny, like a kid, but probably in his late twenties like me, with a square face and good hair that he had gelled down like he was trying to forget he had hair. For a second I thought I knew him, but he just had one of those faces.

My heart leaped and began to race. He had seen the broken lock on the front door. If I came out now, I was likely to catch a bullet. I froze, heart whomping in my chest. Call out to him? Or keep quiet and wait for him to find me? Neither choice was likely to end well. My legs shivered and cramped from trying to keep still, and the close, dusty air was getting thicker. I shifted and tripped on something soft and rolly—one of those annoying Kung Fu Hamsters that were all the rage twenty years ago. It burst into a squeaky rendition of "Kung Fu Fighting." I stomped on it, but it kept screeching and spinning its tiny fists. I swooped down and grabbed it, hammered at it, stabbing at the off switch. Finally, the little bastard squeaked and died.

For an awful second, everything was dead quiet. I looked up through the slats. The cop was gone. When he spoke, his voice was close by. "Step out of the closet, please. Keep your hands up." He had a low, smooth voice.

I slid the closet door open, dislodged a stack of shoeboxes, barked my shin wading through them, and sort of rolled out of the closet with my hands up. A large stuffed panda fell off a shelf and did a slow face-plant in front of me.

The cop was flat against the wall with his gun pointed at me. I had never seen a gun before. Up close, it looked huge. My brain went light and fuzzy, like I was wading through cotton candy. I'd heard of people pissing themselves when they were scared and squeezed everything up tight. "I . . ." A rusty croak came out of my mouth. I swallowed and tried again. "I-I-I'm not armed or anything." I realized I was still clutching the hamster. "Aside from the nunchucks, I guess."

The cop looked at the hamster, then back at me. "Put the hamster down. Slowly." I knelt stiffly and ditched the hamster. The gun didn't move off me. "What's your name?"

I had to think about it. My brain was still fighting through sticky gauze. "Katie," I said. "Katie True. It's my real name." *Shit.* My face got hot. "It's just, I get asked a lot."

The cop didn't blink. "What brings you here today, Miss True?" That mild voice, the polite delivery, like he was helping me choose between Earl Grey and English breakfast. The wide, earnest face, kind of sweet and reassuringly ordinary. And the terrifying do-not-fuck-with-me stillness beneath it all.

He was waiting for an answer. Why was I here? The last few hours whirled past me in fractured bits: Nico's glowing yellow shoes, the weeping woman in the Nine of Swords, BEAST 25 hovering in the blue dark.

"I'm friends with the woman who lives here." *Lived.*

"What's her name?" he fired back.

"Marley . . ." I said. My mouth was open but nothing was coming out. I couldn't remember Marley's last name. He had broken my brain, sent pieces of it sailing out. I straightened up, put my hands on my hips, and said, "I don't remember."

He blinked, clearly wondering if a person who said something so dumb could possibly be dangerous. I stared back at him.

Slowly, he holstered his gun, still watching me. "Did you break the lock out front?"

"No," I said. "The guy who came in before me did that." My breath was slowing, finally. The fight-or-flight floodwaters were receding. "He went out the back when he heard you."

"Did you know him?"

The cop's cellphone rang before I could answer this

deceptively simple question. "This is Jamie," he said, motioning for me to hold on a second. Jamie. Such a nice name for someone who scared the crap out of people for a living. He didn't look like a cop, but he looked like a Jamie. "All right, thanks." He hung up. "Come on," he said, and motioned me out to the living room. "I have some questions for you."

The scarecrow cop slumped down the stairs as we walked into the living room, all stooped shoulders and sad droopy eyes. He must have come in through the back. The card wheel in my head clicked through a few turns and spat out the Three of Swords: a fat red heart, lost in a thunderstorm. In my mind I saw the cop tromping down to a shabby garden apartment after his shift. *Honey, I'm home,* he would say to a goldfish in a mossy tank. Then he would heat up a frozen dinner and binge *Queer Eye*. He would move the tank closer to the TV so the goldfish could watch, too.

"All clear," he said in a loud, booming voice that didn't match the rest of him. "Everything's trashed upstairs, too." He motioned at the totaled living room. "Neighbor says she watched him come right up and break the lock. Says she's seen him around here before, with the woman who lives here." He produced a small notepad and flipped through the pages. "Name of Marley Callaghan."

Callaghan! I gave myself a mental forehead smack.

"Anyway," the scarecrow said, "she said he didn't even ring the doorbell first, probably cased the place before, knew his girlfriend was out of town." *Out of town,* good one. Permanently out of town. The scarecrow nodded at me. "Then this one came in after him."

"I wasn't with him, though," I said quickly. "I just saw him go in and wanted to make sure everything was okay in here." It sounded stupid even as I was saying it. I slumped against the wall, suddenly drained. The old-lady chairs in the living room were looking a lot more comfortable.

"I got a call in to the landlord. Name of . . ." The scarecrow peered at the notepad. "Theodosius Karakostas. That's a mouthful, huh?" His cellphone rang. When he walked away to answer it, Jamie turned to me again, but the scarecrow rushed right back into the room. "I gotta go," he said, running for the door. "This is it."

"It's time, huh?" Jamie said. A bright note entered his voice.

"Sure is." The scarecrow grabbed Jamie's hand and pumped it like a tire jack. "Hey, thanks for jumping in, Jamie."

"No problem, I was driving by. Go on, get out of here."

The door slammed. Moments later, the squad car peeled out through the gravel.

Jamie turned to me. "His wife's having a baby." He dug in his jacket for a small notepad.

"Him?" I blurted out. "I did not picture him as a baby kind of guy."

Jamie flipped the notepad open and looked at me. "How did you picture him?"

"I had a whole lonely bachelor thing going about him. Like, his only friend was a goldfish and they watched reality TV together." I stepped over an upended wicker basket and plopped down in a flowered armchair. It was lumpy and hurt my butt.

Jamie watched me make myself at home. "What gave you that impression?"

I shrugged. "Just a hunch." Relief was making me giddy. I swung my feet onto an ottoman that resembled a bowlegged sheep with two heads. "I used to be a professional psychic." This time I didn't stumble on the word *professional*. "Hunches are kind of my thing."

Jamie reached for a pen. "Officer Bailey is actually having his fourth child right now," he said.

I sat up. "You're not serious."

"He's also head of the social committee and does Officer Friendly at the schools." He was smiling a little, just around the eyes. I got the feeling he didn't smile much. I searched his placid face. Either he was fucking with me or he and his gun had knocked me further off my rocking horse than I thought.

"I didn't say I was a *good* psychic," I said.

For a second, the smile looked like it might spread to the rest of his face, but then it flickered and disappeared. He uncapped the pen. "Do you have a phone number for Marley?"

"No, I don't." Across the room I could see the tiny photo of Marley, staring off into space while Nico gnawed at her. "Anyway, Marley might be kind of tough to get hold of right now."

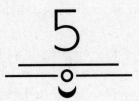

5

*T*oday's the day, I thought, clutching a plastic fork over my paper boat of fried rice and waiting for Marley to appear in the courtyard with her own lunch. *You want to go get a drink this Saturday night,* I would ask her, *or tacos or something?*

We'd been running into each other in the courtyard for a month now, whenever she needed to smoke. We'd started bringing pizza slices and grease-bottomed bags of fried rice out there for sweaty, windy lunches perfumed by diesel exhaust and wildflowers. She worked Mondays, Thursdays, and Sundays, and if I peeked slantwise down the curved mall court from my perch at the register, I could see her joking with Max and his crew of gloomy slacker minions.

I watched an airplane leave a loosening wake in the blank sky. I knew sooner or later Marley would be gone. She drifted along a cross-country trail of tough, fast jobs in tattoo parlors, strip clubs, all-night diners, and low-rent retail. Places my family would have to wash their hands just hearing about. She had an easy, no-nonsense boss quality that should have bounced her straight to the top of any heap, but she never stuck around long enough. If she had another part-time job aside from Stone Blossom, she never talked about it. She was local, but she never mentioned family. I had no idea where she lived. Her boyfriend sounded as temporary as everything else in her orbit. She had no future and no past.

Don't you want to start on a path? my mom would say, nodding like she did when she wanted you to think her idea was your idea. *Lay down tracks for the future?* And then my sister, chiming in with the second verse: *Or would you rather live in a cardboard box next to a burning trash can?* This duet rang out in my head any time Marley talked about some job she bailed on, some deal she cut short, some shot she missed for a better shot that never panned out. She moved by fits and starts along footpaths and backroads that dead-ended and doubled back, instead of slogging ever forward toward some princess-castle mirage of a future. No overthinking, no regrets.

Strength? The Empress? I'd given up trying to slot Marley into the Minor Arcana, and now the Major Arcana clicked past me when she talked, wheeling toward a stopping point that never came. For as big a fan as she was of Sbarro slices and mustard-drowned Polishes, she knew an awful lot about how much sunlight makes the ideal chardonnay grape and had more than once eaten that toxic puffer fish that kills you if it's cooked wrong. She rocked outfits from Discovery and T.J.Maxx, but knew by smell which perfume counter we were walking past and could feel the difference between Coach and Tory Burch leather by touch—all of which she waved away with breezy stories about hitchhiking up and down Napa, or hanging with a bunch of club-hopping chefs while she bused tables at Gibson's. Stories that held up until, like a fake coin or a flat 3D illusion, you looked at them up close.

I didn't look up close. I didn't want to. When she wasn't working, I scooted and fidgeted all day at the register, taking unnecessary trips to the water cooler and watching Stone Blossom like I could make her magically appear. She lit up the mall like a ray of light stabbing through dusty air, showing how empty it was all along.

I knew it wouldn't last. One morning I'd show up at the mall with coffee—cream and sugar for me, black for Marley—and Max would tell me she had quit. Had it with Chicago weather, or dumped her boyfriend, or just *needed a change* and split. Shrugged Lake Terrace off like a shapeless sweater. I'd stand there with the stupid eager-beaver grin still pasted on my face, then shuffle down the mall to work. The coffees would cool in front of me on the counter until I tossed them into the trash.

No. I stabbed the rice. We'd just have to stay school friends, like in third grade. For however long it lasted.

"Holy freakin' Moses." A greasy paper bag plopped down in front of me on the table. Marley folded her long legs under the bench. "Cajun Grill was a zoo today. I had to wrestle a toddler for the last of the bourbon chicken." She dug a Styrofoam container from the bag, then dumped out an avalanche of plastic silverware and sauce packets. She looked up and saw me staring. "I'm kidding. He was probably in middle school."

"Do you want to go out this weekend?" I blurted. "Get some food, or drinks maybe?"

Marley opened the container. Grease splashed her fingers, and she picked up a napkin. Slowly, one by one, she began wiping her fingers. She did not look at me.

I screwed my eyes shut and bit the inside of my lips until I tasted blood. I could still hear the rough squeak of paper against skin—the sound of someone looking for a nice way to say no. *Shit.*

I was glaring at my lunch, trying to think of some plausible excuse to leave early, when Marley said, "Okay."

I stared at her. She took a bite and chewed thoughtfully, then grinned at me. "I'm free Saturday night. What do you want to do?"

"I don't know." I blinked, feeling the blood rush back into my body. "Nothing."

Nothing was exactly what we did, but it was a blazing, breakneck nothing that contained everything.

First, we did not eat dinner at Lindo Mexico because we were too busy snorting and guffawing over the chips and sugary margaritas the annoyed teen waitress kept refilling for us in the hopes that we might order some goddamn food already. When we realized we were full, we sneaked out the back and Marley threw a hundred on the table. *What?* she said when I gaped at her. *Would you want to serve a couple of jerks like us?*

Then, we did not go bowling at the run-down alley on 176 because Marley recognized the sword-wielding angels on the bikes parked outside and said we wanted no part of what was about to go down in there, and before I could ask, she peeled out and set off for a dive bar she knew in Knollwood, but we never made it because she screeched to a stop at a mini-mart she said was the only place in the county that still sold Red Dog beer. We got a six-pack and drank it on the highway overpass on 120, watching cars streak south to the city or north to Wisconsin, people going anywhere but here. *You like it?* she asked, and I said,

Gee, I can't believe they don't sell this stuff anymore, and she laughed and tossed hers back with one hand while she flicked stars of ash into the sky, the same hazy Lake Terrace sky as always, but completely different, and I squeezed my eyes shut and threw them open: *Am I still here? Am I still me?*

After that, things got patchy. I was stumbling after the white circle of the heavy-duty flashlight Marley just happened to have in her car, up a winding forest preserve path, dragging the last of the beer in its plastic six-pack ring, the cool metal bumping my feverish skin.

"Watch out for the bear traps," Marley tossed back at me from up ahead, and I laughed out loud until I realized she was serious. I bent over, huffing. The path widened into a dim glow.

"It's how they protect the weed they grow out here. It's huge money," Marley said. "You don't watch where you're going, you could lose a leg."

I burst after her into a small clearing ringed by twisted trees. "How do you . . ." I leaned against a tree, breathing hard. "How do you even know that?"

Marley shrugged. "I used to come here with my friends in high school."

I scratched my back against the tree like a dog. "That explains it."

But she wasn't listening. She had her hands on her hips, staring out from a high grassy slope overlooking Lake Ruby. Headlights from 176 splashed the shuttered strip malls on the far shore, and when they hit the glass just right they exploded in tiny white supernovas. Off to the side, warehouses hunched in the industrial park under ghostly overhead lights so high the dark ate them before they reached the ground. A high moon splashed light across the lake.

Marley wedged herself into the fork of a low tree branch and held out her hand. I whipped one of the two remaining Red Dogs at her and missed by a mile. She'd been outdrinking me two-to-one all evening, ever since the syrupy margaritas and the tiny bottles of wine in the parking lot of the mini-mart and the abominable Red Dogs on the overpass. Result: I was ripped to the tits, and Marley was as cool and razor-sharp as ever.

I slumped against the tree and watched her retrieve the can. "What is your deal?"

Marley snapped open the beer. "My deal?"

Sober, I would know that this kind of lazy, point-blank question was the surest way to get someone to clam up. "I know what you're doing." I got up and wobbled in a circle, swinging the last beer. "I invented this game." A tree root popped up in my path, and I menaced it. "I ask you a question, you give up just enough about yourself to get *me* talking, and then all of a sudden I'm one of those assholes who talks about themselves all the time." I ripped the beer out of the ring. "You know my whole life story, and I still don't know dick about you."

"How about you sit down before you fall over?" Marley parked her blue cowboy boots up the other side of the branch and wedged the can into her crotch. "I'm getting the spins just looking at you."

I pointed at her. "I'm not an asshole."

"Okay, fine. You're not an asshole. What do you want to know, asshole?"

"I dunno." I yanked at the pop-top of the can. It refused to pop. "Everything. Where'd you grow up? What was your family like? You got brothers and sisters?" I manhandled the can open, took a sip, and was immediately sorry. "What did you want to be when you grew up?"

Marley squinted at her beer. "Ukrainian Village. One brother, one sister. Big dumb Italian family full of uncles and aunts and cousins." She pursed her lips. "Marine biologist."

"You're kidding." I plunked down on an angled tree stump and promptly slid off. "A marine biologist, really?"

"I loved the ocean." She stared at the diamond path in the water. "When I told my dad, you know what he said?" She dropped into a low, thick Chicago accent. If I hadn't been looking at her, I would have been convinced a fifty-year-old guy with a beer gut and a dirty White Sox ball cap had appeared behind me, scratching his balls. *You see any oceans around here? Nobody from Chicago ever became a marine biologist.*

I hiccupped. "More of a freshwater biology person, your dad?"

Marley's face was white stone. "He beat the shit out of me every chance he got. Me and my mom both." She traced a path in the dew on the can. "My brother and sister he left alone because they were his. I was just my mom's bastard kid that he adopted so we could all have the same last name." She smirked. "Because, you know, *family values.*"

"Oh God." The beer went sour in my mouth.

"He was a grade-A piece of shit." She tossed her hair and silver stars flashed in her ears. "A kleptomaniac. And it's not even like we needed the money. He was a union truck driver, made good cash." She took a long swallow and wiped her mouth. "He wasn't doing it for us. He just always had to have some hustle going."

A glowing stick-figure family sketched itself in my mind, like decals on a minivan: run-down mom, slickster dad, three scowling kids. "Did he ever get caught?"

She snorted. "All the time. Any time things started going well for us, he'd pull some shit and get busted and we'd have to move or go back on food stamps. That's why we moved up here." She waved the beer can around. "So we could live in public housing while he did federal time for crossing state lines with a truck full of frozen salmon." She tore the tab off the can and tossed it into the water. A silvery arc and a distant splash.

"Five thousand dollars. That's how much he was getting, to fuck over our whole family." She raised the can and drank for a long time. When she spoke, her voice was a deadly rasp. "He would have done it for less."

"Wow." I pulled myself back up to the stump, landing hard. "I'm sorry."

"I'm over it." Marley shrugged. "He's been dead for years." She ran her finger around the rim of the can. "I do have him to thank for one thing. If we hadn't moved up here, I wouldn't have started acting."

"Acting?" *Of course.* An odd thought skittered through my mind.

"I ended up in a drama class by mistake," Marley said, "and loved it. All of a sudden, I had friends. I had a *thing*. I went full-on theater dork. Lead in the spring musical two years in a row. Drama department award. The works."

My butt was getting numb from being crushed against the tree stump, so I struggled to my feet and went to the drop-off. A freight train drew a splintered note through the woods. The card wheel flashed through the sky. *Nine of Pentacles,* I thought. *Top dog.*

"I actually won this big-deal acting scholarship in New York," Marley said behind me. I turned to catch her eyeroll. "I thought I was going to take Broadway by storm."

"New York." In my mind, a younger, wilder Marley slipped through the faded photographs on the walls of Firebird Imports. *Page of Pentacles. Go forth and do your thing, young one.* "That sounds amazing."

"It sucked," Marley said. "It was all these kids from the Hamptons who had agents and had been doing commercials since they were in diapers. Classic big-fish-small-pond stuff."

"So what then?" I took another mouth-puckering gulp. The beer was even worse warm, but I didn't want to waste it and I didn't want the night to end. "Did you stay in New York?"

"Nope." Marley spun the can like a shiny basketball. "I came crawling home with my tail between my legs." The can fell and she snatched it out of the air. "Worked for my uncle. Did other odd jobs for a while."

She stared at the can and something I'd never seen before crossed her face—regret, maybe, or guilt, or the vapor trail of a dark memory.

"How long is a while?"

"Too long." She shrugged and tossed the can away. "It was easy."

A shiver ripped through me. She was making excuses—something else I'd never seen her do. I peered over the edge. Twisted tree roots poked through the terraced shore, reaching down to the black water. I knew what she meant by *easy*. Too easy. The kind of easy it's hard to break out of. Like Firebird Imports, and before that the year-round Christmas store, and answering phones at the machinery company, and on and on, all the way back to the miserable strip mall shoe store job I got when I first moved back to Lake Terrace, because I couldn't stand another second of lying on the couch at my parents' house talking out loud to the Food Network. One tripping step after another.

A wave of dizziness rocked me and I stepped back. *The Devil. Trapped, stuck.*

"Sounds about right," Marley said. The card melted in the air.

I spun toward her. "In case you're wondering," she said, "yes, you have in fact been saying the cards out loud."

"Sorry." I rubbed my forehead. "Sometimes when I'm thinking, I see cards. You know how some people think in words, and some people think in pictures? I think in cards."

"Do they, like, pop up on a screen or something?"

"They roll up like panels on a slot machine. At least the Minor Arcana do—those are the suit cards. They just ding, ding, ding! Fall into place. Sometimes I even hear the sounds. The Major Arcana, the trump cards—those are on a roulette wheel. The little ball goes round and round until it clicks into place."

Marley rubbed her nose. "Are you a gambler?"

"My aunt Rosie was. She taught me to read the cards. Sometimes she would take me out to the boats in Indiana. I held her gin and tonics while she worked the slots." I took a swallow. "I think she had a problem."

Marley cackled. "One of many. You ever think about opening your own shop? Like that old lady you worked for?"

Eddies of ice swirled through the boozy halo around my body. "I actually went as far as scoping out stores at the mall." I stared into the can. Bubbles winked at me like eyes out of the dark. I took a gulp, to drown them. "I went to the library and checked out a stack of books on starting a business."

Marley sat up in her tree chair, listening.

"I couldn't make it past page one. You needed an MBA to even read the thing." I drank faster, taking angry gulps to drown the murk flowing up from the well I usually kept cemented shut. "Can I remind you I only made it through a year of college?"

"So what?" Marley said. "You don't need a college degree to look at some shit ball and know he's cheating on his wife." She swung her legs down and straddled the fork of the tree. "You've got a feel for this stuff, man. It's—and I mean this in the best possible way—not normal."

"If I could have clients just appear out of the blue, I could do it," I said. "Like, if all I had to do was read. But there's so much other shit to keep on top of. Advertising. Marketing. Accounting." My head spun and I buried it in my hands. "I don't *keep on top of things* very well." My arms and legs went rubbery. The lights blurred in my eyes. "I know I'm not stupid," I said in a small voice. "I'm smart. I always have been. I should be . . . *further along*." I couldn't stand up anymore. I cleared away a small grove of crushed beer cans and cigarette packs and lay down on the ground. Water splashed close by. The sound swelled to the roar of a sunlit waterfall.

"All right, Princess. Let's get you home." Marley's voice shook me awake. Dead leaves crunched by my head. "This ain't the Palmer House." Big arms slid around me and pulled me up. Marley slung my arm around her shoulder, and we lurched back down the path, away from the lake.

"When I was eight," I mumbled. "I was really into those Sparkle Fairies books. There were, like, a thousand." I pulled the mangled plastic beer rings out of my pocket and handed them to Marley. "I went online and searched all the library catalogs in Lake County. I made an Excel spreadsheet and made my parents drive me around until I found all of them."

Marley thanked me for the garbage. "See? You kept on top of some shit."

"I just wish I could pull it out when it matters," I said.

"Matters to whom?" She stopped short and my face mushed against her shoulder. The firebird tattoo leaped at me, eyes blazing.

"Listen," Marley said. "You're not going to remember much

tomorrow, but try and remember this." Her voice slapped me awake, cut through the cotton blurring my sight. "It's not enough to have a *thing*. You've got to figure out how to do that thing *your way*."

"How?" I mumbled and when I looked up she was gone. The firebird yawned at me with Marley's wide, gleeful grin.

"You'll know it when you see it," the firebird said. "Just keep doing what you're doing." Flame and shadow swallowed its face until only the smile was left. We started moving again, picking our way down the bumpy slope. I looked back at a photonegative flash: bright water, black sky. Everything was inside out.

"Did you ever . . ." My tongue was furry in my mouth. "Did you ever act again?"

I didn't hear what she said, and then I was lying down, and she was telling me not to barf in Max's car or she'd get fired, and then I was in bed with the room spinning around me, and then it was morning and I was at the mall again, and everything looked the same except it was all spinning and lit up like a carousel, and I knew that someday soon, maybe not today, maybe not next week, but soon, in some way I couldn't yet see, everything was going to get better.

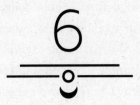

6

The police station sat in a grassy bowl in Lake Terrace's old downtown, a windy intersection you'd blow right by unless you were going to the Stardust Lanes (closed), the Dollar General (open), or the SplashWerks car wash (open but looked closed). Trucks thundered by on their way to the highway or to the warehouses on the far side of Lake Ruby. You could see them crowded in the fog behind the low, flat station building, dark shapes over glittering water.

At Marley's, I'd given Jamie the SparkNotes version of the evening's events, minus the part where I snooped on Nico's phone. The picture of Marley's body became, in my account, *a strong indication* that she was no longer among us. Jamie listened to everything, took notes, and then asked me to come back to the station for "a few more questions," which I think was Cop for "I don't trust you." He was waiting for me in the station parking lot, leaning against his car.

"Did you get lost?" he said when I got out.

"No," I lied. "I just took a shortcut."

He blinked slowly and waved me inside. A squad car pulled around the corner in front of us and he put his arm out so I didn't get creamed. I didn't think he even knew he was doing it.

We walked along beige hallways plastered with announcements in all caps and pictures of cops doing nice things for kids and animals. Jamie stopped for a new pen in a windowless office space crammed full of desks facing each other. The one across from Jamie's was a jumble of papers and files. A framed crayon portrait titled MY DADY hung on a corkboard—a stick figure in a blue uniform and an old-fashioned brimmed police hat. Jamie's desk had nothing on it, not even a coffee cup.

He left me in a small room with a fake-wooden table and a loud ticking wall clock that skipped a beat every seven seconds. I counted. There was a poster of the Chicago skyline on the wall, and another one of a little blond kid flying a kite. FOLLOW YOUR DREAMS, it read. Sirens kept bubbling up and howling away outside. The AC was cranked, and I shivered in my thin T-shirt. I wished I hadn't left my hoodie in the car.

Jamie came in with a manila folder, a notepad, and a small bottle of water, the kind they give to kids at birthday parties. He put the water in front of me, sat down across the table, and opened the folder. I took the opportunity to stare at him. White button-down shirt, black blazer, like he'd rather be wearing a suit but this was the closest the dress code would allow. Clean, closed-up, blank. Swords energy, all sharp angles and parallel planes. He reminded me of an old-time cop from one of the black-and-white movies my dad was always watching.

I downed the lukewarm water in one gulp and wiped my mouth just as he was looking up at me. "Katherine Amelia True," he said. "Are you still at 4200 Shady Pine Drive, apartment 1B?"

"Yep." I eyed the folder, squirming in the plastic chair with the holes in the back. It reminded me of being in elementary school.

"Huh." He scanned the sheet. "But you grew up in Silvergrove?"

"Yeah, so?"

He shrugged. "We don't see a lot of west side kids sticking around after high school."

I made a face. "Yeah, I know, I'm not realizing my potential. Say hi to my family when you pick up your check." My stomach growled. My pre-dinner snack of flat Coke from my car had not prepared me for a long evening. I wished we could move this along.

He put the folder aside and pulled his notepad close. "I was hoping you could clarify a few things for me." He was being really polite, which seemed like a bad sign. "You work at"—he checked his notes—"Firebird Imports, over at the old mall?"

"That's right."

"The place with all the . . ." He waved his pen around in flouncy circles.

"Trinkets?" I suggested. "Bric-a-brac? Tchotchkes? Crap?"

He tilted his head. "You don't like working there?"

"The boss is a little eccentric." I shrugged. "But she's never around and there are no customers, so it's actually kind of ideal."

"You don't get bored?"

"I find ways to amuse myself."

"Like doing tarot readings for customers?" He clicked the pen. It had a blue LTPD logo on it. "How do you learn to do that, anyway? Do you take a class or something?"

"My aunt showed me the basics when I was a kid, but mostly I just kind of wing it."

"A family tradition, that's nice." I looked up to see if he was kidding but it was hard to tell. He said everything in the same pleasing undertone, so you kind of had to watch him. I didn't mind. "You said you used to do it professionally?"

"That's right." I put my hands behind my head and tried to lean back in the chair, but the seatback was too short. "I worked at a shop in the city a few years back."

"No kidding." Perking up, interested. "One of those places with the neon sign in the window?"

"Incense, crystals, beaded curtains. The whole deal."

"You know, I've always been curious about those." Casual now, like he didn't really care, but keeping his eyes on me the whole time. I had the crazy urge to reach over and mess up his hair. "What type of people did you get in there?"

"Well, it was Wrigleyville, so we got a lot of drunken bros wandering in after Cubs games." I squished the empty water bottle and produced a satisfying crunch. "Lots of tourists, people from downstate in the big city for the first time, that kind of thing."

"And the rest of the time?"

"Just regular people, I guess. There was no 'type.'" Where was he going with this? "Nurses, mechanics. Stay-at-home moms. But, you know, Lincoln Park stay-at-home moms, so." I rubbed my fingers together. "We did have a cop come in once."

He raised an eyebrow. "Really?"

"Yeah. Does that surprise you?"

"It does, actually."

"Cops don't worry about the future?"

Just the tiniest lift at the corner of his mouth. "They don't like to admit they worry about the future."

"Well, that's the genius of going to a psychic rather than, say, a friend or a therapist." I shifted around, trying to get comfortable. "You don't have to admit anything. You can go in there and treat

the whole thing like a big, dumb joke." I tossed the crushed bottle and caught it like a ball. "And if you happen to hear something that makes sense and might help you, you just say it was a
coincidence."

"What if you don't hear anything that can help you?" Still
looking right at me, trying to get me to trust him. I knew it was an
act but I liked pretending he was interested.

"You can say, 'See, I knew it was all fake.'" I shrugged. "It's
totally safe. Either way, you don't have to admit you believe in
fairies. Or, more important, that you have a problem you can't
handle yourself."

"You've given this some thought." The table was sloped and
the LTPD pen rolled toward me.

"Not bad for a west side girl who stuck around town." I caught
the pen before it fell and rolled it back to him.

"So what do you get out of it?"

"Besides the cash?" I had to think about that one. "I get to be
nosy. Poke around in people's lives. Tell them what to do,
without—"

"Taking responsibility." Definitely messing with me now, but I
kind of liked it.

"You say that like it's a bad thing."

Voices floated by in the hallway outside, loud, louder, then
soft. Jamie picked up the pen and glanced at his notepad.

"So. You and Marley." Dropping words now, slipping into a
chatty, informal rhythm. "Pretty good friends?" He didn't
believe me.

"For sure." I scooted back and forth in the chair. "She was my
best friend."

"You guys hang out together a lot?"

"Yeah, we hung out." I licked my lips. "Occasionally."

"Movies? Coffee, that kind of thing?" He looked like he was about to veer into *Mani-pedis? Cosmos?* I would have had to chuck the empty water bottle at him. But he stopped.

"Actually, we mostly saw each other at work." Jamie raised an eyebrow. "Like, a lot. We had lunch together up to, like, three times a week." My hands crept to the cards in my back pocket. "And we went to the same high school."

"Ah." Jamie nodded agreeably. "Friends from way back, then."

I shrank in the seat. "No, we weren't there at the same time. We just met two months ago." I told myself to shut up, but I couldn't stop talking. "The thing is, we both left town for a while and came back. And now we were both working at the mall." *The difference was, I was probably going to do it for the rest of my life,* I didn't add.

Jamie watched me, then clicked his pen. "So you didn't know this boyfriend of hers? This Nico?"

"Nope. I knew she had a boyfriend, but I didn't know his name. I thought Nico was just a normal customer. I mean, as normal as you can be with a bleeding head wound."

"You said you talked to him. What did you talk about?"

"Just 'Hi, how are you' kind of stuff. He saw me playing with the cards. That's when I offered him the reading."

"See anything interesting in his future?"

"Yeah, prison." This was the part of the story I'd glossed over because I wasn't eager to come across as a slimeball or a lunatic. I sat there, running my fingers over the ridged underside of the table. It sounded like a small animal farting. "Anyway, it's not about reading the future." I forced myself to sit up straight and look at him. "It's about reading the person."

Jamie watched me placidly, then checked his notes. "At what

point did he tell you Marley was dead?" He looked up at me. "That seems like kind of a conversation-stopper."

Marley's bloodied face flashed into my mind. "Well, he didn't *tell me*, exactly." I had a sudden itch on the back of my neck and swatted at it. "I looked through his phone and saw a picture of her. With a bullet-sized chunk missing from her temple."

"You looked through his phone," he repeated.

"Yes, I looked through his phone, all right?" Busted. "He came in looking like he'd just had his ass handed to him, but when I asked what was wrong, he gave me all this stoic man-crap. I was just trying to help him." My hands crept back under the farting table again, and I squeezed them together in front of me. "But he needed to *believe* I could help him. I was just . . . helping him believe."

"By cheating him out of twenty bucks?"

I grunted. "Look, I could have done the reading cold. He wasn't exactly Mysterio. I just wanted to give him his money's worth."

Jamie put his pen down in front of his notepad, perfectly straight. "Okay, Katie," he said. "Here's what you're telling me. Jump in if I get something wrong." He sat back and folded his arms. "A guy comes to your store. Kind of a strange guy. In some distress. You find pictures of a dead body on his phone, but when you go check it out, there's no body."

"Oh! I almost forgot." I dug Marley's necklace out of my pocket. "I found something better than a body."

Jamie eyed the necklace, then looked at me. "How is that better?"

"It's Marley's necklace." I shook it at him. "She wore it all the time. Like, every day. She loved that necklace." I twitched my eyebrows at him meaningfully.

"And?"

"Don't you see? It proves she was there. And she'd never leave that necklace behind—unless she was dead." I bit back any speculation that Marley had left the necklace there as some kind of message because I was trying to sound *less* crazy.

Jamie rubbed his forehead like he had a headache. "Okay, let's table that for now. Here's the part I'm not clear on. You see him in the parking lot afterward. In the dark. A perfect stranger. Who"—he motioned to the necklace—"may or may not have just killed your . . . best friend." I caught the pause. He leveled a skeptical look at me. "And you follow him?"

I shifted in my seat. "Well, sure, when you put it that way, it almost doesn't make any sense."

"He drives to a house." He ticked off points on his fingers. "He breaks in. And again, you follow him. Why didn't you just call 911?"

"I wanted to, but my phone was dead." I was not enjoying this highlight reel of all my poor decision-making over the past few hours. "Look, he was right there. I couldn't just let him get away, could I?"

"Because Marley was your best friend."

"That's right."

"Do you always forget your best friend's last name?"

"I do when I have a gun in my face."

"You didn't have her phone number either."

That one I did not have a response to. In retrospect, it did seem odd that we'd never exchanged numbers, even to link up for an evening out. By then I was used to her weird privacy issues, so I hadn't even noticed.

The clock skipped a beat. "Okay," Jamie said. "Want to hear *my* explanation?" He arranged the folder and notepad in front of him like he was staging a battle. "You and Nico already knew each other."

"*What?*"

"He goes to Marley's house one day and sees something he likes. Diamond ring, gold jewelry, whatever. He says, Hey, Katie, help me out with this and I'll cut you in. Marley would never suspect her boyfriend, right?"

"That is insane." I actually laughed out loud. "I'm not a criminal."

"Really?" Jamie opened the folder. "June 12, 2012. Apprehended by LTPD for removing a tube of nail polish from Hot Topic." He looked up at me and waited. This highlight reel went back further than I thought.

I sank into my seat. "It was a set of alien-head fake nails, first of all, and second of all, middle child syndrome is real, okay? It was a cry for help."

"December 8, 2013. Underage consumption of alcohol in Deerhaven Park." He gave me a pointed look. "*After* the park was closed."

"I feel nature should be enjoyed twenty-four hours a day. You know, if you're going to dig up every—"

"Here's one from just a few years ago. Public indecency. Forest Park Beach, Lake Forest."

"Okay, that was a religious thing. I got involved with some Wiccans and they did a lot of stuff skyclad." I craned my neck at the file. "There aren't any pictures in there, are there?"

He glanced at the file but said nothing. *Made you look*, I thought.

"Look, Katie," he said. "One way or another, we're going to find out what happened here." He closed the folder and patted it with his palm. "And then you can add home invasion and theft to your little collection." He was still talking in the same soft voice, but it was like I had blinked and someone else had sat down in his place. The guy with the gun at Marley's house. The still, blank one underneath all the nice. I couldn't believe I fell for his good-cop bullshit. I even knew it was bullshit and fell for it anyway.

"I didn't know Nico." I looked down at the table and traced a whorl in the fake wood. "I never met him before in my life. He came in, and he was all busted up, and acting weird. I just . . ." I shrugged. "I wasn't trying to cheat him. I didn't care about the money." I slumped in the chair. "I was just trying to get him to talk. I wanted to know what happened to him." I squelched a little smile. "Getting stuff out of people, especially when they don't want you to—that's, like, the best thing ever, isn't it?"

Jamie said nothing, but I caught a flicker of that ghostly smile around his eyes.

"When I read cards at Miss Lucille's, I could figure out what a person's problem was just like that." I snapped my fingers. "Just from watching and listening for a few minutes. Asking a few questions. Even when they thought they were hiding it from me. Or from themselves." I sat up straighter. "So when Nico showed up, he made me want to do that. I wanted to feel like I was still . . ." I trailed off.

"At the top of your game," Jamie finished quietly.

"At the top of my game." I looked up at him, and his face was still impassive but there was something sad and tired in it. That odd familiarity flashed through me again, like it had when I first saw him through the slats of Marley's closet. It wasn't exactly that I felt I knew him; it was more that we were feeling the same thing. The eerie Six of Swords filled my mind: a pair of hunched figures crossing still waters. Sadness you've felt so long you don't even notice it anymore.

"When I saw the picture of Marley, that's when things kind of got out of hand." My throat went dry, and I swallowed. "Fine, maybe I didn't know her as well as I thought I did." I picked up the crushed water bottle. The damage lines in the plastic sparkled under the fluorescent lights. "But I liked her. A lot. She wasn't like other people. She didn't judge me, or give me a bunch of shitty advice." The patterns in the wood wavered in front of my eyes. "She didn't expect anything from me, so I knew I wasn't going to disappoint her." Tomorrow morning, I would go back to work—blank hours at the cash register, the flies-in-amber JCPenney ladies down the court, a carton of fried rice for lunch, the squishy alarm code buttons on the back door, my car sitting alone in the dark parking lot. Everything the same again as it was before Marley, and would be every day after.

I heard Jamie shift in his chair, but I didn't look at him. I didn't want to see his fake sympathy. This highlight reel had turned into a Hallmark movie. Roll credits, already.

"How sure are you that she's dead?" Jamie asked quietly. I looked up at him. He didn't look sympathetic, or even fake-sympathetic. Just curious.

"Well," I said. "Nico pretty much sat in front of me and told me he killed her."

"Wait a minute." Jamie sat up. "He *told* you he killed her? I thought you were just going by the photo."

"I believe his exact words were 'I didn't mean for her to die.'" I tossed the mangled bottle at a metal wastebasket in the corner. "I pretended I could see what happened in the cards. Rolled my eyes back in my head, put on the whole psychic show." The bottle missed the wastebasket and knocked a framed certificate off a file cabinet.

Jamie didn't even turn around. "And he fell for it?"

"Yep. He freaked out, said he didn't mean for her to die, kind of lurched around like a beached whale, and took off." I yawned and stretched, suddenly exhausted. "That's the whole truth, Officer Jamie." I slumped in the elementary school chair. "Take it or leave it."

"I'll take it," he said slowly. "I'm just trying to decide if you really had no idea you could get hurt, or if you just didn't care."

I wasn't sure either. "So . . . are we good here?" I reached for my backpack. "Can I go home?"

"Of course." He shook his head and started gathering the paperwork. "Thank you for sticking around. We've had a string of home invasions up in that area and I wanted to make sure this wasn't related." He tapped the manila folder. "Sorry to open up old wounds."

"No, it's fine, I love talking about everything I've ever screwed up." I got up and fixed the destruction I had caused next to the wastebasket. "You sure you don't want to look at my Presidential Fitness Test score from third grade?"

"Actually, I can't look at anything from back then. Juvenile records get expunged at eighteen." He folded over the cover of the manila folder and held it up for me to look at. In it was a page ripped out of a notepad with some hastily scrawled notes: *Retail theft—Hot Topic. Drinking—Deerhaven Pk. 2012–2013?*

I goggled at him. "Then what— How did you—"

"One of our officers has a creepily good memory. Remembers every call he's ever had. He gave me a few basics and I filled in the rest." He stood and picked up the files. "The beach thing was real, though. Because you were an adult at the time." His eyes sparkled. "Presumably."

We stared at each other. "Not bad," I said. "You ever consider switching teams? You're a pretty good liar."

"Thanks." He stood and opened the door for me. "You're not."

"You sure about that?" I hoisted my backpack on my shoulder and walked into the hall. He followed me. "I think you're just jealous because I got a confession tonight and you didn't." I milled around, pretending I knew where to go until he started walking. "So, how long do these murder investigations usually last?"

Jamie exchanged nods with a short blonde in a bulky bullet-proof vest walking toward us. "Technically, this isn't a murder investigation."

"It's not? What is it?"

"We could open an investigation into the break-in."

I heard a *but* in there somewhere. "So open an investigation into the break-in."

He gave me the look doctors have when they give you bad test results—part *I'm sorry* and part *Boy, would I rather be anywhere else*. "We'd need the property owner's go-ahead, and we haven't heard from him yet."

"I can't believe this." I stopped walking and stared at him. "You're not going to do *anything*? I just told you that guy said he killed Marley."

"Look, Katie, I'm going to be honest with you." I caught a whiff of his former bureaucratic slickness. "I'm not ruling out that something happened to your friend, but it's pretty difficult to initiate a murder investigation without a body." He looked away for a second. "Or any other reliable evidence that a murder actually occurred."

"Reliable evidence?" My backpack slid off my shoulder and I yanked it back up. "Oh, you wanted *reliable* evidence? Well, why didn't you say so?"

"We're a small department." He put his hands in his pockets. "We don't have the resources to follow up on every—"

"Then why'd you sit there and grill me for an hour if you weren't going to do anything about this?" The worst part was, I knew he was right. That just pissed me off even more.

He took a business card out of his pocket and offered it to me. "If you think of anything else, please don't hesitate to call."

"Yeah, sure thing." I grabbed the card and shoved it into my backpack. "If Marley's body falls out of the sky on me, I'll be sure to drag it over here and dump it on your desk." I turned away and stalked off down the hallway.

"Let me walk you out to your car," he called after me.

"I can find it," I shouted back at him.

I couldn't find it. I wandered around in their stupid maze of hallways for a good twenty minutes before I even found the exit. When I stumbled out into the lot, the hot air closed around me like a fleece robe. It felt good after the Arctic interview room.

I climbed into the car and wrapped myself in my hoodie. Two thoughts twisted around each other in my mind: *Finally, I get to go home.* And then: *Great, now I have to go home.*

I leaned my head back, closed my eyes, and stuffed my hands into the hoodie pockets to warm them up. Something rough grazed my fingers. I dragged it out and held it up.

Marley's necklace. The stones winked and shone in the dark. If Marley had left the necklace by the dumpster for a purpose, I was doing a piss-poor job of figuring out what it was.

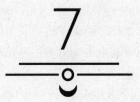

7

The Pizza Pandemonium car was in my parking space again. I lay on the horn, but the delivery guy was already on his way out, waving *okay, okay*. There could be a whole desert of empty parking spaces and he would still park in mine.

Shady Pines was a set of mottled-brown apartment buildings with boxy black roofs like woolly British soldier hats. It was jammed between the Metra tracks, the industrial park, and the back of the Chicago Asian Foods supermarket. The nicer apartments on the top floors had balconies, but mine just had a scraggly patio with an ugly lawn chair I couldn't throw away because my sister gave it to me when I moved in. When we were younger, she referred to the place as Sketchy Pines and probably still did, just not to my face. Jessie lived in a giant house in Long Grove with her pharmaceutical sales rep husband and their daughter, both of whom were way too nice and well-adjusted to be related to her. I suspected she had ordered them illegally through a human trafficking pipeline. She and I talked only a few times a year because she kept offering to "show me the ropes" of real estate, and I was running out of polite ways to say I'd rather stab my eyes out with a fork.

I wrestled the front door open just as a giant laundry basket full of kids' clothing bounced down the hall toward me. Mrs. Ortiz from 1D was somewhere behind it. She tripped on a piece of uneven carpeting, stumbled, and fell. Tiny superhero T-shirts flew everywhere.

Mrs. Ortiz made a soft noise, like this was the latest indignity in a whole evening's worth. I knew how she felt. I helped her up and got to work stuffing the laundry back into the basket. She joined me on the floor, thanking me in English and Spanish.

"I asked Bear to fix it last week." She pointed at the offending bump in the brown carpeting. "He said don't worry, I'll get to it. And did he get to it?"

"Well, it is summer." Bear, the building manager, spent any available good weather days outside washing and waxing his midnight blue 1984 Camaro. I tossed a pair of tiny Wonder Woman underpants into the basket. "I'll remind him if I see him."

We got the basket upright and back in her arms and she started off toward the laundry room, then stopped. "Ah, Katie." Her round face peeked around the side of the basket. "I'm working an extra shift next Saturday evening."

"Want me to stay with the kids?" I spent the night in 1D whenever Mrs. Ortiz picked up late shifts at the gastropub at the new mall. Mr. Ortiz drove a forklift third shift somewhere in the industrial park. They were always trying to pay me, but I felt like an asshole taking money for sitting around watching TV and eating a far better dinner than I'd make for myself while the kids fed themselves and did their homework without having to be told.

"Please, if you can?" Mrs. Ortiz looked sheepish. "You have plans?"

"I'll check my calendar," I said, because I wanted to be the kind of person who had a calendar and plans. "But I'm pretty sure it's okay."

Mrs. Ortiz put down the basket, walked back over to me, stood on her tiptoes, and gave me a kiss on the cheek, which for a brief moment made me want to be nice to people more often. I watched her bounce off toward the laundry room.

I unlocked the door to my apartment and snapped on the lights in the entryway. I had already dumped my backpack and jacket on the floor and was tossing my shoes onto the pile next to the empty shoe rack when I heard tapping noises coming from the bedroom. I froze. The tapping was scattershot, like mice scrabbling over a rooftop. Too irregular to come from the AC unit. Someone was here.

I sank to the floor, heart pounding. Nico had followed me home. He knew I had talked to the police.

I reached into my backpack for my cell but remembered that it was still dead. I looked around for a hiding place, but my apartment was essentially two big rooms, one of which I was now trying to avoid. A red plastic flyswatter hung on the far wall of the kitchen. I crawled over and snatched it up.

The tapping in the bedroom stopped. I scuttled under the kitchen table and raised the flyswatter. "I have a gun," I said in a cracked voice.

The kitchen light snapped on. I squeezed my eyes shut, then forced them open. A stoop-shouldered, carrot-topped beanpole with freckles and gold-rimmed glasses on his nose stood at the light switch. He looked at me, at the flyswatter, then back at me. "Where's the gun?"

"I don't have a gun, you dope." I climbed out from under the table and tossed the flyswatter at him. "I thought you were . . . never mind, it's a long story." I brushed bits of petrified food off my jeans. "How did you get in?"

"The back door was unlocked." He pointed to the sliding glass patio door.

"I should have known," I said, straightening the *Song of the Lark* print I'd had since an eighth-grade class field trip to the Art Institute. It went cockeyed on its nail any time someone opened or closed the patio door.

"You should keep that door locked," Owen said.

"Yeah, I know. The lock's broken. I need to call the super, but it's summertime." I slid the patio door open. My unit backed up to the loading docks of Chicago Asian Foods and I never knew what aroma would greet me out there. Sometimes it was kimchi and sometimes strawberry soda and sometimes rotten fish. Tonight it smelled like some kind of spiced cake, so I left the door open.

"What are you doing here, anyway? Besides scaring the crap out of me." I sank into a corner of the giant green-and-gold flowered couch that took up most of the living room. The Ortizes gave it to me after Mr. Ortiz made shift supervisor and they got a better one. This one smelled like Play-Doh and fried food and I loved it.

Owen had gone into the bedroom to retrieve his laptop and was now perched crisscross applesauce on the far armrest of the couch. I eyed his laptop to gauge how long it would be before he bought himself a new one and gave me the one he was currently using. The last laptop I got from him had conked out a month ago. "There's a power outage in my building. They said it could be out until tomorrow and I have a biodiversity seminar I need to prep for." He balanced the laptop on his knees. "I tried to call you, but your phone is dead."

"Apparently, you have to recharge it *every* time it runs out of juice. When are you going to get a new one so I can have yours?"

He was already typing again and had forgotten all about me. My brother was doing postgrad at Northwestern, studying evolutionary biology. He paid for his crappy overpriced Evanston apartment by working as a lab assistant and having no social life. He would be the Page of Wands forever, pure action and ideas, unhardened by the layer of fakery that came with growing into a Knight or Queen.

"Why didn't you go stay with Mom and Dad?" I said. "At least they have food."

"You have food." Owen motioned to an empty jar of grape jelly on the pair of milk crates I was using as a coffee table. "Besides, Mom and Dad ask a lot of questions."

"And we know what happens to people who ask too many questions." I went to the pantry to check for anything edible. There were eight identical tin cans of corned beef hash that I didn't remember buying and that I suspected were actually meant for cats. I took one out, pried it open, and dumped the contents into a saucepan. It came out in a can-shaped glob.

Owen put down his laptop and came into the kitchen. There was no point in asking him if he wanted to eat. If there was food, Owen would eat. If there was no food, he would not eat. Sometimes for days.

He leaned on a chair, tipping it toward him and balancing it on its back legs. "You look weird," he said. "Were you crying?"

"Yes. I heard 'Sweet Child o' Mine' on the radio."

"Oh. I thought maybe you got fired again."

"No, not today." I mashed the hash-shaped goo down in the saucepan. "I kind of got mixed up in a murder, though."

"A murder, really?" He said it like some people might say *A yoga class, really?* "Were you a witness?"

"No. A guy came into the store, and I snooped on his phone because I wanted to wow him with my psychic powers, and he had a picture of . . . of someone I knew, and she was dead." I wasn't sure I was up for another set of verbal gymnastics explaining my relationship with Marley. "She was a friend of mine. Kind of."

"You have psychic powers?"

I glanced at him. "Not yet. I'm working on it." Too much information at once tended to fry Owen's circuits. In school, he had been a math god, except when it came to word problems, because he would overfocus on where the two trains were heading when they left the station and whether they were steam or coal powered.

"You should go back to doing readings," Owen said. "You're good at it."

"Well, thanks, Owen." The hash had started to hiss and bubble, so I squished it into two bowls and brought them to the table. "It's nice to be good at something."

"I could never do a reading." He sat down and stared into his bowl until I got up and got forks.

"Sure, you could. Maybe you could bring a cheat sheet." I rummaged in the cupboard for plastic cups. "Those little smiley face flash cards the social worker used to give you." I pulled an exaggerated frown. "I'm *sad* . . . because I just killed someone."

Owen emitted his shocking hoot of a laugh and started eating. "Well, I think you should go back to it when you lose your job again." I had learned to take Owen's compliments in the spirit in which they were meant. "Did you detain the murderer until the police got there?"

I filled a couple of plastic Chuck E. Cheese cups with water and brought them to the table. "No, but I followed him. He broke into my friend's house and I went in after him." I sat down and picked up my fork. "He trashed the place looking for something. I don't think he ever found it. He ran when the police got there."

Owen stood up, circled the table, then sat back down and kept eating. I had his attention now.

"I talked to this detective and he thought I was in on it." I stared out the patio door at the lights from the back of the market. "Let me ask you something. Have you ever looked at somebody you just met and felt like you already knew them?" The Six of Swords floated through my mind again on deep, still waters.

Owen picked up a forkful of hash, but it was too hot to eat so he put it down. He eyed his fork malevolently, then shoved it in his mouth anyway. "Like déjà vu?"

"No, not exactly." I twirled my fork in my bowl. "You know how you see someone on the train maybe, or in the store, and you think if you got to know them—"

"I don't ride the train."

"Well, whatever. The bus, the street. The lead-lined aquarium where you socialize with others of your kind."

"Oh. I know what you're talking about," he said, letting out big breaths of steam and trying to talk at the same time. "That feeling is your body responding to a potential sex partner with a favorable genetic makeup." He waggled his fork at me. "This detective. You want to have his babies."

"What? I do not."

"Your body does." Owen popped a foot under him in his chair and bounced up and down. "Preferably male babies, sexually attractive and extremely promiscuous. So they can scatter their seed as widely as possible."

"Owen." I dropped my fork. "I'm trying to eat."

"Immortality." He thrust his fork at me like a corned beef hash–covered sword. A brown glob fell off and splatted on the table. "Your genes are looking for other genes that will ensure the highest chances of reproductive success for as many generations as possible." We'd hit Owen's *thing*. We'd be here awhile. "You want to live forever."

"That sounds exhausting." I watched him pick up the runaway glob of hash and pop it into his mouth. "Who the hell wants to live forever?"

"Everyone. They just don't know it. So they make up things like love at first sight."

"Wow. You know, if this whole research scientist thing doesn't work out, maybe you can write greeting cards."

Owen slurped at his water. "So, why did that guy kill your friend?" Not once had he asked why I chased Nico or called me crazy for doing it. Either he had a refreshing disregard for extraneous details or his decision-making was as damaged as mine.

"I don't know," I said. "Why do people kill each other?" In the apartment next door, a loud, warbling opera snapped on and then snapped off again.

"It's usually money," Owen said. "Or sex."

"My money's on sex," I said. "It turned out he was her boyfriend. She told me last week she was going to break up with him, so maybe he went crazy from heartbreak."

"I think it's money *and* sex," Owen said. "I think they broke up because she stole a large amount of money from him. That's what he was looking for at her house." He nodded, satisfied at having solved the case. "Are you going to help the cops find him?"

"No, why would I do that?" I pretended the thought had never occurred to me. "I told them everything I knew. The rest is their job." I took a bite of hash. It was salty and tasted like smoke and plastic. "Although they're not exactly falling all over themselves to get started."

"Why not?"

"Blah-blah busy, blah-blah resources, blah-blah I'm probably a crazy person who's making the whole thing up."

Owen stuffed the last piece of hash in his mouth and contemplated his empty bowl. I got up, brought over the pan, and dumped the rest of the hash into it.

"So, about this detective," Owen said, and for a wild second I thought he was reading my mind. "Did he have good teeth?"

"You know, I didn't check. Because he was not a horse."

"Hm." Owen nodded. "Unusual upper body strength? Did you see him lift anything heavy?"

"Why, do you need help moving a piano? Where are you going with this?"

"I'm just trying to evaluate his genetic staying power." He got up, circled the kitchen, and sat back down. "Superior physical strength is just a basic ask. How about intelligence? Night vision?" He stared off into space dreamily, twiddling his fork. "Disease resistance?"

"I mean, he was in okay shape," I said. "And you can't be dumb and be a detective." I thought about it. "You know what? He did offer to help me find my car in the dark." I leaned toward Owen and flicked my eyebrows at him. "And the whole time I was there, *he didn't sneeze once*."

"If you really did have psychic powers . . ." Owen perched in the chair and bounced up and down. "You guys could start a race of super-strong, super-intelligent nocturnal precogs that never get sick." He picked up his bowl and upended it into his mouth.

"Mother of Supermen," I said. "I like it. Do I get, like, X-ray vision or a plaque or something?"

"You get to have as many babies as you can for the rest of your life," Owen said. "Until your uterus gives out and you die in childbirth."

A thrumming car stereo from a passing car pounded through the room, like an ogre lumbering by on his way home.

"What else do I have to do for the next thirty years?" I raised my plastic cup to Owen and we clinked. "Live forever."

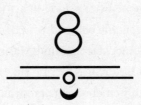

8

saw Kurt Cobain again on my way to work. He was wearing a short-sleeved dress shirt and skinny tie and had a badge on a lanyard around his neck. Blond stringy hair down to his chin, just this side of an uncomfortable conversation with HR. Smoking like he was trying to get it all in while he could, and listening to something loud and screamy. He was wedged into a rusty Honda with a forest of old bumper stickers on the back, and he always turned in to the gated Abbott Labs campus.

I threw Kurt a metal salute he didn't see, yawned, and stretched my sore back. I had given Owen my bed last night and slept on the couch, which was not meant for overnight accommodations. Plus, Owen kept coming out every five minutes to get water, or go to the bathroom, or just blurt out whatever he was thinking.

I glanced in the rearview mirror and was startled at my own black-lined eyes staring back at me. This morning, on a whim, I had put on Marley's necklace. It was the kind of accessory that bossed the outfit around, and before I knew it, I had switched my stretch pants and T-shirt for an uptight little sundress I never wore. Then I had to run a few extra combfuls of gel through my hair to make it all textured and shiny instead of hanging around my face in a brown sheet. That led to some heavy eyeliner and dark lipstick, which led to a pair of big, angry boots. I ended up with a Girl Scout–gone–wrong look that I kind of liked. *Okay*, the necklace said. *Now you can go.*

I had last seen the necklace around Marley's neck last Thursday. The food court bakery was getting rid of their old stuff, and I knew I would score free chocolate croissants if I let Casey, the old Vietnam vet who ran the place, show me pictures of his grandkids. I was just gloating over my haul when Marley dropped onto the bench opposite me at the picnic table. She had sort of a punkabilly look going that day, hair swept up in a messy beehive with crimson tendrils reaching for her face, and a skintight red halter-strap tank. The necklace sat neatly in her décolletage. Underneath her usual swaths of black eyeliner, her face looked pink and raw.

She blew her bangs out of her face with a sharp little huff and checked out the giant paper bag of croissants. "What did you do, give Casey a hand job?"

Cranky Marley was here. There were other Marleys, a whole army. They moved through quickly, like clouds racing through the sky, and I'd already figured out that even the darker ones didn't stay long, usually leaving with an apology. I looked down, pretending to search my pockets for a scrunchie. The day was boiling with sudden violent outbursts of wind. My hair danced around, smacking me in the face.

She peeked inside the bakery bag, then pushed it away and fished a lighter and a pack of cigarettes out of her pocket. "I'm not hungry," she said.

"Everything okay?" I said.

She flicked the lighter over and over in her fingers. Sparks flew up and disappeared in the wind. "You know how you make up your mind to do something, and you can't do anything else until it's done?"

I gave up on the scrunchie and grabbed my hair in my fist. "Are you going to break up with your boyfriend?"

Marley dropped the pack of cigarettes. Surprise flickered in her eyes and disappeared. Then it came back, big and glossy, like she'd tried it on and decided *Yeah, okay, let's go with this.*

"Nailed it as usual." She tipped an imaginary cap. "How'd you know?"

I shrugged. "You don't talk about him much. That's always a bad sign." I put a croissant on a butter-stained napkin. "And when you do, it's usually because he screwed something up."

"I'd say a breakup is definitely in the cards tonight," she rasped, shaking a cigarette out of the pack. Cranky Marley had a lower voice than regular Marley, almost a man's voice. It was like she was channeling all the shitty dudes that had passed through her life. She scanned the table. "Speaking of which, no cards today?"

I patted the velvet bag in my back pocket. "Too windy."

"Too bad, I could use some head-clearing." She twisted her hands around the lighter and cigarette, hiding them from the wind. The cigarette wouldn't light. She gave up and tossed them both onto the table.

"What happened?" I broke off a bit of crusted chocolate and popped it into my mouth. "Between you guys, I mean?"

She glanced over her shoulder at the stone barrier that separated us from the highway. "He's a fucking thief is what happened. I can look the other way on a lot of shit, but stealing?" She shook her head. "Fuck that."

Bleary bits of the drunken night at Lake Ruby floated through my memory. Marley's face, stone-stuck in her rage-smile, talking about her kleptomaniac dad.

Marley packed her smoking stuff away, watching me. Her face had snapped back to a bland curiosity. "Got big plans for the weekend?"

I let her change the subject. "Not really. I'm guessing my brother will show up on my doorstep like a stray." My throat was burning from the sugary pastries. I wished I had brought water. "He doesn't have cable and there's a *Star Wars* marathon all weekend, so I'm just putting two and two together."

"Cool." She was still watching me. A wild gust of wind raised my hair in thick sheets around my face. I grumbled and pulled it back again.

"Listen," Marley said. "I have to go." She stood up, patting her pockets. "Sorry I'm such shit company today."

"No way." There it was. Bye, Cranky Marley. "You've got stuff going on." I rolled the croissant bag closed and handed it to her. "Here. You'll need your strength for tonight."

She stared at me. "What?"

"For the big breakup." I shot her with some finger guns. "Taking out the trash!"

"Oh." Marley gave me a little smile. "Yeah." She rummaged in her pocket and pulled out a worn black hair scrunchie. "Here."

"Thanks." I took it from her. "I'll give it back to you Sunday."

"Keep it," Marley said. She stood there for a second, then pulled open the door and melted into the dark entryway.

I put down the scrunchie to clean up my pastry mess. The little piece of black cloth shook on the table, caught by the wind. I lunged, but I was too slow. It danced out of my fingers, skittered across the stone highway barrier, flew out into the emptiness, and disappeared.

When I got to work, Larissa and her grandnephew Sam were hunched over a laptop, shouting at each other in Russian. They stopped and turned to me when I walked in.

"What are you all dressed up for?" Sam said. "You got a job interview?" Sam was a skinny guy with wire-rim glasses, a sharp nose, and a receding hairline that he downplayed by growing his hair long so it stuck straight up from his head. His self-appointed mission was to find ways for Firebird Imports to stop hemorrhaging money, all of which Larissa shot down.

My hand shot to Marley's necklace. "I'm not dressed up."

"Hm." Larissa looked me up and down. She was a short, squat designer-fashion addict in her seventies. She mostly ignored me, which I preferred to her volcanic flare-ups of interest. "You look good," she said. "You need to do this all the time." She was like a second mom to me, meaning she never said anything nice without meaning something else.

Larissa and Sam resumed their argument. I tuned them out and peeked into the mall. Firebird Imports was in the JCPenney court, a circular jumble of shops prone to sudden openings and closings, like a business-sized Whac-a-Mole. The current lineup: a vitamin store selling pills that promised to *punch, pound, shred,* and *destroy*; a tween bauble-o-rama begging you to take six when you bought one; two metal-shuttered vacancies; and Stone Blossom, where Marley had worked.

He's a fucking thief is what happened. Whatever Nico was looking for at her house, it wasn't his to take. Pieces started clicking together in my mind. Something had happened last Thursday night after I saw her, something that led to her death. *I didn't mean for her to die.* Nico did look like the kind of dope who didn't know his own strength, but my gut told me it didn't come from simple rage at being dumped. Nico, Marley, and the missing object: three points on a circle, surrounding a murder. The card slot machine whirred to life in my mind, wheeling through cups and pentacles, love and money, all twisted around each other.

I peeked down the curved mall court at the distressed metal awning of Stone Blossom. Marley was missing her second straight day of work, but I didn't sense any unusual curiosity about this over at the store. Just Max and his anemic staff milling about under the strobe light they used to either attract passersby or cause seizures. Could it be Max didn't know what had happened? I ticked off the minutes of the morning, waiting for my shot to go over there and ask a few innocent questions.

At lunchtime Larissa put on her Italian supermodel sunglasses, reapplied her bright red lipstick, and left, telling me to finish checking the inventory and close up early. Sam disappeared shortly afterward. When I was sure I was alone, I sneaked over to Stone Blossom.

The place was bigger inside than it looked from the outside, like a horror movie house that some unsuspecting family moves into by accident. It branched off in odd directions that ended in nooks full of jewelry trees displaying skull necklaces, mannequins in bondage gear, and racks of leather and velvet clothing. It smelled black and purple in there.

Max sat at the counter pounding his head to "Sweet Leaf" and poking through a product catalog. A tall guy with a long gray ponytail and a Jesus Lizard T-shirt was using a tape gun to price T-shirts reading SHUT THE FUCK UP.

"Katie-pie!" Max shouted when I came in. "Just the person I wanted to see. Come here." He thrust the catalog at me. "Which one do you like better? The skull on a background of roses or the skull on the background of dollar signs?"

I peered at two thumbnail photos of cigarette lighters. "I like the roses. It says *I'll kick your ass but I still believe in love.*"

"That's what Danny said, too, man." He nodded toward Jesus Lizard. "You guys got impeccable taste." Max was wearing his waist-length black hair in a high ponytail so you could see the shaved sides underneath. He was rocking a blood-red silk shirt under a double-breasted overcoat with metal studs down the front—a tiny guy in clothes that made him look tall. I liked him. Everyone he saw was just the person he wanted to see, and everything they said was just the right thing at the right time. Knight of Cups all the way, white horse, red roses, the guy who loves everyone and whom everyone loves.

"Speaking of impeccable taste," he said, "you look good today, man." His eyes stopped on my necklace. My stomach did a little flip-flop when I realized he would probably recognize it, but he didn't say anything.

"Thanks, Max." I turned away from him, pretending to examine a rack of Bettie Page wallets. "Hey, is Marley in today?"

"Oh, she's actually not working here anymore, yeah." Max ended everything he said with an additional yeah or no, like he was answering the question ahead of the one you were asking. "Yeah, she quit."

"She what?" I gaped at him. "When?"

He scrunched up his face to remember. "Thursday? Was her last day? Yeah."

I stared at Max. Marley hadn't said a word about quitting when we saw each other on Thursday. The windy croissant day. "Is she— Do you know why— I mean, is she . . . okay?"

"She went to the Bahamas, man." He zoomed an airplane hand into the air. *"Neee-yowm!"*

"The . . . Bahamas?" I wondered if "the Bahamas" was some kind of death euphemism I'd never heard.

"Yeah, she said she was about to come into a little extra dough, know what I mean?" Max said. "Said it was time for her to move on, yeah."

There was a metallic crash. Danny the stock guy had managed to overturn an entire rack of motorcycle boots and was standing in the middle of them blinking. "Aw, shit," he said sadly. Max hurried out from behind the counter to help.

"Hey, I'll catch up with you later, huh? Yeah!" Max said over his shoulder. I stood there for a second, then left them to scale Boot Mountain.

Back at Firebird, I sleepwalked through the rest of the afternoon, picking up painted wooden spoons and teapot cozy dolls to check their item numbers, then forgetting them immediately and having to do it again. The few rickety connections I'd made about the events of last Thursday night came crashing down. Now Marley was expecting to "come into some extra cash"? Whatever shady deal went down that night, it now appeared she was a willing participant . . . except things hadn't turned out the way she planned. I tried to remember her face, but all I could picture was the photo of her ruined body. My mind bubbled with dark possibilities.

And under all of them, a thought like a low, unpleasant drone. Maybe she didn't know she would die, but she did know she was leaving. And she didn't tell me.

She didn't say goodbye.

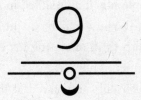

9

On my way home from work I hit the traffic light at the water treatment plant half a mile from my apartment, the one that lasts forever. I rolled down the window and took a big breath of hot air laced with bus exhaust and fried chicken grease. *I should learn to cook,* I thought, knowing I never would.

I glanced in the rearview mirror. The stylish stranger from this morning was gone. My hair was a wild tangle, my clothes were sticking to me, and my eyeliner was smudged. I had a pounding headache. I had spent the afternoon squinting at my phone through internet searches of every conceivable spelling variation of "Marley Callaghan" with nothing to show for it except an Irish grandma's Facebook page, a profile of a teen soccer star from Boise, and offers to shop for "Marley Callaghan" in my area.

The traffic light glared red. Marley's death, her skirting the law, her quiet plan to skip town—it all popped to the surface of my mind and sank again like twisted ingredients in a poisonous stew. But what bugged me most, the noxious distillation at the bottom . . . was me.

I told myself I didn't see it coming, but I did. All the gaps in Marley's sunny, easy chatter. The loose story threads I could never weave into a whole. The glimmers of big money washing up in her hardscrabble life. It all pointed in red neon to danger, but I wasn't looking. Too busy soaking up the freedom I felt being around her, the selfish thrill of closing my eyes and diving into the roller coaster tunnel blind.

I chewed my fingernails and stared at the plaza across the street—three empty storefronts, a Dairy Deelite, and a Ref's Whistle. If I had paid more attention, gotten to know her sooner, listened more instead of talking, I could have . . . what? I bit down hard on my finger and a tiny ball of blood welled up from its corner. Untangled Marley from whatever mess she was trapped in? Or just gotten stuck in it myself? I sucked on my finger, feeling the tiny secret beat coursing through it. All I knew was that I'd had a shot to do things differently and blew it. And now it was too late. Marley was gone.

In the window of the Ref's Whistle, a jock-y model grinned ear to ear from a life-size poster. GET YOUR SPORTS ON! He was wearing the Ref's Whistle getup—yellow-and-blue-striped shirt, black pants, yellow shoes.

Yellow shoes. Something went *ping* in my brain like a pinball hitting a target.

Car horns blared behind me. I woke up, did an illegal turn in to the plaza's outbound turn lane, and screeched into the parking lot. There they were—Nico's shoes, with their blue-winged RW logo. No wonder they'd looked familiar. They were part of the Ref's Whistle employee uniform and I saw them every day on my way to and from work.

I threw the car into a space in front of the store and hopped out. VISIT US AT OVER TWENTY CHICAGOLAND LOCATIONS, read a decal on the glass door. The next closest store was twenty miles away, in Niles. If Nico worked at a Ref's Whistle, this had to be the one.

My heart popped a wheelie in my chest. I whirled outward and scanned the lot, eyes darting through the aisles. It was a small lot. If he was here, I'd know it fast. A drop of sweat crept down my neck like a tiny, insistent bug. There. The black truck was two rows away from me, taking up a space and a half next to a grassy curb. BEAST 25.

My legs wobbled and I dropped to a squat next to my car, breathing hard. A young mom pushing a stroller hopped back and quivered in place, unsure whether to help the heatstroke victim or run from the crazy lady. I gave her a cockeyed grin and she moved on.

I crawled into my roasting car and slammed the door, fumbling at my backpack. The business card with the LTPD triangle logo was crushed all the way at the bottom. OFC. J. ROTH, INVESTIGATIONS. I stared at the card, then tossed it onto the passenger seat. What good would calling him do? He would politely write down what I told him and stick it in a file, where it would sit forever.

I dug around for my tarot deck. Two shuffles and a cut: the Wheel of Fortune. Now, *that* was more like it. I looked up at the Ref's Whistle, the blazing sunlight blanking out the window. I'd never gotten the chance to talk to Nico—*really* talk to him. First I scared him off, then Jamie did. And now, cycling up on the great golden wheel of too-good-to-be-true coincidences was another chance to find out the truth. I patted down my dress, smoothed my hair, and climbed out of the car. Nico wouldn't be thrilled to see me, but this time we weren't alone in an abandoned mall. Killing me would be frowned upon, as would running out on his work shift. I had him.

Inside, the store was cool and smelled pleasantly of new rubber. I let my eyes adjust and headed toward the counter between aisles of bright gym shoes like fancy pastries displayed on round trays. A teenager tried on a pair of Nikes while his little brother ran up and down the aisles. Two employees in Ref's Whistle colors wandered around: a short guy with a tall fade and a middle-aged blonde. And leaning on the unattended front counter, like he was waiting for a piña colada at a swim-up bar, was Ofc. J. Roth, Investigations.

I stopped short, nearly tripping over the amok toddler. Jamie turned to me. "Katie," he said. "What a surprise." Again I couldn't tell if he was messing with me, so I tried to look pleasant and outraged at the same time. "Shopping for shoes?" Not smiling but not displeased to see me either.

"Nothing," I said. "I mean, no. I was just going home from work." I twisted my fingers in my backpack straps. "Taking the scenic route." I gestured weakly at the entrance behind me.

Jaime looked through the window at the brown weed-strewn hulk of the sanitation building, then back at me.

"All right, fine." I lowered my voice. "I was driving by, and I recognized the shoes these guys wear." I motioned to one of the salespeople. "Nico was wearing a pair last night," I said. "So I figured I'd stop by and . . ." I trailed off.

"Stalk him?"

"Ask him a few questions." I had not actually thought about what those questions would be. Somehow it hadn't seemed important, like I'd know what to say when the moment presented itself. The trick was getting the moment to present itself. I tried to distract Jamie from my glaring lack of preparation. "What are *you* doing here?"

Jamie picked up his notepad. "We put a BOLO on the plate you gave us for Nico's truck. One of our road guys spotted him here and ran it. I said I'd check it out."

I clutched an imaginary set of pearls. "Slow day for you and your small department in a small town?"

He gave me a steady look. "Not really."

There was an interesting silence that was cut short by the emergence of a manager from the back room. "He'll be just a few minutes," she said. I took the opportunity to ogle Jamie. Dressed to the nines again in khakis and a blazer in this heat, but still looking neat and cool and well-put-together. I was suddenly aware of my sweaty dress and wild hair.

"Did you get his full name?" I said when Jamie turned back to me.

Jamie looked like he was deciding if he should tell me to fuck off now or later. He glanced at his notepad. "Dominick Battaglia," he said. "I'm going to have a little talk with him."

"Great." I folded my arms, dropped my backpack, and leaned against the wall next to the counter. "That's a great idea."

Jamie watched me get comfortable.

"Yeah. I'll just, you know, I'll stick around in case you need backup," I said.

"I think I can handle it," Jamie said.

"Oh." I briefly considered running next door and setting something on fire to distract him. "*Oh.*"

"But I'll let you know if anything comes out of it," he said. So sweet. So pleasant. Such a pain in my rear. We stared at each other, not blinking, while I fidgeted with my backpack.

"Look, Katie," Jamie said. "You wanted me to look into this, and I'm looking into it. But I think considering the nature of your previous interaction with Mr. Battaglia, it would be better if I talked to him alone." He put down the notepad. "Don't you think so?"

I chewed my lip. "Fine. I'm going. But you wouldn't even be here if it weren't for me." I made a sour face at him. "You know that, right?"

This time he smiled for real. "It was good to see you again, Katie."

I had to take a breath. He had a killer smile. "You're welcome," I shouted back at him, heading for the door. He gave me a mild glance and turned back to the counter.

Outside, I blinked in the sun for a few seconds, then climbed into my car. The Wheel of Fortune stared up at me from the passenger seat. What goes up must come down. I shoved it into the deck and stared at the Ref's Whistle window, peering around the smiling jock. If I angled myself right and squinted, I could just see—

Jamie's face appeared in the murky window. He gave me a pointed goodbye wave. I replied with my most luxurious eyeroll, then backed out of the space and pulled around into the next aisle, heading toward the road. A flash of yellow darted in front of me, moving fast under wide, staring eyes and bared teeth: Nico, aka Dominick Battaglia, running like hell for his truck. He looked up and his eyes went dark as he recognized first me, and then what was about to happen.

"Hey!" I said out loud, like that was going to stop him. I stomped my foot but I must have hit the wrong pedal because the car zoomed forward and Nico's face flashed white in front of me. I screeched and jerked the steering wheel. Too late. My bumper clonked him and he went down like a sack of wet noodles. The car veered toward a lamp post and there was a metallic crunch. I squeezed my eyes shut just before my head bounced off the steering wheel.

"Ow," I managed to say.

Jamie appeared in time to catch me wobbling out of my car. Nico was on the ground, holding his side. When he saw me, he pointed and tried to say something, but I had knocked the wind out of him.

"Are you okay?" Jamie asked, taking me by the arm. I nodded.

Jamie reached down to help Nico, who ignored him and pointed at me. "You!" he wheezed. "You're that witchy chick from the mall. What are you trying to do, kill me?" He staggered up and tried to limp away. "Is that why you gave me the Death card?" He turned to Jamie. "She gave me the Death card."

"I'm not trying to kill you," I said. "Quit acting like a baby."

"Acting like a baby? You hit me with your car!"

"No, I didn't," I said. "I mean, I did, but it was an accident." I turned to Jamie. "He ran out in front of me. You saw him, right?"

"Mr. Battaglia," Jamie said. "I thought we were going to talk."

Nico glowered at Jamie. "I suddenly remembered a previous engagement." He turned to leave.

"It'll have to wait," Jamie said, and glanced at me. "Otherwise I'll need to write you a citation for leaving the scene of an accident."

Nico looked at him, then at me. "Aw, come on. I'm not even hurt. She barely touched me."

"Oh, now I barely touched you?" I cried. "How about the Death card?" I wobbled my fingers at him. "Woo!"

"Katie, get in your car, please," Jamie said.

It was safe to say my car had lost its battle with the lamppost. The entire right-front corner looked like a rhino had used it as chewing gum. When I tried to start it, it gave a sad whine and died. I dialed the guy who fixes my car, wishing my phone had a category besides Favorites for numbers you hated calling but did all the time anyway.

Across the lot, Jamie and Nico were talking. Correction: Nico was talking, shuffling, waving his arms, and clutching his gut. Jamie was listening to him in that way he had that was somehow chill and intense at the same time. I paced, inching closer to them with each pass until Jamie shot me a warning look. I plopped down on a curb, watching the pair out of the corner of my eye, shuffling the deck. I pulled one card after another, but my mind was roiling and they showed me only image after image of discord and confusion—the Eight of Wands, the Two of Swords, the Moon.

Finally, Jamie and Nico shook hands. Nico went to his truck, giving me a wide berth. Jamie walked over and sat down next to me. "You okay?" He glanced at my forehead. "You're looking at a pretty good bruise."

"Now I finally get to say 'You shoulda seen the other guy.'" I touched my forehead and felt a small, sore lump. "Well? What did he say?"

"Nothing much, yet. I'm meeting him at the station." Jamie watched BEAST 25 sweep past us and out onto Lake Street. He turned to me. "Off the record, did you hit him on purpose?"

"Off the record, were you really going to give him a ticket for ditching an accident?"

Jamie gave me his almost smile. "I owe you one," he said.

"I'd say you owe me more than one." I nodded at the tow truck pulling up to my trashed car. "How about a ride home?" Jamie gave me a gracious nod. "*After* you take me to the station and talk to Nico."

Jamie gave me a skeptical look.

"I'll stay out of the way, all right? Just tell me later what he said." I shrugged. "I was going to take the bus, so I'd be waiting anyway. You owe me a little air-conditioning."

Jamie looked like he was about to either laugh or scream. "Deal," he said.

"Good." I wanted to tease him more about magically finding time for something he was supposed to be too busy for, but he was staring across the street. I followed his gaze. Sunlight flashed across the reservoirs of the waste treatment plant—emerald green pools under a pink-and-violet sky.

"You're right." Jamie tilted his head. "That is actually kind of nice."

10

There was a half-eaten sheet cake in the police station's break room on a round table surrounded by plastic chairs. A glob of blue frosting shaped like a baby shoe sat on the edge of the cake. The TV blared the evening news for no one.

I waited five minutes after Jamie left to sneak out and look for the interview room, but the station's labyrinth of pus-colored walls defeated me. When I got tired of wandering in circles, I headed back to the break room to drink sour coffee and peruse the self-professed PARTY WALL next to my table, a bulletin board chronicling the LTPD's robust social life. I scanned the wall for Jamie and found him looking shell-shocked in an indoor shot where everyone wore hideous blue T-shirts with elephants on them. The elephants held signs in their trunks reading STOMP OUT CRIME! Behind the group, a whiteboard read, inexplicably, NEW CHOMPER CODE, DO NOT ERASE.

Officer Bailey, depressed bachelor–turned–father of four, walked into the room and headed for the cake. He didn't see me.

"Hi, Officer Bailey," I said. He turned to me, holding a fork. I watched him try to figure out how he knew me. "I'm Katie. We met yesterday. Right before your wife had the baby." I took my feet off the chair across from me. "How is the baby, by the way?"

"Great! Thanks for asking." He anchored the fork in his piece of cake. Then he came over, sat down, took out his phone, and punched up a thousand pictures of a tiny red-faced squid named Angus. Then he moved on to pictures of his other three kids, narrating each one in his foghorn voice. "Always something with these guys! I get home the other day, find out my eight-year-old shaved my three-year-old's head. Just ass-bald. That kid was not going to win any beauty contests anyway, and now he looks like a fucking bowling ball with teeth." He burst into deep guffaws. "Man, I love those little fuckers. You don't have kids, you don't know dick about life, no offense."

He got up and cut me a slice of cake that I did not ask for but was not stupid enough to refuse. His weepy Three of Swords was morphing before my eyes into the Nine of Cups, a squat grinning dude surrounded by cups brimming with all of life's dainties. He was quite the chatterbox. I wondered if I could pry anything useful out of him.

"You guys have a really nice station here." I looked around at the peeling walls, crusty industrial coffeepot, and screeching fluorescent lighting. "I mean, not that I've seen that many."

"And that is a good thing!"

"So, Jamie and I talked in this conference room last night? It was just past a room with a bunch of desks and a plant in the corner?" I licked frosting off my fork. "Where is that room, anyway? I might have left something in there."

"Jamie!" Bailey mumbled around a mouthful of cake. "Oh, man, what a super guy. Always ready to help out. Like yesterday.

It was my call, but Jamie picked it up for me when Laura went into labor."

"Yeah, I remember." Talking to this guy was the conversational equivalent of walking a giant slobbery Saint Bernard. "So about that room—"

"Not much of a talker. Works like a dog. And so serious! We haze the new guys a bit. Ex-lax in the coffee, that kind of thing. And if you let these assholes get to you, they do it even more." He shook his head. "Jamie, though? That guy is like Fort Knox." He chopped his hand in front of his face. "They left him alone after a week."

I paused with the fork on the way to my mouth. "Wait, Jamie's new?"

"Not new-new. He lateraled in from LAPD about a year ago." He scraped his plate for the last bits of frosting. "He's a good guy, but he kind of keeps to himself. I keep inviting him over to meet the family, but he hasn't made it out yet."

Can't imagine why, I thought, remembering a glossy professional shot of Bailey's kids, a gang of glowering boys with identical blond crew cuts and grins showing varying degrees of dental disrepair. "Did you say LAPD? Like Los Angeles?" I couldn't think of a shade-free way to ask why anyone would leave LA for Lake Terrace, Illinois.

"Oh yeah. We couldn't pass him up. You kidding? The guy who caught the Blue Sky Strangler?" He got up and poured himself a Styrofoam cup of coffee. "They were flying out criminal psych experts from all over, and then this hotshot, first time out in Robbery-Homicide, gets the guy in nothing flat. You probably heard about it on the news."

I nodded like I spent all my time keeping up-to-the-minute on obscure law enforcement gossip. I was torn between pumping Bailey for more juicy tidbits about Jamie and trying to wrestle him back to the more pressing subject of the interview room.

"If I had a job with the LAPD, I'd hang on to it like a fucking piranha, you ask me," Bailey said, echoing my earlier thoughts. "But I heard something about a shooting he was involved in." He shrugged. "Shit happens, you know?"

He came back to the table, stirring the cup with a plastic straw. "Hey, that guy ever turn up, the one who broke into the house? Heard them on the radio saying they spotted him."

"Jamie's talking to him right now." Perfect segue. "Probably in the same room I was in last night. I thought maybe—"

"Nah, he's got him in the Box. I just heard Jamie in there. Didn't know that's who he was talking to."

"The Box." I sat up. "That sounds so cool. Like something from a TV show."

"Oh yeah." Bailey puffed himself up like a peacock. "It's got the one-way glass and everything."

"Wow! I have always wanted to see that." I dropped into a conspiratorial whisper. "Any chance I could sneak a peek?"

"Sorry, little lady, not when it's *ocupado*, know what I mean?" He knocked me off-balance with a shoulder cuff. "I'd show you, but then I'd have to feed you to the Chomper!"

I took a huge bite. "What is this Chomper I keep hearing about?"

"That's what we call the door to the inner station, where the Box and the cells are." He downed his coffee and got up. "It is the heaviest goddamn thing. You punch in the lock code and run through it like hell if you want to keep your limbs. Had a guy a few years back got his foot stuck in it—chomp! Eighteen stitches."

I stopped chewing and went still. *Lock code.* My eyes itched to glance at the bulletin board, but I glued them to Bailey and swallowed the glob of cake.

"Jamie told you about the Chomper, huh?" Bailey said.

"Yeah. Yep. He . . ." I sneaked a glance at Jamie's beleaguered face in the STOMP OUT CRIME photo. "Yes, he did." I shot up from the table, jittery with excitement but trying to look like I had to pee. "Say, this has been real nice, but do you think you can point me to the bathroom?"

"Sure thing! Down the hall, make two lefts and a right." He tossed his coffee cup in the trash. "If you get to the Chomper, you've gone too far."

I gave him a huge smile and hurried out. "Not likely," I muttered.

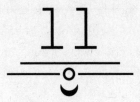

11

Bailey was not kidding about the Chomper. It was a bitch to drag open and slammed shut the instant I sneaked through. I gave a quick mental thanks for his warning, and for the code still being current. And for the empty hallway on the other side. It was really a gift sometimes, not to think too hard about everything that could go wrong before you did something stupid.

The hallway beyond the Chomper was a twin of the one I had just left, empty, with doors on either side. One door had voices leaking from behind it, so I squeezed it open and crept in, trying to keep the light out. Inside was a dark room with a wall-size window in the middle looking into another tiny room lit by buzzing fluorescent lights.

In the inner room, Jamie and Nico sat across from each other at a foldout table. Jamie had his chin propped on his elbow, listening to Nico, who looked like he hadn't stopped talking since the Ref's Whistle parking lot. I scrunched in close to the window so I could hear over the humming lights.

". . . saying some wackadoo shit. Wackadoo stuff, excuse me," Nico was saying. "Stuff like she could see the future, and I was going to die." I growled under my breath. I never told the idiot he was going to die. I hoped Jamie would skewer his lying ass.

Nico stopped to take a gulp from a Styrofoam cup. The edge looked like it had been chewed. "I don't think she was playing with a full . . ." He snapped his fingers, groping for the word.

"Deck," Jamie filled in.

"Deck. Not playing with a full deck, if you catch my drift." Nico looked around the room.

"I think I do." Jamie shifted in his chair. "But I was hoping you could help me out with something else." So genial about it, like Nico was doing him a favor. "We've got a couple of people who saw you last night at"—he checked the notepad in front of him—"8436 Maplewood Lane. You remember being there?"

Nico blinked. "Oh yeah, yeah, that was me." He clapped his hand on the table like he had just remembered a good story. "That's where my girlfriend lives. I went there to pick up some of my stuff."

Jamie nodded agreeably. "Do you have a key?"

"I do," Nico said, nodding in time with Jamie as if hypnotized. "I mean, I did, but I couldn't find it. At the time." He ran his hands through his hair. "I broke the lock. Someone saw me, huh? I must've looked like I was trying to rob the place."

Jamie joined him in a short laugh. "Yeah, the neighbors called us." Nico opened his mouth, but Jamie cut him off. "What were you looking for?"

"What was I looking for?" Nico settled back in his chair. "Oh. My gym bag. I forgot it there."

"You work out, huh?" Jamie said. "I can tell. You're in great shape, man."

"Yeah, you know." Nico looked wary. "I take care of myself."

"Where do you work out?"

"Chicago Body Pros."

Jamie whistled. "Hard-core. Isn't that the place what's-his-name owns? The old Bears quarterback? I wouldn't last a week at that place."

"You work out, too?" Nico perked up.

"Yeah, at that place on Milwaukee, what's it called . . . ?" Jamie closed his eyes and frowned.

"XSport?"

"XSport, that's it. I've got to tell you, though, the biggest work-out I get is writing the membership checks every month."

They both laughed. I might have made a retching noise. Jamie's eyes flicked toward the window.

"Of course, you've got to keep in shape, with the work you do," Jamie said.

Nico stopped laughing. "What do you mean?"

"You said you also work part-time for Battaglia Bros. Moving and Hauling." Jamie checked his notes again. "Guessing there's a family connection there?"

"Oh yeah." Nico relaxed. "My uncles got a little business. Built it from the ground up, years ago, down in the city. They got a second place now, up in Gurnee."

"Doing good for themselves, huh? Love to hear it." Jamie had smiled more in the last five minutes than he had since I'd met him. "What do they have you doing?"

Nico stiffened. "Nothing too big. Just driving or moving stuff. You know, when they need a little extra muscle." He picked up his cup and drank noisily. "We do office moves, residential, junk hauling, stuff like that. Deliveries."

"Deliveries," Jamie said. "Of what?"

Nico blinked. "All kinds of stuff." He took a savage chomp on the cup and a hunk came off in his teeth. He stared at it then tossed it onto the table. "You know. Whatever people need." He started talking faster. "We work all over. We got customers in Waukegan, Gurnee, Grayslake. We go as far north as Wisconsin."

Jamie stared at him.

Nico turned pink and manhandled his hair. "I'll tell you what they *don't* have me do, though, is answer the phones in the front office, you know what I mean?"

Jamie waited a beat. "So your girlfriend. Marley," he said. "Where'd you guys meet?"

"Marley? Oh. At the gym." Nico took a breath and slumped in his chair. "Where else, right? I'm over there in the corner one day doing squats, got my pods in, I'm in the zone. And then I just see this flash of red hair. She's lifting on an inclined bench, and she's got the weight set really high, kind of a lot for a girl, but she's killing it, you know? I look over there again and I can see she's got her hands too close together on the bar. She is about thirty seconds away from blowing out her pec minor." I wondered what the hell a pec minor was.

"Ugh," Jamie groaned. "Had a buddy of mine do that once. That is not good."

"Right?" They made some man-noises. "So I go over there, and I'm like, 'Hey, I don't mean no disrespect, but can I show you a way to do that where you won't end up in the hospital?' And she laughs. I mean, I'm a funny guy. And it just kills me when a girl has a sense of humor, you know? So she says, 'Okay, tough guy, show me what you got.'"

Nico straightened the collar on his Ref's Whistle shirt. "So I showed her how to do it, and we got to talking, and then I started seeing her there all the time. I said, 'Are you spying on me or something?' And she was like, 'Yeah, you wish.' She was so funny, man." He stopped talking, and his smile faded.

Jamie waited.

"She was older than me, but that was okay." Nico was talking quietly now. "Not really my type, with that weird hair and all that jewelry and stuff. And real smart, too." Nico glanced at Jamie. "I mean, that's cool, I can handle a smart girl." He tugged at the gold chain under his shirt. "She was always, like, really interested in me. You know how most girls are, in one ear and out the other and then back to *me, me, me*." He flushed and his eyes twitched. "But she wasn't like that. She asked questions. She remembered stuff." I imagined Marley listening to Nico's harebrained ruminations on manhood and pec minor blowout stories, the way she used to listen to me. Either she was one of those rare people who found everyone interesting, or I wasn't as interesting as I thought I was.

"It was like opposites attract, you know? We had so much in common. Like, one time we were hanging out and this old song came on, 'I'm Not in Love,' and I was like, 'This is my favorite song,' and she was like, 'Me, too!'" His face fell. "It was kind of our song."

I shoved my fist into my mouth. *Marley?* The same Marley who had broken some dude's teeth in a Circle Jerks mosh pit?

Jamie must have looked skeptical, too, because Nico said, "I know, right?" He snorted. "I told her, 'Are you listening? The dude is not in love.' But she explained to me how if you kind of look under the surface, he *is* in love." He sat back in his chair and his eyes went soft.

Then he made a strangled noise, put his large head down on the table, and began to weep.

Jamie waited. Then he reached for a box of tissues and set it in front of Nico.

Nico lifted his head, yanked a tissue out of the box, and blew his nose loudly. "I didn't kill her," he said.

"But you know who did," Jamie said, not missing a beat.

"No, no, I don't." Nico started to cry again. "If I did, that son of a bitch would be dead by now." He ripped the crumpled tissue in two. "You'd have to lock me up for real."

"When was the last time you saw her?"

"Last Thursday night. At the warehouse. My uncles' place. She helped us out sometimes."

"You remember anything unusual happening that night?"

Nico's face crumpled with fresh tears. "We, uh . . . I guess you could say we had a falling-out." Aha. So at least the dumping had proceeded as planned.

"I'm sorry to hear that," Jamie said. "What did you fight about?"

"It wasn't a fight exactly." Nico looked down. "I just . . . found out some things." Shiny tears rolled down his cheeks. "It turned out she'd been lying to me all along. About everything." The last word was a rough whisper. Nico swiped at his eyes with a meaty hand, like he was trying to erase the memory.

Shivers wound down my spine. Something didn't match up. Who had dumped who?

Jamie tapped the desk with his pencil. "And you never talked to her again?"

"I kept calling, but she wouldn't pick up." Nico shivered. "So I went to see her at work. She works at this weirdo place at the old mall, where they sell all this devil stuff." He shook his head. "But she wasn't there. The little dude who runs the place said she quit." He huffed in annoyed surprise. "She didn't tell me nothing about quitting." *That makes two of us,* I thought. I was actually starting to feel a little sorry for him.

"So I'm standing there wondering what the hell is going on, and I get this . . ." He fought to control himself. "This text. It was just a photo of her. She was . . ." He closed his eyes, took a breath, and started over. "She was dead." He pointed to his temple. "Shot in the head."

The humming lights got louder, then went quiet again. "Who sent the text?" Jamie said.

Nico shook his head. "I don't know. The number was hidden."

"Would you mind if I took a look?"

"Oh." Nico looked down. "I trashed the picture." He sniffled. "And emptied the trash," he added quickly. He swiped for another tissue and knocked the box on the floor. "I was upset, you know?" He leaned down to recover the box.

"Of course." Jamie gave Nico a grim stare. "What happened after that?"

"I went nuts." Nico gave a hollow laugh. "I ran into a door or something. When I got the text." He pointed to the Band-Aid on his forehead. "Didn't even know it until later. I was just kind of wandering, trying to get ahold of myself, and I ended up in that Russian place where that chick with the cards works." He picked up a new tissue and blew his nose again. "I was so screwed up, I thought she knew Marley was dead. Crazy, right?" He did the loony head twirl on himself.

Jamie folded his hands in front of him. "Why didn't you call the police, Dominick?"

Nico stared down at the tissue. "Like I said, I wasn't thinking straight."

"You were in denial," Jamie said. "It's the first stage of grief."

"Fuckin' A." Nico pointed the snotty tissue at Jamie. "I was totally in denial."

"I get that." Jamie nodded, leaning back in the chair. "So, here's what you're telling me, Dominick. Let me know if I get anything wrong." *Here it comes*, I thought. "You just found out your girlfriend was dead. You were upset. Confused. Possibly scared." Steel flashed in his voice. "And the first thing you thought to do was go to her house and toss the place because you wanted your gym stuff back?" He leaned back in his chair and crossed his arms. "Do I have that right?"

Nico shrank in his chair and his eyes went animal-blank. "I . . . had really bad denial," he stammered.

Jamie made a noncommittal noise. His eyes never left Nico's. "So, did you find it?"

"Find what?"

"The gym bag." Jamie's voice was cool, patient. "Did it ever turn up?"

"No." Nico narrowed his eyes. The shock on his face turned to mulish obstinacy. "I never found it."

The two men stared at each other across the table. The lights hummed and flashed.

"Look, Officer," Nico said. "You want to write me up for break-ing into Marley's house, go ahead. But I didn't take nothing, and I didn't kill her. I was never going to kill her." He tossed the sec-ond tissue on the table. "So if there's nothing else, I'd like to go home." He sniffed. "I've had kind of a rough few days, if you catch my drift."

———

When Jamie walked into the break room, I was back in my spot at the table, pretending I hadn't just hauled ass across the station.

Lights were turning on in the parking lot, filtering through the blinds in pale, dusty streaks. The news was over and the TV was showing an infomercial featuring a food processor that looked like a large sex toy.

Jamie walked to the coffee station and stood there, staring at the pot. He poured himself a cup, brought it to the table, and dropped into the chair across from me. He had dark circles under his eyes. I thought about Bailey saying he worked all the time.

"How'd it go?" I said carefully.

"You tell me," he said. "How'd you make it through the Chomper, anyway?"

"I don't know who's more full of shit, him or you. You're just better at hiding it." I crossed my arms. "Do you really work out at the XSport on Milwaukee?"

A flash of light in his eyes. "I didn't even know there *was* an XSport on Milwaukee."

"I have to say, I did not see the waterworks coming," I said. "Was he faking it?"

Jamie shook his head. "He doesn't have the acting chops. That was real. He didn't kill her." A silver-haired guy in uniform walked in, got coffee, and left. Jamie watched him. "I wouldn't call him squeaky-clean, though. Did you see him when I asked about the family business?"

I liked how he said that, like he was counting on me to pay attention. "He about soiled himself. What do you think they're into?"

"Stolen electronics. Counterfeit luxury goods. Drugs. Who

knows?" Jamie shrugged. "Whatever it is, it's not just moving and hauling." *If you catch my drift,* Nico added in my mind. "How does a guy who works part-time at the Ref's Whistle and lifts a few boxes for his uncles afford Chicago Body Pros? That place is all fifty-year-old Silvergrove guys in Maseratis."

I knew the guys he was talking about. I'd seen them driving around the neighborhood when I was a kid—fit, good-looking older guys in expensive sweats who hosted weekend beer bashes for their high school kids so they could get next to teenage girls. Nico would definitely be the oddest duck in that flock . . . and Marley would be even odder. Was she there to hook up with rich dudes? If so, why would her arrow stop on Nico? Every logical path I tried to follow hit a brick wall.

Jamie stirred his coffee. "Whatever they're doing, it looks like Dominick dragged your friend Marley into it, too."

My friend. I felt a stab of guilt from earlier. "I'm not sure *dragged* is the right word," I said. "I saw Marley that day. Thursday. She told me she was going to break up with Nico, but she made it sound like he was the one hiding stuff from her, not the other way around. She said he was a thief."

"And he called her a liar." Jamie shrugged. "Breakup stuff. He said, she said."

"I think it was more than that," I said. "Something else happened that night." I filled him in on Marley's plans to jet off to the Caribbean.

Jamie rubbed his chin. "You think *she* was the thief? It would certainly explain why he was looking for this alleged 'gym bag' at her house."

"No way," I said. "The one thing I know for sure is that she hated stealing. Her dad went to prison for it, and it kind of traumatized her." I watched steam rise from Jamie's coffee. "I think maybe she and Nico had some agreement or deal, and it didn't turn out how either of them planned."

"She didn't plan to die, that's for sure," Jamie said. The plastic straw went around and around. "Dominick said something weird at the end. Did you catch it? He said, 'I didn't kill her, and I was never going to.' Like he was *supposed* to kill her. Or he knew someone else was." He picked up the straw, shook it off, and folded it in two.

The infomercial ended and a crime drama with sneaky music flashed onto the TV.

"I'm going to send a couple of techs out to the mall," Jamie said. "Just in case there's still something out there." He drained his cup and looked up at the TV screen. "We're swamped right now, and this isn't even an official case." He crumpled the cup, tossed it at the trash, and sunk it in one smooth shot. "But now you got me hooked."

I had him hooked. I knew I wasn't supposed to take that personally, but I did anyway. Someone screamed, and I flinched, but it turned out to be the wife being murdered on TV by her husband while she folded shirts in the laundry room. A flash into the past: now the wife was stirring an evil-looking white powder into the husband's morning coffee. Another flash, and then another, back and forth, layers of guilt, one on top of another.

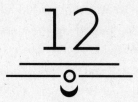

12

By the time Jamie drove me home it was almost eight-thirty, and the sugar high from the cake was wearing off. I was tired and jumpy at the same time.

I thought Jamie would pull up in front of the main entrance to my apartment building, but he parked in guest parking and turned off the car. "I'll walk you in," he said.

We stopped at the front door. "Thanks for letting me stick around today." I was trying to think of a way to invite him in that wasn't creepy or dumb. Jamie said something, but it was drowned out by the screech of the Pizza Pandemonium car pulling into my parking space. The usual sweaty delivery guy jumped out and yanked a giant stack of pizzas from a warmer case.

"Apartment 1B, right?" He thrust the stack at me.

"All of them?" I struggled to keep the pizzas upright and Jamie stepped in to help me. "Who ordered pizza?"

The pizza guy looked at me like I was a five-year-old asking him why the sky was blue. "It's paid for," he grumbled. Then he got in his car and peeled away.

Jamie helped me get the pizzas inside the building. When we opened my apartment door, a sour stench smacked me in the face, making my eyes water and my nose itch. I stumbled in and Jamie followed me, politely wrinkling his forehead.

Owen was perched on the armrest of the couch, typing. He was wearing a pair of worn tighty-whities and nothing else. The TV was tuned to one of the classic movie channels, blasting the screechy opening music of *Psycho*. Owen looked up. "Hey," he said, and kept typing.

I threw Jamie a glance and turned back to Owen. "I have some questions," I shouted over the TV.

"What?" Owen tore himself away from the screen. I watched him struggle to make sense of our facial expressions. "Oh. Yeah. It's formaldehyde. I spilled some on myself at the lab." He motioned to a pile of clothes in the middle of the floor. "It's okay, my brain has habituated to it. I can't smell it anymore." He bent back to his work, then glanced up again. "Your brain will habituate, too." Then he saw the pizza. "Oh, good, dinner's here." He hopped up from the couch, marched up to Jamie, opened the top pizza box, took out a slice, and started chewing.

"Owen!" I said.

Owen looked back and forth between us. "Do you guys want some, too?"

By the time the lady in the movie drove off with the money, my living room looked like the site of a great cheesy massacre. Owen was right—no one remembered or cared anymore that the apartment smelled like a mortuary. I kept stealing glances at Jamie, shocked each time to find him stretched out on the far end of the couch, leaning on his elbow like someone had loosened the strings that held him together all day. This morning I didn't think I was going to see him again. My brother's gross inability to estimate food had finally come in handy.

Owen's favorite commercial came on, the one where the old couple travels the world holding hands and gazing into each other's eyes because they've invested wisely. Owen put down his slice of pizza, planted himself inches from the TV, and burst into a high, clear, pitch-perfect rendition of the commercial's background song.

> See the pyramids along the Nile,
> Watch the sunrise on a tropic isle

Jamie sat up. "That is incredible."

"He sang before he talked," I said. "We had this game. I would start singing, and because I'm generally acknowledged to be the worst singer in the family, Owen would join in just to shut me up. It was pretty useful when he got dysregulated and we needed to calm him down quickly." I glanced at Owen, swaying in front of the TV. "Sappy love songs are his specialty. Remember 'I'm Not in Love,' Marley and Nico's song? He does a pretty great version of that one."

Owen's eyes were closed and if you didn't know better, you might believe he was pining for someone lost across the ocean. Jamie cocked his head, watching Owen. "What do you think he's seeing right now?"

"I think he's seeing himself singing," I said.

The commercial ended and the movie lit the room again with its soft white glow. Owen hopped over the milk crates and back onto the couch. He picked up his slice of pizza and took a huge bite, staring at Jamie. I stayed sharp to head off any surprise poking or sniffing. Owen liked to explore with all his senses.

"Are you married?" Owen asked Jamie.

"Owen." I elbowed my brother in the ribs.

"It's okay," Jamie said. "No, I'm not married." He was watching Owen with a sort of dreamy indulgence. They seemed equally taken with each other. Earlier, after we settled the initial pizza confusion, Owen got in Jamie's face like a curious toddler and started leading him around by the elbow, chattering about school and work. Then he plunked Jamie down in front of the phylogenetic tree he had programmed on his laptop to bloom with every living organism on Earth. I knew by now Jamie was a genius at faking interest, but he had watched the tree for a long time, the screen branching in front of him into luminous birds and fish.

"Why aren't you married?"

Jamie considered the question. "Because being married to a cop sucks," he said. "And the women I spend time with are smart enough to know that." The way he said *women*. These were women with functioning cellphones who read the news and managed to keep their hair neat all day long. I smoothed the disheveled mop on top of my head and hid my chewed-up fingernails.

"Don't you want kids?" Owen pressed.

"You don't have kids, you don't know dick about life," I said. "According to Bailey."

"So I've heard." Jamie linked his hands and turned them inside out for a long stretch. "Did you get the baby slideshow, too?"

"I did, along with some pro tips." I stopped the top pizza box from sliding off the milk crate. "Don't leave your coffee lying around in the break room."

Jamie's cellphone rang. He excused himself and stepped out the front door.

"What are you doing?" I whispered to Owen. "You can't just ask people stuff like that."

"Why isn't he married?" Owen said. "He's of above-average intelligence. Gainfully employed."

"You sound like Mom."

"His face is unusually symmetrical." He balanced on his knees on the armrest of the couch, still holding the slice of pizza. "Did you notice that?"

"No, I didn't. I haven't tried to fold his face in half." I glanced at the door. "Didn't you say the power came back on at your place?"

The door opened and Jamie came back in. Owen fell off the armrest and dropped the pizza on his chest. Jamie stepped around him and sat back down. Owen popped up next to him. "Who was that?" he asked.

"The tech team," Jamie said absently. On the screen, the lady was arguing with a cop in mirrored shades. Jamie stared at them blankly, watching some private movie in his own head.

Owen stood up, tossed his half-eaten pizza slice back into the box, and wiped his hands on the oversized sweats I'd given him. "Okay, good night." He walked into the bedroom and closed the door.

Jamie turned to look after him. "Was it something I said?"

"Nah, he was just done. His meter was full." I hiccupped. "Don't worry, he liked you. Not everyone gets to see the tree, you know."

"The tree was pretty amazing." Jamie broke into one of his rare smiles, and it knocked a hiccup out of my face. "You guys seem close."

I was dying to ask him what the tech team said, but something in his voice stopped me. He looked lost in some dusty corner of his past, and I didn't want to pull him out of it. I wanted to ask if he was an only child, but I wasn't sure I had the same nosiness pass as Owen.

"He drops in whenever, and I can't get rid of him for days," I said. "Other times I don't see him for months." I shrugged. "It's cool. He has a narrow attention window and it kind of opens and closes without warning. I don't take it personally."

"You're lucky," Jamie said. I wondered what he heard in what I had just told him. He gestured to the destroyed pizza. "Thanks for letting me crash your party."

"Thank *you*. I wish you'd been here for the great Bundt cake debacle of '15."

Jamie looked around, taking in my rickety secondhand bookshelves, the sun-faded *Song of the Lark* print, last night's dirty plates still on the counter in the kitchen. "Have you lived here long?" *In this shithole?* I added automatically, then told myself to stop it. Jamie looked relaxed and happy. He wasn't trying to bait me. The judgment was coming from inside the house.

"I've been here about eight years." I squirmed on the couch, and a wistful reminder of fried meals past drifted out. "After I couldn't afford to live in the city anymore."

"And you've been working at the mall since then?"

"Ha! You are grossly overestimating my ability to hold down a job. Let's see, there was the tarot place in the city, you already knew about that. After I moved up here there was the shoe store, the car dealership . . ." I scrunched up my face, trying to remember. "The heavy machinery sales company. The year-round Christmas store." I brushed a cluster of crumbs off my knees. "That one was actually not bad. Too bad the owner got busted for child porn."

Jamie flicked away a lock of hair that had busted out of its gel prison. "You ever think about starting your own place? To read cards?"

My muscles went stiff. He had such a bright, generous look on his face I felt sorry for him. He thought he was paying me a compliment, not shining an industrial-size floodlight on my failures. When Marley had poked at this particular sore at Lake Ruby, I'd been too drunk to care, plus I knew that she—in a good way— didn't give a shit one way or the other. Jamie, like me, hadn't earned his nosiness pass yet.

"That's a really good idea." I made my voice thoughtful and chipper, but it came out sounding like I was stuffing meat through a grinder. "I don't think it would fly around here, though. If you have your own therapist, personal trainer, and life coach, you probably don't need a psychic." I folded my arms and glowered at the screen. Out of the corner of my eye I watched Jamie wonder who the surly teenager was who had suddenly appeared next to him.

"Okay, your turn." I tried a ham-fisted subject change. "Worst job ever. Go."

"This is only my second one." He shrugged. "I've only ever been a cop."

"You're kidding." I turned back to him. "Did you work in high school?"

He shook his head. "I did the Explorer program. It's a volunteer thing for kids who want to be cops. My parents were horrified." He caught my curious look. "Nice Jewish boys don't become cops." He brushed pizza crumbs off his shirt. "I'll never forget my graduation from the academy. My dad came up to me and said, 'Well, you'd better be good at this.'" He pursed his lips. "Not congratulations, not good luck, just"—he raised his hand, flat, to eye level—"here's the bar."   ·

The card wheel spun in my head and spit out cards, one by one: Knight of Wands, Five of Cups, Six of Swords. *Inspiration, Disappointment, Perseverance.* I searched Jamie's face for clues about what it felt like to know, early and for dead certain, who you were. Even when no one around you agreed.

"How come you left LA?" I blurted out, and immediately cursed myself.

Jamie turned away, as if from a sudden blast of cold air. "It was just time for a change," he said, watching the screen. I stared at him, wondering if I should apologize, although I didn't know for what. Now there were two surly teenagers sitting on the couch. On TV, the lady and the nice young man who did not seem stabby at all were talking about getting stuck in their own private traps.

"Do you want a beer?" I asked Jamie. The thought of beer kind of turned my stomach ever since the Red Dog night, and I wasn't even sure I had any. I just wanted to clear out the last vapors of whatever had quietly exploded in the room.

"Sure." He gave me an unreadable look. "Thanks."

I got up and went into the kitchen. "So what did the tech team say?"

He raised his voice over the TV. "They didn't find anything at the dumpster."

"Nothing at all?" I stuck my head in the fridge and rooted through ancient bottles of salad dressing and mustard.

"No body, obviously. No blood, no signs of a struggle. No drag marks, no gunshot residue. Nothing you wouldn't expect to find in a dumpster." He sat up and closed the lid on the pizza box nearest to him. "It was a slim chance anyway, big outdoor area like that."

"But we know she was there." I poked my head out of the fridge and pointed at the necklace around my neck.

"Doesn't mean she was murdered there." Jamie stood up and gathered the empty pizza boxes. "The photo could have been faked." He squeezed past me and stacked the boxes on the counter in the kitchen.

"Can you search her house?" I fished an ancient MGD out of the vegetable crisper and paired it with some ditzy blackberry thing my sister once brought over. "Find whatever Nico was looking for?"

"Not until we hear back from the landlord." Jamie shook crumbs off his hands and stared into the garbage like he was looking for clues. "Trying to solve a murder without a body is like doing a jigsaw without the box. Most departments won't even touch something like this." I dug in a drawer for a bottle opener, strategically blocking Jamie's view of the chaos inside. He thanked me for the opened beer and went back to the couch.

The living room was dark now, pulsing with white TV light. I crossed the room to pull back the blinds and expose the patio door. The lady in the movie was having problems. She wasn't sure anymore that she wanted to keep the money. She looked pretty and sad. I made my face sad, wondering how actors did it, faking things that were supposed to be uncontrollable.

"What we need is Marley's real name," Jamie said. "Then I could run her through the system, check for priors."

I choked on a gulp of wine cooler. The sweet bubbles burned my throat and I bent over coughing. "Marley wasn't her real name?" I squeezed out, turning to Jamie.

"There's no Marley Callaghan with her parameters in the system. No driver's license, no social, nothing." He swished his bottle and watched the beer glitter inside. "It's an alias."

The beads of the draw chain dug welts into my fingers. No wonder my Google stalking had come up empty. I just figured

Marley was a technophobe; it never occurred to me she was using a fake name. *When I was dancing at the clubs,* Marley told me, *there was always some guy trying to get my real name.* The ugly twist in her smile. *I'm not your girlfriend, dude. We're not even friends. I'm just here for the cash.*

But she was working then, right? Hustling an extra buck out of some sad sack with more money than brains? I had no money. I was nobody. I had nothing for her to hustle.

My fingers traced the necklace, looking for exits in the maze of beads. There was a break in the clouds, a black fragment of sky with stars wheeling through it. You thought you were standing still, until something punched a hole in your wall and you realized you were spinning through space at a thousand miles an hour. If she didn't actually like me, what was in it for her to keep hanging around? Why would she look for me on her breaks? Take me where she took her high school friends? Push me, when no one else did, to *keep doing what you're doing*?

The gap in the clouds moved off and the sky went still again. No. Whoever she was, she was my friend. Nothing else made sense.

"It was there for a reason," I mumbled.

"What was?" Jamie said behind me.

"The necklace." I had forgotten he was there. "I just had this feeling. This hunch, when I picked it up, like it was there for me to find."

"You think she left it there intentionally?"

"I don't know." I turned to Jamie. "But I want to find out." That's what you did, right? For a friend in trouble? You helped. Even when they were beyond help.

Blood swirled through the shower, and the black circle of the drain rose to fill the TV screen. The room went dark. Jamie drained his bottle and got up. On TV, the worst had already happened, and now the air was full of loud, emotional questions. "Make a list," he said. "Anything she said that might lead us to her identity."

I gave him an arch look. "Us?"

He grinned. "I'll help you when I can." He went to the kitchen and put his bottle in the sink. "But you have to promise me something. No more chasing people. No more walking into strange houses. No stakeouts." He leveled a clear, steady look at me. "You are not a cop. Leave the police work to me."

After Jamie left, I lay awake on the couch, staring into the dark. Marley's necklace was on the milk crate next to me. Up close, the spade looked like the shadowy slope of a mountain.

I picked up my phone. It was dying again, beeping and popping up frantic boxes begging me to plug it in. I ignored it and checked my email, trashing for the third time a blast from the LTHS alumni association about my upcoming ten-year high school reunion. Then I dragged the email out of the trash again because you never know.

I opened a browser and typed *Blue Sky Strangler* into the search box. A dozen links popped up—the *LA Times*, *LA Weekly*, and a law enforcement journal. I found a flashy article with a lot of pictures: a dilapidated house with smashed windows, a mug shot of a dead-eyed guy with long hair, two cops walking the crime scene.

I stopped, then scrolled back to the cops. One was a tall guy in his fifties with dark hair going gray. The other was a young guy, eyes locked away behind sunglasses. The expression on his face landed somewhere between a smile and a snarl. His hands were up, acting out something that had gone south but turned into a great story: *You believe that shit?*

It was Jamie. I looked closer. Same squarish face, same glossy hair, same everything . . . and totally different. If I had passed him on the street, I would have thought, *Who the hell does this guy think he is?*

I typed in *Jamie Roth LAPD.* More Blue Sky Strangler articles popped up, and a more recent one, from a few years ago. "Tragedy at the LAPD," the headline read. I clicked on the link and started reading:

> An early morning raid turned deadly on Tuesday when an LAPD Major Crimes team raided a Cahuenga Pass residence suspected of housing a ring of illegal arms dealers. LAPD Officer Tyler Frank, 28, sustained gunshot wounds that would eventually prove fatal. No other officers were harmed, and five arrests were made. Team lead Detective Jacob "Jamie" Roth was unavailable for comment.

I scanned the rest of the article but it was full of vague news-speak that carefully avoided answering any important questions: Who was Tyler Frank? Were he and Jamie friends? Who shot who? *What happened?* I flipped back to the Blue Sky Strangler photo. The grinning, self-satisfied Jamie in this picture faced death—and worse—every day. What about the death of Tyler Frank was bad enough to make him decide he'd had enough?

My phone trumpeted its death tune and went dark. A white box danced in the air in front of me. Between the smug over-achiever in the picture and the poker-faced ghost that had just left my apartment there was a blank, a break like the split in a flower stem refracted in water. One thing in two places, with no path in between.

13

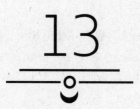

"Is Jamie coming over again tonight?"

I slumped in the passenger seat of my parents' old Subaru Outback with my head against the glass. I had dreamed early this morning that we were late for Marley's funeral because Owen couldn't find his *Star Wars* pajamas. I told him to wear the Lego *Star Wars* ones because really, was anyone going to be looking that closely, but he said, *No, it's a funeral, I need to go more formal.* The funeral was in the courtyard on the Four of Wands and by the time we got there everyone was already drunk, celebrating something big that had just happened or was about to happen. Jamie, in funeral black, passed the beer I had given him back and forth with Aunt Rosie. *Did you check the lighthouse?* Rosie motioned to the red-tipped tower behind her. *Check the lighthouse.* The dream hovered around me like a haze of gnats that Owen kept scaring away with his questions.

"I don't know if Jamie is coming over tonight," I said. "I don't think so."

"Why not?"

I pried my head off the window, leaving a grimy spot. "It doesn't work that way. Trust me." Explaining how to calculate the proper time to hit someone up again after a successful hangout was beyond my articulation abilities right then.

"When are we going to see him again?"

"As soon as I do something stupid or illegal." I rubbed at the grimy spot with my fingers, making it worse. "Don't worry, I'll come up with something."

Owen stopped for a light. I watched cross traffic move through the intersection in slow motion. It was another hot day, overcast and hazy. At least my parents' Subaru, now Owen's, had AC, unlike my car. A pearl gray Lexus slid into the lane behind us. I wondered what their marketing stooges had dubbed that color in the catalog. *Charcoal Mist. Asbestos Sunrise.*

"When is your car going to be fixed?" Owen asked.

"I don't know," I said. "They said they would call me."

"How are you going to get home?"

"Bus."

"How about tomorrow morning?"

"Owen, I don't know! One thing at a time." A rusty Honda pulled up next to us. "Hey," I said out the side of my mouth. "Look over there, but don't look like you're looking over there."

"What?" Owen swung his face to the window with all the subtlety of an industrial searchlight.

"Look at the guy next to us," I said.

"Who?"

"That guy in the gray Honda. It's Kurt Cobain. See him?"

Owen looked at me. "Kurt Cobain died in 1994 of a self-inflicted gunshot wound."

I blinked. "Yeah, I know that, Owen. I'm just saying, doesn't that guy look exactly like him? I see him every morning." Owen looked unconvinced. "Wouldn't it be funny if everyone thought he was dead, but he's actually been working in IT at Abbott all these years?"

Owen frowned. "Don't you think he would find employment more suitable to his talents?"

"Well, that's just it. Maybe he wants a new life. Maybe he doesn't want to do what people expect anymore. Maybe he just wants to sit in a cube and drink shitty coffee and reinstall Windows for people all day long."

Owen thought about it. "Except he wouldn't look the same. He would have aged."

"That is actually a really good point." We passed the sanitation plant and the Ref's Whistle plaza. I peeked into the parking lot, running my fingers along Marley's necklace. Today it had forced me into a short plaid skirt and thigh-high boots I had worn once to a rave.

I tugged on the necklace and it came apart in my fingers. The netting on one side tore and spilled its cargo of black stones and charms into my lap.

"Shit!" I scrambled to gather the broken pieces as Owen stopped for a light. "Shit, shit, shit!"

Owen took the ruined necklace from me and squinted at it. "I can fix it."

"You can?"

"I'll need to take it with me." He handed it back to me as the light turned green. "Is it valuable?"

"Doesn't look like it." I dug a crusty Ziploc baggie out of my backpack and put the necklace in it carefully. "I just like having it around. It's the only thing I have left from Marley."

"So it has sentimental value."

"I guess you could say that." It also, I didn't say, kind of made me feel like a different person when I wore it. Or maybe more myself. I didn't want to blow up Owen's brain trying to explain. "Anyway, thanks." I looked up at the street. "Also, don't forget the mall's torn up at the main entrance. Use the north entrance."

Lake Ruby glided into view, a white sparkle behind dark trees. A small boat prowled the far shore past a small lighthouse-style tower. The dream flashed through my mind again. "Hey Owen," I said. "Are there any lighthouses around here?"

"The closest one is in Waukegan Harbor, 14.3 miles away. Lake Terrace and the surrounding suburbs are completely land-locked." The lake and its lonely little boat disappeared behind us. "Which is why as a sophomore in high school I mounted a cam-paign for student council president, on a platform of changing the yearbook name to something more regionally appropriate." Owen looked at me. "I didn't win."

"They weren't ready for your bold style of leadership," I said. "Anyway, they'd never go for it because they love that LTHS looks like an abbreviation for—" Plug met outlet in my mind, and the light snapped on. I grabbed Owen's arm. "The *yearbook* is *The Lighthouse*."

"That's what I just said."

"Owen, that's it. That's what the dream was trying to tell me!"

"What dream?"

"I had a dream last night that we were all at Marley's funeral and Aunt Rosie was there. She said if I wanted to find Marley, I should check the lighthouse." I tapped my forehead. "I forgot Marley and I both went to LTHS. But my brain remembered."

"I miss Aunt Rosie," Owen said. "Where does she live now, anyway?"

"In California, I think," I said. Rosie also kind of lived in my head. When I thought of her she rolled up as the Star, a skylit naked chick with no use for coverings or disguises, answering to no one but herself, but she also showed up in other cards, flickering through every card in the deck. She *was* the deck. "I miss her, too," I said.

"She smelled funny," Owen said. "Grassy."

"That was grass," I said. "All right, let's think about this." I rubbed my temples. "Jamie said if we knew Marley's real name, he could look her up, see her history. Stuff that would help us figure out who she was and who killed her." I gripped my knees. "I can find her in the yearbooks. *The Lighthouse.*"

Owen frowned. "But you said she was older. She wouldn't be in your yearbooks."

"I can get more yearbooks. The school would have them, or the library. They can't be that hard to find." Owen was showing inadequate enthusiasm for my brilliant idea.

"How do you know which ones to look at? Do you know how old she was?"

I pictured Marley's face. She was one of those women who could be either thirty or fifty.

"And even if you have the right yearbooks, are you going to look at every single picture? What if she doesn't look the same, like Kurt Cobain? This is not an efficient—"

"You know what, stop pissing on my parade! You can't solve every problem before it . . ." I sat up. "Wait, where are you going?" Owen had missed the turnoff to the mall. "Are you going to the Macy's door? I'll have to walk through the whole mall." I hooked a thumb behind me. "Why didn't you take Industrial?"

"Industrial takes you to the west entrance. You said use the north entrance."

"Ugh!" I groaned and waved him into the old public works

parking lot to turn around. "You knew what I meant. Do what I *mean*, not what—"

My stomach leaped. Rounding the turn behind us in the rear-view mirror, dark against the white Lake County fleet cars, was a pearl gray Lexus.

Asbestos Sunrise.

Owen said something, but I didn't hear him. "What did you say?"

"I said I was just doing what you told me," he said. "Are you mad? You look mad. I can't tell."

I glanced at the rearview mirror. The Lexus swung out of the lot, backtracking after us.

"No, I'm not mad." I patted Owen's shoulder. "You did good, Owen."

The power-walking seniors in matching sweat suits were on their second pass of the morning. They rounded the fake tree, passed JCPenney, and headed down the other side of the court. I followed them with my eyes from my perch at the counter. The store had been empty all morning and Larissa was in the back, clackety-clacking at her computer and shouting on her cell in Russian.

By the time Owen dropped me off at the mall, the Lexus had disappeared. I never got a good look at the driver. Now I slumped on my stool in front of the cash register, wondering if I'd been seeing things. Or if I was still rolling around on my stinky couch, trapped in uneasy dreams. I screwed my eyes shut and flung them open. *Is this real?*

I reached into my backpack and pulled out an old Dollar Store receipt and a chewed-up pencil. Owen was right: my yearbook idea, as genius as it had seemed in the car, was too broad. Staring at a thousand tiny pictures of teenagers with acne and bad hair was exactly the kind of giant repetitive task that would defeat my already meager attention span. I bent over the scrap of paper, doing Jamie's assignment from last night: dredging up anything I remembered about Marley that might point to who she was.

Fifteen minutes of pencil chewing and staring into space yielded a modest list:

1. Ukrainian Village
2. LTHS—drama
3. Truck driver
4. Theft—federal—frozen salmon—$5K

It wasn't much. Most of it was stuff I remembered from the night at Lake Ruby, which, even though I was wasted, stood out better in my memory than most of the time Marley and I spent in the dismal courtyard at work. Marley was different that night— sharper, more in focus. Maybe she thought I'd be too drunk to remember anything. I got out my phone and texted Jamie the list, along with a few explanations. He texted back immediately. Perfect spelling, no abbreviations. Definitely no emojis.

A small square sheet of notepaper slid toward me across the counter. There was a drawing of a girl on it, a perky sort of comic book girl with a round face and huge eyes, sitting at a table or desk. A puffy thought cloud hung over her head. In it was a distant castle, tiny flags waving in an invisible breeze. The expression on the girl's face landed somewhere between hopeful and sad. More than anything, she wanted to be somewhere else.

It was me.

I put down my phone and looked up. For a second I thought Nico was trying to pull a Clark Kent, showing up in a suit and glasses and hoping I didn't recognize him. Then I realized the man standing in front of me, with the cute picture and bashful smile, was not Nico. He just had Nico's face.

A silvery warning note chimed in my mind. Like Nico, he was a big guy, and no stranger to the gym. But he was slighter, less obviously pumped. Instead of rumpled sweats, he was wearing a shiny charcoal-gray suit. It fit perfectly and looked like it cost more than my car. His hair was the same dark blond as Nico's, but there were actual elements of style in it, unlike Nico's utilitarian brush cut. He looked like someone had taken Nico, shaken him down into his component parts, and put him back together straighter, sharper, smoothing out the rough edges and erasing the uncertainty and fear. Nico got bounced around like a ping-pong ball by his circumstances, but not this guy. This guy would never get upset enough to walk into a door without realizing it. He wouldn't want to bleed on his suit. He was a pentacle, I thought, slick and down-to-earth; I just wasn't sure yet which one.

Nico 2.0 smiled. "Do you have a minute?" He looked around at the empty store and chuckled. Not in an obnoxious way, but in an inviting *we're both smart enough to recognize irony* sort of way.

"Sure." I smiled despite myself. "Did you draw this? It's really good."

"You like it?" He pushed the drawing toward me. "You looked so thoughtful. I got inspired. Sorry, I hope that's not creepy."

"Yeah, no, it's fine." I stared at his almost-Nico face. The picture was the least creepy part of all this.

"What were you thinking about?" he said.

I glanced over at Stone Blossom, where Max was chatting with a couple of skateboarders. "I was thinking about a friend."

"That's funny," he said. "I was just thinking about a friend of yours, too." He slipped a hand into his pants pocket, rummaged around, and plopped a key ring on the counter, moving it out of the way.

A Lexus key fob sat on the key ring, smooth and black.

The hair on my arms stood up. I didn't imagine it—he *was* following me. My mind raced, trying to remember if I'd seen him anywhere else today. Did he know where I lived? What else did he know? I set my face in a bland, pleasant mask even though every nerve in my body tingled. "Do I know you, Mr. . . . ."

"I'm Joey," he said, like that explained everything. He took out a small notepad and a heavy gold pen and swept the keys back into his pocket. Then he began to sketch in clean, fast strokes. Seconds later, he tore the sheet off the pad and held it out to me.

This one was a drawing of Nico—the real Nico. It was done in that same old-fashioned comic strip style, and eerily accurate, if not very flattering. In this picture, Nico had a heavy, bovine face and blank eyes. He was practically drooling.

Joey leaned on the counter. A wave of cologne rolled off him, sweet and intense. "Do you know him?" he said.

"He came in a few days ago." I pushed the drawing back at him. "Sunday. Right before closing."

Joey blinked and waited. "And that was the first time you ever saw him?"

Great, this again. I nodded. "He said his name was Nico," I added helpfully. "Is he your brother? He looks an awful lot like you."

"Does he?" His smile stayed solid, but his eyes went black, like a blinding floodlight had snapped off, revealing an empty plain stretching off into the dark. I remembered an old science fiction story I'd read as a kid, about a tiny village where evil spirits took

over people's bodies through beautiful, ornate masks. The villag-
ers called the spirits Not Our Brother.

Now he was flashing his bright dental work again, like the car
salesman who is totally on your side and just wants to get you the
best deal. "I'll get straight to the point," he said. "I don't want to
take up any more of your time." He indicated the empty store
again, but the joke didn't land as well this time. "My colleagues
and I are expecting a delivery of some value from Nico, and we
have not received it. He claims to have it in his possession, which
would be encouraging if it were true. But here's the thing. Nico
is . . ." He stared into space, pretending to go off script. "He's the
kind of guy who is always a bit late with *this*, forgets *that*, mis-
places the *other*." He gave me a knowing nod. "He's that guy. We
all know people like that, right?"

I knew people like that, all right. I was one of them.

"We're actually thinking—and I sincerely hope this is not
true—that he might try to keep the delivery for himself." He gave
me a cool stare. "For himself and whoever is helping him."

I was starting to understand, but I played dumb. "What does
this have to do with me?"

"Good question. I'm talking to all his friends, to see if they
know anything about it."

"We're not friends," I said. "We don't know each other at all."
I felt it unnecessary to mention that I had nearly killed Nico with
my car and then watched him spill his guts in a police station
interrogation room.

He was already drawing again, slashing at the paper in fast,
bold strokes. It came so easy to him, so naturally. Like breathing.
He held the new picture up. This one was an outdoor scene. A
house. Marley's house—I recognized its old-fashioned, sagging

layers—and a girl, sitting in a car outside of it, watching a tiny figure go inside.

Tiny icicles danced on my skin. It was me again. He'd even gotten the rust stains on the Fiesta right. He'd been watching me for a long time.

"I was looking for a friend of mine," I said. Out of the corner of my eye, I saw Larissa come out of the back and stand watching us.

"Of course," Joey said. A third picture: Marley, looking hot and malevolent, like an elf queen on the eve of war. "I'd love to get it straight from the horse's mouth." He leaned in close and lowered his voice. "But we both know she's not available."

The icicles on my skin became stabbing ice picks. "Her boss said she quit," I said. "Left town."

He gave me an icy stare. Then he picked up the sketch and ripped it to shreds and tossed the bits onto the counter. Marley's disembodied eye stared up at me.

"You don't have to explain," he said flatly. We were down to it now, the rock-bottom offer. "Like I said, we just want what's ours." He reached into his wallet again and brought out a crisp fifty-dollar bill. "This is just for starters. Whatever your deal is with Nico, we'll top it. No questions asked."

He thought Nico and I were in it together. Whatever *it* was.

"I'm sorry, Mr. . . . Joey." I brushed the torn pieces of paper into the garbage. "I don't know where your delivery is. I don't even know what it is." I slid the fifty back across the counter. "I can't take this."

The floodlight flicked off again and I could see that cold emptiness in his eyes. "An honest person, huh? So rare." He put the notepad away and tapped the fifty. "You keep this. And if you do happen to hear something, give me a call. Day or night." He scrawled a phone number on another sheet, tore it off, and gave it to me. "Don't wait too long." He picked up the fairy-dream drawing of me and crumpled it in his fist. "I wouldn't want you to go out of town, too."

He tossed the little ball of paper past me at the garbage can. It clipped my ear, bounced off the rim, and landed inside, in a pile of receipts and candy wrappers. Joey gave me an indifferent glance and left.

Larissa appeared at the counter. "Who was that?"

"Not Our Brother," I murmured under my breath.

"Hm," Larissa said. "Good suit." She pointed to her face. "But his face wants a brick." She turned around and went back into her office.

I dug the ball of paper out of the garbage and spread it out on the counter, smoothing the little figure's wrinkled face. Then I folded the sheet into a tiny square and slipped it into my pocket. When I was sure Larissa wasn't looking, I picked up the fifty like a dirty sweat sock, stuffed it into the cash register, and slammed the compartment shut.

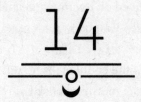

14

The 574 bus was new, with whisper-quiet air-conditioning, padded seats, and air that so far smelled more like pine disinfectant than sweat socks. I was wedged into an aisle seat next to a hipster absorbed in a rapid-fire text convo with his phone sounds turned all the way up. It sounded like volleys of machine-gun fire punctuated by soothing bells. Probably a new relationship. They hadn't started ghosting each other yet.

A gray Lexus pulled up next to the bus, and I sat up. The driver was a bald guy in a pink golf shirt. I sank back into the seat and closed my eyes. Every time I thought about Joey, a musical pounding started up in my head, an idiotic two-tone melody that wouldn't stop and wouldn't let me think. I squeezed the balls of my hands into my closed eyes and waited for the bus to take me home so I could collapse on my bed and stop my brain for a few minutes.

I burst through the door of my apartment, dropped my

backpack, kicked off my shoes, and headed for the bedroom. I just needed five minutes before I went back to worrying about—

I stopped and returned to the living room. Something was off. The pizza boxes on the counter were stacked neatly. I clearly remembered rushing past them on my way out this morning thinking *Cool, I made a ziggurat.* Now the boxes were flush with each other, the way anyone except me would stack pizza boxes.

I slid open the pantry door. The rolls of Life Savers were also in a neat stack, not stuffed in the cracks between everything else. The box of cloth napkins my mom gave me in the hopes that I would develop table etiquette had been opened. Each napkin had been unfolded and refolded. The coat of dust around my stack of ramen noodles had tracks in it.

A jangling pressure rose in my chest, like a force field amping up. My place was a mess, but it was my mess, and I knew it backward and forward. I sniffed the air. There was a sharp, earthy tang winding through it, something foreign but familiar.

That was when I saw *The Song of the Lark* hanging cockeyed on its nail again. Heat rolled through my face. That painting was straight this morning. Someone had come in through the patio door. I swallowed a lump in my throat and picked up the flyswatter.

"Owen?" I bleated. No response.

I crept into the bedroom, although I had pretty much destroyed the element of surprise by then. There was no one to surprise. I flung open the closet door, lifting the flyswatter. No one.

I scanned the room. The cigar box where I kept my collection of crappy chokers and chains had been opened. Everything was still there, but moved around. The pile of headbands, earrings, and miscellaneous junk on my nightstand had been explored.

The explorer had tried—and failed—to put everything back the way it was before.

And yet, nothing was missing. The gold necklace my parents gave me for my high school graduation—the only valuable thing I owned—was still in its velvet box. The wadded-up dollar bills I'd tried to give Owen for last night's pizza binge were still in plain view on the kitchen counter. The only thing missing was . . .

My hands crept to the empty space around my neck. Marley's necklace.

Nothing was missing because what the thief wanted was already gone.

"Boy, they really did a number in here, huh?" the short, round, mustached cop said, looking around my bedroom at the over-turned laundry basket, ruined bedclothes, and boxes spilling from the closet.

I was still holding the flyswatter. "Nah, it's pretty much always like that."

Mustache's partner was this chick Nicole Barton that I had gone to high school with, a girl with a round, bearish face full of freckles and a turned-up nose. She hadn't been super friendly to me or anyone else who lived west of the Metra tracks ever since third grade, when she broke Taylor Privette's wrist for calling Nicole's dad a bum because he'd gotten the family kicked out of subsidized housing for selling weed. I lost track of Nicole after she got expelled for threatening a guidance counselor with a butterfly knife. It was nice to see she'd had a weapons upgrade since then.

Right now, Nicole's tiny eyes were flickering around my

apartment with grim satisfaction. "How about this?" she said, pointing to the mess of bills and junk mail inside my milk crate coffee table.

"Nope, that's been that way for weeks," I said.

Mustache rubbed his chin and adjusted his camera strap. "Can you point us to something that *was* tossed?"

"Well, nothing was tossed, exactly," I said. "It was a reverse tossing. A criminal straightening-up, if you will."

The cops exchanged a glance. "Can you get them back to finish the job?" Nicole said.

"Guys, just do what you can," Jamie said. "Get the jewelry, the pantry, and the back door." He was leaning on the wall next to the fridge, looking at me. I had already filled him in on the Joey situation, and I figured this particular blank, polite expression meant he was worried. Or pissed off. I couldn't tell the difference yet. "Are you okay?" he said.

I nodded and dropped the flyswatter on the counter. He picked it up and hung it on its hook. "What were you going to do with that?" he said.

"I don't know. It was the best I could do. I don't own a frying pan." I plopped down on the couch and put my boots up on the milk crate. I was still wearing my work/rave outfit, which looked weird on me now without Marley's necklace holding it together.

Jamie watched Nicole jiggle the lock on the outer screen door. "How long has that back door been broken?"

"You know, I'm actually not sure it's ever *not* been broken."

Jamie gave me a particularly slow blink.

"Look, if you're going to lecture me, bring your A game," I said. "I can take a lecture like some people can take a punch."

Jamie stared at a stack of expired ad circulars on the kitchen counter. He looked like he was restraining himself from throwing them in the trash. "I don't believe in coincidences," he said. "The same day this Joey guy harasses you at work, your apartment gets tossed?" He circled the kitchen table, arms crossed. "What did he look like?"

"Like Nico's eviler twin," I said. "They've got to be related." I thought of Joey's strained smirk when I suggested as much. "But I don't think they're on the same team."

"They're after the same thing, though," Jamie said. "Did he tell you what it was?"

"No. He was being vague on purpose, to see what I knew," I said. "He didn't know who he was dealing with. Nobody outdumbs me." I took a breath and smelled that odd smell again. Patchouli, maybe, or lavender? It had settled into my nose-brain, and I wasn't sure if I was still smelling it or just a memory of it. I remembered Joey's sickly sweet man-perfume. This was definitely not it.

"Joey didn't do this," I said. "This isn't his style." Joey's neat, bespectacled face floated in front of me. "He crumpled the picture," I added, half to myself.

Jamie looked up from a fridge calendar from May of last year. "What picture?"

I stood up and handed Jamie the wrinkled drawing. He unfolded it and looked at it for a long time. "Is this you?"

I peeked over his shoulder. I barely recognized my own face in the drawing. "The whole time we were talking, he was drawing these cartoons," I said. "Me, Nico, Marley." I pointed to the picture. "He gave me that, and when I didn't tell him what he wanted to hear, he . . ." *I wouldn't want you to go out of town, too.* "He kind of implied I would meet the same end as Marley." It was the first time I had said it out loud.

"Can I keep this?" Jamie said.

I nodded and plopped back down on the couch. "He was try-ing to scare me. But whoever sneaked in here went out of their way *not* to scare me. They didn't even want me to know they were here."

"I'm not sold on your necklace theory." Jamie's latest circuit around the kitchen had deposited him at *The Song of the Lark*. He stared at it for a few seconds, straightened it, and kept mov-ing. "Whatever these guys want, it's obviously valuable." He turned to me. "And that necklace . . ."

"Looks like it cost five bucks at a flea market. Yeah, I know." My hands crept to my neck again, and I held them down. "But it could have sentimental value."

Jamie narrowed his eyes. "Did Joey strike you as a sentimental guy?"

"I meant Nico," I said. "We already know he's a weeper. And he's been known to break into people's houses."

"Dominick turned Marley's place upside down." Jamie ges-tured around the room. "This isn't his style either."

"True. If Nico did this, your friends wouldn't be acting like I just made this whole thing up." Nicole, dusting for prints in the bathroom and pretending not to eavesdrop, gave me a dirty look.

"It could just be some jerk walking around trying doors," Jamie said.

"And not actually stealing anything? Like a big wad of money?"

Jamie picked up the big wad of money. "It's six dollars." He let it fall back on the counter.

"I don't buy it," I said.

Nicole and her partner trooped into the living room with all their equipment. "I think we're done," Mustache said. "There's not a whole lot here."

"Unless you have some carpeting that was mysteriously

vacuumed," Nicole added. Jamie gave them a clipped *Thank you* that meant *Get out*, and they left.

"So, what happens now?" I said.

"We'll send everything out for processing. Don't count on much. I'll find out what Dominick was up to today." Jamie checked his cell. "Does this building have security cameras?"

"*Security* cameras? Sure, let me just call down to the bell captain."

"Well, if nothing else, I have this to work on." Jamie unzipped his messenger bag and produced a stack of paper the size of a Stephen King novel.

"What's this?" I leafed through pages of tiny, dense names, dates, and addresses clumped together into blocks.

"A report of all federal thefts in Illinois over the last thirty years. I need to go through and flag any record where the claimant matches the offender's employer and is also a trucking company." He pointed to the top of the first sheet, at a set of penned numbers so neat they looked typed: 60612, 60610, 60622. "And where the offender lives in one of these zip codes." He looked at my confused face. "Basically, I'm looking for a Ukrainian Village trucker who stole from his company."

My eyes widened. "Marley's dad. Or stepdad or whatever."

"Wait, he wasn't her biological dad?" Jamie said. "That's a problem. I was thinking if we found him, that would give us her last name at least. But they might not have the same last name."

"They do, though." I snapped my fingers, remembering. "She said he legally adopted her so the whole family would have one name." I looked at the pages with a new appreciation. "Once we find her dad in here, then we'll just need her real first name." I hefted the stack. "This is how the magic happens, huh? Through busywork?"

He gave me a wry look. "Welcome to the glamorous world of investigations."

"What if I take a look at it?" I said. "Busywork is kind of my jam." The stack was heavy, and I set it on the table. "I always have a few free hours at work. Or six." My yearbook idea sounded a little junior high bake sale compared to this, and I was itching to get started on something, anything that would lead to Marley. If the report gave me her last name, it would make searching the yearbooks go a lot quicker.

Jamie looked doubtful. "I'm not comfortable letting this stuff float around," he said. "Besides, this"—he gestured around the room—"is getting more complicated than I expected. Now that you've got guys like Joey threatening you, I don't like you getting any deeper into this than you need to." He walked over to the patio door and looked out into the deepening twilight. "Do you have somewhere else you can stay tonight?"

For a second I thought he was inviting me over. I pictured him living in an immaculate new-construction condo by the new mall with rows of neat coffee cups next to a spotless sink and no art on the walls. "You really think it's that bad?"

"I don't know." Headlights from the street flickered over him and moved on. "But whatever this thing is, you're in it now." He turned to me. "I know that much."

My heart sank. I'd been secretly hoping that if Jamie wasn't worried, I didn't have to be either. "I can go stay with my parents," I said glumly. "Or my sister."

Jamie picked up the flyswatter. "Which one is preferable to defending yourself with this?"

"Give me a minute," I said. "I'm thinking."

15

My mom watched me stuff eggs into my mouth. "How long has it been since you've eaten a complete breakfast?" She was eating a grapefruit half from a grapefruit bowl, with a grapefruit spoon.

"I eat a complete breakfast every day. It says so on the box." I picked my face up out of my plate and sniffed the air like a badger. I had forgotten that kitchens can have nice smells like coffee and frying butter, and not just burnt Styrofoam and bug spray.

Jamie had talked me into leaving for the night, and in return I had talked him into parting with the report. *Whatever this thing is, you're in it now.* He had meant it as a warning, but the spike of fear I'd felt when he said it was gone. I felt wired and sizzly, like a circuit had closed inside me. Last night I sat down at the desk where I used to struggle through my homework, under a framed clip from the *Lake Terrace Observer* of an eighth-grade me holding an ugly vase that came in fifth in the Lions Club's art competition. I'll just look through a few pages, I thought, spreading the report over the scratched-up desk. The next thing I knew, it was two in the morning, and I was asleep with my face drool-stuck to the page I was on. I had gone through thirty pages and marked up two names. Now I was sitting in the breakfast nook of my parents' Disney castle house on the west side of town, feeling a queasy mix of nostalgic inertia and spazzy impatience.

"Will you be back tonight?" my mom said. My dad flipped a page in his issue of *Wood*. He ladled spoonful after spoonful of sugar into his coffee cup until my mom took the spoon away from him. My dad owned a small construction business and generally preferred building materials to people. He was a man of few words, most of which got talked over.

"No, I'm good," I said. "There was just . . . some stuff going on in my building and I needed to be out of there." Being vague was okay but lying was out. My mom was VP of sales at FunDamentals (the Fun Learning Toy Company!) and spent her days in joyless meetings with old men debating what constitutes fun and whether or not paranoid new parents would pay $29.99 for it. Her experience with bent truth—on both the giving and receiving end—was not to be discounted.

"You know you can stay as long as you need to, right?" She nodded expectantly, like I was a toddler standing in a pile of broken crockery. *You're not in trouble, okay? I just want the truth.*

"Really, it's fine." I struggled to keep the edge out of my voice. What she was really asking was, did I lose my job again. My parents accepted me as their slightly squished middle child whom they loved but had no expectations for. It was very nice and supportive and smacked a lot of giving up. My sister, on the other hand, had decided she was *not* giving up, but her only solution for improving my life was to plumb the well of my (deeply) hidden talents for selling real estate. I had chosen my parents last night over Jessie because I decided I'd rather be sad than pissed off. "Just waiting for my ride," I said, folding and refolding the napkin in my lap. "And then it's off to work."

"You're still at the gift store at the mall?" My mom got up and filled the electric teakettle on the spotless granite counter. I nodded, my face blazing. "Wow, still?" She crossed her arms and looked proud. "It's been a while. Good for you!"

Ugh. I should have gone to Jessie's. At least her disappointment was all out there in plain English, no translation necessary. "I won't be there forever," I said tightly. "Just until I find something more, you know. Fulfilling." The words tasted sour in my mouth. I'd said them so many times they no longer had any meaning.

"Of course, honey." She didn't believe me. I'd never given her any reason to. She brought two sleek white mugs to the table and put one in front of me. The mugs read *Welcome* in different languages. She hadn't asked if I wanted tea, but watching her go through the familiar motions, I realized I'd never wanted tea so much in my life. When I was a kid she would read to me from *The Snow Queen*, and the part I loved best was when the nice old witch keeps Gerda in her house with her magic flowers and cherries and comb until Gerda forgets that what she wants above all else is to find her beloved missing brother. I was always a little sad when the spell broke and Gerda left the kind old witch all alone again.

I watched my mom wind her tea bag on her spoon and squeeze it out into her cup—exactly three squeezes, always, for as long as I could remember. The Queen of Pentacles, safe and secure. It would've been so easy to give up. To move back here and eat real food and not have to schlep my laundry to the spider-infested basement in my apartment building. Also, to be around people who loved me even when I didn't do much to deserve it. This was the real reason I avoided coming here—not because my family drove me crazy but because I was afraid I might never leave.

Outside the bay window, a fire-red Porsche Cayenne zoomed around the circular driveway. Moments later, the back kitchen door banged open and my sister, Jessie, flew in like a spooked parakeet. It must have been time to update the billboards because she had straightened her hair. It swished around her face in long shampoo-commercial streaks, just quivering to explode into the curly mass Jessie had always hated. My parents greeted her.

"Katie! Hey!" Jessie did an exaggerated double take. "I didn't see your car outside." She gave me a silly pout. "Is it in the shop again?"

"Fender bender," I grumbled. *Just ran over a murderer, NBD.*

"Why didn't you call me?" Jessie handed my mom a bag of evil-looking pikes and tourniquets that were barely recognizable as borrowed cooking equipment. "We would have lent you a car." Her tone was playful and mock-accusing with undertones of deep and lasting resentment. "We still have Mom's old White Camry of Death, remember? It's just sitting there."

"Yeah, I didn't think of that," I lied. Favors from Jessie were carefully tabulated and applied against any future offenses, real or imagined.

"Really, now," my mom said. "It was just a squirrel."

"Plus two sparrows," my dad added. "And a skunk. Want some coffee, Jessieface?"

I didn't think Jessie needed to be in the same room as coffee, but she grabbed a mug and bounced over to the coffeepot. I knew I had mere seconds to change the subject before she recommenced bullying me with her generosity. "How's business?" I asked, knowing I would immediately regret it.

"*So busy!*" Jessie chirped. "Just rocking and rolling." She did a hip-shaking jig that I had to look away from. "We could really use some hee-e-elp," she singsonged. "Next time you . . . next time you're free." *Next time you lose your job*, is what she almost said. "Are you still at, um . . ." She snapped her fingers.

"Firebird Imports," I said. "Still there."

"Oh." She made an *oopsie* face. "Still?" My mom had used the same words, but Jessie's was a completely different question. "What are they, working you to death? You look exhausted. Great big rings." She underlined her eyes. "I've got a cream. You want some?"

I crumpled my napkin and tossed it on the table. "I am a little tired. I was up late last night." I sat up straight. "Working on a project."

Record scratch. Everyone stared at me. My dad put down his coffee cup.

In the triumph-over-adversity epic film I imagined would be made of my life, a glossier, better-dressed version of me creates an artistic word collage out of all the school progress reports describing my persistent failure to focus, stay on task, and generally achieve anything. "Not living up to potential" features prominently. Also "easily distracted," "lacks follow-through," and, my all-time favorite, "catastrophically disorganized," as if thousands would die in a tsunami because I couldn't keep my locker clean. Teachers, guidance counselors, and team coaches were consistently baffled that I showed "profound intelligence" and tested "off the charts," but then "barely scraped by," "gave less than 100 percent," "underperformed," and "literally failed to show up all semester." The word collage would win a prestigious art prize, allowing me to retire and live a life of reclusive genius in a warm place full of colorful birds and weird fruit. (In real life, by the time I found the art supplies and cleared off a workspace, I would be hungry, and after I ate I would probably binge a bunch of space documentaries and fall asleep on the couch.)

The teakettle turned off with a snap that made me jump. "What kind of project, Katieface?" my dad said.

"Oh. It's, well, I'm sort of working with the police on an investigation." My fingers started to tingle. The magic spell was breaking, and suddenly I remembered who I was and what I was supposed to be doing.

"An investigation." My mom knitted her brows. "Is this some kind of volunteer work?"

"Something like that." If sticking my nose where it didn't belong counted as volunteering.

"We had to call the police the other night." Jessie used small silver tongs to pick a slice of coffee cake off a glazed ceramic serving tray. The eye of a huge yellow Mexican folk art sun stared up at us. "We heard screaming, but it was just the Gilberts next door watching TV. One of those crime dramas that's been on forever." She took a bite and dabbed at her mouth with a napkin. "What was the name of it? Ugh, I can't remember."

"Well, that's wonderful, Katie." My mom brought out a wooden box of tea bags. We'd had it for years. When Owen was a kid he liked to open it up, dump the tea bags out, and lick the velvety inside. "Volunteer work is a great way to get your foot in the door." She poured the water in a neat steaming cascade. "I just never figured that police work was"—she glanced at my dad, who was already reading his magazine again—"a door you wanted to get your foot in." My mom sat down and dug at her bowl. A grapefruit-scented mist rose into the air.

The kitchen door slammed open and Owen barreled in, swinging his laptop bag like a battering ram. My mom and Jessie sprang out of their chairs and started talking over each other like the goddamn president had just parachuted in from Air Force One. I dunked my tea bag and tossed Owen a grumpy nod. My mom was already fixing him a plate.

"Oh, good, I'm glad you're here," Owen told me. He rummaged in his backpack and brought out Marley's necklace, all fixed up.

"Thanks, Owen." Now I felt like an asshole for begrudging him my family's slobbering. I slid the necklace around my neck, where it clashed with my outfit in an ugly New York Fashion Week sort of way.

"Oh." My mom tilted her head. "That's . . . an interesting piece."

"How'd you manage to smuggle that out of Dracula's tomb?" Jessie said.

"Dracula does not have a tomb because he is not dead," Owen said. "He sleeps in a coffin during the day to avoid sunlight." He took a monstrous bite of toast. "That belonged to Katie's friend Marley. She traveled around the country working in bowling alleys and fast-food dining establishments until she was murdered last week in the mall where Katie works. Just yards away." He shoved a forkful of eggs into his mouth and grinned. "Katie's trying to find out who killed her."

My mom's spoon froze halfway to her mouth. A slab of grapefruit plopped into her bowl.

"Now, that is interesting!" My dad looked up and brandished his fork at me. "A murder! Right here in Lake Terrace. Isn't that interesting, honey?" He turned to my mom and she glared at him until he looked back down at his plate.

"Why does Owen know all this stuff and I don't?" Jessie said.

"Hey, Owen." I clutched my fork. "Remember how we talked about not saying *everything* out loud?"

"Oh. Right." Owen thought about it. "Because your friend's apparent social status coupled with the danger of involving yourself in a murder investigation might make everyone uncomfortable." He looked very proud of himself for puzzling it out.

"Yeah, like that. That didn't need to be said out loud either."

Jessie clapped her hands and leveled both index fingers at me. "I know this great little start-up that will send hot meals to your friend's family for a week while they're dealing with the funeral stuff." She started rummaging in her giant logo-covered purse. "This woman I do Pilates with started it up when her cousin's husband died." She dropped into the tragedy whisper. "Cancer." The purse disgorged bits of paper that Jessie peered at one by one, then slammed on the table. "It's really taken off for her. Talk about an evergreen market, right?"

"I don't know her family." I took a swallow of tea, shocking and hot and satisfying. "I don't know much about her at all. That's part of what I'm investigating. I'm trying to find out who she was."

Jessie gave an annoyed little huff and started shoving the purse's guts back in. "I thought you guys were friends."

"We were." I stopped there. My relationship with Marley fell into a friendship gray area, and Jessie didn't do gray areas.

My mom placed her spoon on her folded napkin. "Well, it's nice that you want to find out what happened to your . . . friend, but I don't see why the police can't handle it."

"The police don't care," I said sharply. "Not enough, anyway." I picked up the silver tongs and moved a slice of coffee cake off the sun's other eye. The other eye belonged to a dark sleepy moon. "Some part of me knows it's not my place. That I should just let it go." I moved slice after slice out of the way, revealing an arcane celestial smile, half light and half dark. "But I can't." I looked up to see everyone watching me. Even Jessie had stopped molesting her purse. "It just feels like there's something I can do here that no one else can," I said.

Jessie clapped her hands. A slow, warm smile bloomed on her face. "*NCIS*," she said. "Now I remember. They were watching *NCIS*."

A car pulled into the driveway. "There's my ride." Not a moment too soon, or Jessie might have received a piece of coffee cake in the face. I downed the rest of my tea, put my plate in the sink, and gave each of my parents a quick kiss. "Thanks, Mom and Dad. I'll call you later." I fully meant this, and also knew it would never happen. "See ya, Jess. Owen, thanks again."

Owen leaped up and ran to the window. A smile blazed on his face. "Jamie!" he shouted.

"Who's Jamie?" My mom got up and went to the window. I hoped Jamie would just honk instead of trying to come to the door. No such luck. He turned the car off, got out, and headed toward the house, looking even more freshly scrubbed than usual.

"Jamie is a police officer," Owen intoned. "He is not married and has trouble maintaining relationships due to the dangerous and inconstant nature of police work. He has a very symmetrical face."

My mom's eyes grew wide, then narrow. "I can see that." She turned to me. "Well, that clears a few things up."

"What things?" my dad said.

"That is totally unfair," I said. It wasn't. I had a long history of getting absorbed in weird shit for the sake of some dude, as evidenced by the mountains of "gently used" fencing equipment, coin collecting albums, and fusion cookbooks moldering in my parents' attic. "It's not like that this time." *Is it?*

"How long is this going to last?" my mom said. I froze with my hand on the doorknob and turned to her. Up close, I could see cracks in the ceramic sheen of her makeup, hardened tracks my siblings and I had worn there. "How long is it going to last this time?" she repeated.

"It will last until she cracks the case." My dad looked up from his gluey coffee and smiled at my mom. "Don't you remember the fairy books?"

My mom ran her hands through her hair, already looking tired at nine in the morning. Her hair settled back into the same perfect silvery-blond bob as always.

"Thanks, Dad." I gave him another kiss, cuffed Owen on the shoulder, and ran out the door before I got any more questions I couldn't answer.

16

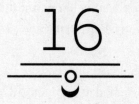

hurtled into the driveway and nearly knocked Jamie over. "Is that your family?" Jamie raised his hand to the kitchen window. My parents, Owen, and Jessie were pasted to the glass like tigers at feeding time. Owen waved exuberantly, and Jamie smiled and waved back.

"Yes. Let's go before my mom comes out and offers you coffee cake." I tossed my backpack into the back seat. "If a crumb passes your lips, your soul is forfeit." I stifled a yawn.

"Late night?" Jamie pulled out of the driveway.

"I got through thirty pages." Jamie's car was junk-free and smelled like pine disinfectant. His messenger bag sat alone in the back seat. "I think my eyes have calluses."

We pulled out of the subdivision onto Park Avenue across from the entrance to Lake Terrace Estates, the new mall that was killing the old mall. It was an outdoor ring of bright brick stores in fashionably odd shapes around a small green space with walking paths that led to more stores. Not 10 A.M. yet on a weekday, and the parking lot was already packed.

"I forgot you and Marley went to the same high school," Jamie said.

"I did, too." I switched into a low, mysterious voice. "Until it came back to me in a dream." I left out the part of the dream where he was wasted at Marley's funeral.

"I guess you really are psychic."

"I knew you were going to say that." We passed the new downtown—the library, the new public works complex, and the park district gym—cream-colored brick-and-glass buildings glittering in the midmorning sunlight. "How about you? Did you find anything?"

"Still waiting for a call back from Dominick." We passed the police station, its flags drooping in the sluggish morning air. "But I found out some interesting things about Joey."

"Such as?"

"I assumed he was a Battaglia, and sure enough, he popped right up." We'd left downtown and stopped at the tracks for a Metra train. "Joseph Battaglia, thirty-four years old. Also known as Joey the Nose."

I groaned. "You are not serious. He has a crime name?"

Jamie shook his head. "Boxing name."

"*So much better.*"

He wrestled his phone out of his pocket, swiped on it, and handed it to me. "Is this him?"

It was a publicity photo. Shirt off, gloves up, five-hundred-watt smile. He was just a kid—smooth face, tightly gelled hair. *Brylcreemed.* The word popped into my head, a vapor out of my dad's old black-and-white crime thrillers. The photo couldn't have been more than twenty years old but it looked ancient, an artifact from a vanished age of finned cars, scheming dames, and handsome brutes.

"That's him." My voice cracked. Jamie looked at me, but the train moved off and we started moving again. "He looks really young here."

"He wasn't even eighteen. His boxing career was short and pretty unremarkable. I think he figured out quick he was better on the money side, so he moved into management. I'm guessing that's where 'The Nose' comes from." We crossed into the strip of forest around Lake Ruby.

"Has he ever been busted for anything?"

"His name pops up in connection with bookie stuff, but nothing's in black-and-white. With guys like him, you have to read between the records." The forest thinned out and we plunged into the sunlight. "One incident stands out, and I would have skipped right over it if it weren't for you." He looked at me. "This is after Joey's boxing years were over, when he was off the radar, probably running books.

"There was a boxer, a guy named Buck Stillwell. Golden Gloves middleweight champ two years running, total rising star. His neighbors found him in his apartment with a bullet in his head, still holding the gun. Apparent suicide." I held my breath. I could tell this was not the end of the story. "Something about it didn't quite add up, but nobody looked too closely."

"Why not?"

"I'm getting to that. Now, Buck had just come off an amazing run. He was on fire, couldn't lose. The rumor was, he was supposed to throw his last fight, but he didn't. He won. Which of course created problems for whoever had money riding against him."

I sat up. "Joey."

"Or some big client of Joey's." He motioned for me to scroll to the next picture on his phone. "They found that in Stillwell's apartment. It reminded me of the sketch Joey gave you."

It was a drawing of a family, on a familiar scrap of tiny notepaper. A smiling mom and two kids, a boy and a girl, with round cartoon faces. The mom, from behind the wheel of a minivan, waved the kids off into a classic old Chicago red brick school with a chimney in the courtyard.

My mouth went dry. "Are they . . ." It came out whispered, and I started over. "Are they . . ." I couldn't finish that time either.

"They died in a car accident the week before Buck's apparent suicide." Jamie's voice was flat. "Hit-and-run. Somebody rammed them into the oncoming lane on I-94, into the path of a semi."

I looked at the picture again. The younger child, a boy, looked to be five or six. There was a circle of white in his eye, a tiny speck of light. It made him look curious, charmed by everything. To understand so well what makes people special, what makes them alive, and still be able to destroy them without a second glance . . . It was something the shell of a human would do.

Jamie watched me study the picture. "That's another reason nobody looked too deeply into his 'suicide,'" he said. "The guy's whole family was just wiped off the face of the earth. Who *wouldn't* want to put a bullet in his own head?"

We stopped at the T intersection at the end of Park Avenue. "Do we know what Joey's up to now?"

"You'll love this," he said. "Battaglia Bros. Moving and Hauling lists him as their CFO."

"You're kidding. So Nico and Joey *are* on the same team. Sort of. Are they brothers?"

"Couldn't tell, it looks like a big family. Sounds to me like

Dominick went rogue with some company assets, so they sicced the big dog on him. I also read up on Battaglia Bros. to see if they've had any brushes with the law."

"Anything interesting?"

"No." He looked uncertain. "Not exactly. They had a traffic stop earlier this year for an overweight truck."

"They have big, beautiful trucks? That's it?"

"It wasn't their truck—it was headed to them with a shipment of medical supplies. The origin point was in the Bahamas." The light changed, and Jamie turned onto Lake Street. He gave me a pointed look. "But I'm guessing it started off somewhere else before that."

"Should I know what that means?"

"Customs keeps an eye on packages from certain international locations. Russia, China. There are labs over there that will cook up anything you want and sell it to you right over the internet." We flew by the Ref's Whistle and the smiling jock in the window. "What a lot of these labs do is, they'll ship your package first to somewhere that U.S. Customs isn't watching. The Bahamas. Cuba."

"So you think the Battaglias are bringing in drugs?"

"It's just a theory. More like a hunch." He looked at me. "Check your dreams. I wouldn't turn down a good psychic tip at this point." The glass facades of the Abbott campus came into view. We were passing through later than I usually did. Kurt Cobain was probably already at his desk.

I wanted to ask Jamie if he thought Joey killed Marley, but I was afraid of what he would say. I gave him his phone back and squeezed my hands together. If I let them go, they would start shaking.

"Jamie." I turned to him as he nudged the car onto the mall access road. "Why are you doing all this? This isn't your case. It's not even *a* case. You've got to have better things to do."

A white mall security truck meandered through the empty aisles on the far side of the lot. We drove past Max's crappy bumper sticker–covered hatchback. Jamie pulled up in the drop-off lane at the mall entrance. He put the car in park and followed the security truck with his eyes. "I do have better things to do," he said. "I just got a new case this morning. A woman called in and said someone had smeared dog feces all over her car. I can't wait to tackle that one."

I had the urge to snicker but stuffed it. Jamie looked lost, staring out the window like he had woken up in a place he didn't recognize with no idea how he'd gotten there.

"Hey," I said. "Take it from an expert. If you're going to use humor as a defense mechanism, you need to look a little less like someone died."

The instant the words left my mouth, I regretted them. The news article I'd looked up flashed through my mind and a whisper out of the blank space of Jamie's past brushed by me. "I'm sorry," I said. "Did someone . . . ?"

Jamie kept staring out the window. "My friend Tyler died. In LA. There was a raid and he wasn't supposed to be there and . . ." He waved it away. "It's a long story." *Four of Swords*, I thought. *Loss, regret, withdrawal.* The real Jamie was peeking out now, as if through a crack in a locked door.

Jamie watched the security van make its way across the parking lot. There was a bearded dude inside texting with one hand on the wheel. "Sometimes the closer you get to someone, the less clearly you see them," Jamie said. "It's like looking through a window on a rainy day. When you get right up to it, you don't see through it anymore. You don't see the street, the cars, the houses." His mouth twisted. "You just see yourself."

He shrugged, like he was waking up, and turned to me. The real Jamie was gone, locked back up. "I wasn't a good friend to him," he said. "And now it's too late to do anything about it. But maybe it's not too late for you. She's gone, but you can still be a good friend to her."

I knew I was going to be late for work, but I didn't move. "What if I can't do anything? What if we don't find anything?"

"Well, then the dog shit emergency will have to be the highlight of my week." He gave me a lopsided grin and I felt a wave of dizzy joy and also fear, because as the seconds ticked by and neither of us moved or spoke, I knew we were about to cross some boundary between wondering and knowing, and I almost didn't want it to happen, wanted that moment to stay forever possible instead of definite, because I was afraid everything afterward would be a letdown.

"Thanks, Jamie," I managed to say. I don't remember what he said next—*Don't mention it*, maybe, or *See you later*.

I stumbled out of the car and watched him pull away. Then I dragged open the entrance doors and raced through the mall toward JCPenney. I was almost to Firebird Imports when that smell hit me again, that sweet musk I'd smelled in my apartment after the break-in. I stopped dead in the middle of the court, sniffing the air. The power walking seniors gave me a dirty look and stepped around me.

The smell was gone except for a faint echo in my mind, but I didn't have time to think about it because it was 10:06 and I was late.

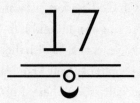

17

was wrapping a set of tea glasses with engraved removable metal holders when my phone, nestled underneath the counter, lit up: JAMIE CELL.

I stuffed the half-wrapped glasses into a waiting plastic bag and thrust it at the customer on the other side of the register. "Here you go," I said. "Have a nice day." Watching my phone ring and ring and waiting for the guy to get the hell out.

"Brings back memories." The guy stared fondly at the bag. He was an older guy with a full head of silver-blond hair, fit and well-dressed, like an actor in an ad for a country club or a hair-replacement procedure. In the course of the ten minutes he had now spent at the cash register, he had told me the story of his many years in Novosibirsk as a bigwig at a multinational aircraft manufacturer. All the while making me unwrap and rewrap the glasses because I wasn't doing it the way they used to do at Barney's in New York, where he lived half the year. "See, the way you use these glasses is, when you're on the long-distance trains up there in Siberia, and you're drinking your tea, the little holders . . ."

"Keep the tea from spilling?" I guessed, trying to move the conversation along.

"Exactly!" He acted like I had just translated the Rosetta stone. "I tell you," he said. Oh God, he was just warming up. I glanced at my phone. One more ring would send it to voicemail, and I had forgotten my password years ago. "I wish there were more honest, hardworking young people like you." He leaned in and dropped into a whisper. "Especially around here. Know what I mean?"

"I know exactly what you mean." I shook the bag at him. "Mind if I take this call? It's my parole officer." I answered my phone with a flourish.

The man blinked at me, then squeezed his lips together in a bloodless line, grabbed the bag, and stalked out of the store.

"You're going to want to see this," Jamie said without preamble. People were typing and talking in the background. "I called Chicago Asian Foods. The good news is, they have security cameras on the loading docks right where they back up to your patio."

"What's the bad news?"

"The bad news is the loading dock cameras are crap. The real top-of-the-line stuff is out front. But it's not a total waste." More typing and a duck quacking alert sound. "I'm sending you some stills."

My phone dinged. I put Jamie on speaker and swept through the snapshots. They looked like all security footage did—black-and-white and grainy and crappy. The first was a shot of the whole alley from a high angle. Two trucks in the near loading bays filled most of the screen, and in the upper left-hand corner was my patio door. I could just make out Jessie's wicker chair. The time stamp at the bottom of the screen read 1:08 P.M.

The next shot showed a figure in black walking toward my

patio, hood pulled down. In the next picture he was opening my patio door and stepping inside. In the next, he had pulled the door closed.

An invisible hand squeezed me around the middle. I let out my breath with a noisy whoosh. "How long was he in there?"

"Half hour. Not long."

"He looks like he's wearing gloves."

"And a mask. So you can forget about prints or face ID. I zoomed in on his clothes but I didn't see any logos or markings."

I squinted at the figure. In one screenshot his face was angled toward the camera and I could see white eye, nose, and mouth holes shining against a dark ski mask. "Joey and Nico are both big guys. This guy is on the smaller side."

A pause, then more typing. "I'm sending you a couple of videos. They could take a sec." Two tweens walked into the store, both carrying skateboards. They were holding hands like they hadn't figured out how to do it yet. Nobody in the store all day long and now the whole world needed Russian souvenirs right this goddamn second.

A couple of files dinged through on my phone, and I opened the first. It showed a bright, clean parking lot. "Is this out front?"

"Yes. About thirty minutes later."

The full-color video looked more like a TV commercial than security footage. A little girl walked by clutching a stuffed unicorn. Every sparkly pink sequin was clear.

A figure in black swayed into view. His hood was off now, and his long jet-black hair streamed behind him in loose waves. My heart did a painful leap, hammering the inside of my chest.

"Classic move," Jamie was saying somewhere far away. "Park the car somewhere else so it doesn't get on camera. This guy knows what he's doing."

The man came closer. His hoodie was half zipped, revealing an Iron Maiden T-shirt. He was wearing a pair of round blue-tinted sunglasses. There was no mistaking who it was. The video was too good.

"It might not be the same guy," Jamie said. "But the clothes and the timing—"

"That's Max," I said.

Jamie stopped talking. "Who?"

"Max!" I barked. The tweens swiveled toward me. I turned away, grabbing at a half-empty bottle of water I had left on the counter, draining it noisily. "Max. The guy who owns Stone Blossom. Marley's boss." I lowered my voice and looked around wildly, like Max was hiding behind a shelf of samovars.

Silence on the line, interrupted by a distant sneezing fit. "Are you sure?"

"Hang on." I left the skaters gaping at me and took my phone into the back, past the fitting rooms, and into Larissa's office. My legs felt hollow. I fell into Larissa's chair and watched the rest of the videos, one by one. The second video showed Max getting into his car and driving away. The car reared back toward the screen and I zoomed in until I could see the stickers clogging the little hatchback's rear fender: Celtic Frost, Shellac, and a grinning rainbow skull.

"It's him, Jamie." Sweat pooled at the neck of my T-shirt. "I know his car. We drove right by it this morning when you dropped me off." The spicy perfume from the atrium drifted past me again and everything fell into place, like heavy tumblers clicking aside in a cracked safe. I fell back in Larissa's chair, straining its ancient springs. "And the smell."

"What smell?"

"The smell in my apartment after the break-in." I drew a line in the dust on top of an ancient desktop PC with a floppy drive. "I didn't realize what it was, until just now."

"You didn't say anything about a smell."

"I thought I was imagining it, but when I walked by the store this morning, I smelled it again. It's the incense he burns at the store."

There was a long pause, then Jamie started talking. "Okay, Katie, listen to me."

"Sandalwood, I think, or patchouli, although that's more hippie than goth. He uses a grim reaper incense burner, though. You put the stick of incense right in his teeth." I got up and started circling Larissa's desk.

"Are you listening?"

I sat down, then got up again. "I'm listening."

"No, you're not. You're thinking. Stop. Don't even think of going over there and poking around." He was talking fast now, like he was afraid I would drop the phone and leave it hanging in midair with speed lines next to it. "Don't confront him, don't follow him, don't go near him. If he is the guy who broke into your house—"

"*If?* Who else could it be? Everything fits. I bumped into Max like three times yesterday. He saw that I didn't have the necklace on, so he must have figured it would be at my house." I picked up a pen and drew shaky circles and figure eights all over Larissa's desk calendar. Ideas were standing out in my mind in sharp relief where a moment ago there was only a blank, impenetrable wall.

"How does he know where you live?"

"I don't know! He probably has, you know, like, ways of finding stuff out."

Jamie started over calmly. "*If* he is our guy, we could be dealing with a pro. Not someone to mess with. Plus, you don't want to tip him off that we're on to him." He paused. "Let me handle this, okay?"

"Okay. Fine. I'll let you handle it," I said through gritted teeth. My fingers danced around Larissa's desk, picking up pens and receipts.

"Are you going home or back to your parents'?"

"Home. I don't think I can survive another night with my family."

"Is your patio door going to be fixed anytime soon?" Jamie said.

"I left a message with Bear, so, no."

"All right." Jamie sighed. "Just go home and lay low. I'll send a car to keep an eye out."

He launched a few more warnings and directions at me that I ignored, and we hung up. I sat at Larissa's desk staring at her 1980 Olympics bear clock. The bear said I had a few more hours until closing, but I didn't want to go back out on the floor. I wasn't scared, although I probably should have been. I just didn't trust myself not to barge across the atrium to Stone Blossom.

And do what?

I picked up my phone and scrolled through the patio images, squeezing and pulling at the screen for a better look. The face in the hoodie and sunglasses blurred into a pixelated wash. Why would Max put on crime-wear and bust into my apartment for Marley's chintzy necklace? I couldn't think of a reason . . . unless he killed Marley and the necklace somehow pointed to him. The hair on my arms stood up. When I walked into Stone Blossom on Monday morning, Max had noticed the necklace; I was sure of it. But he played dumb. I almost wished Owen hadn't been so quick to fix the thing so that it would still be safe, somewhere else.

Not that it mattered. I was still here, and so was the guy who wanted me out of the way.

18

The White Camry of Death had buttons for everything, and each one of them worked. Every time I stopped for a light I delighted myself by activating whispery wipers or turning on a snooty classical music station or popping open some secret compartment. Jessie, not to be outdone in the generosity Olympics, had brought the car to the mall earlier in the afternoon. I tried to scare her off with mostly fictional horror stories of the wrongs perpetrated on innocent cars in the Shady Pines parking lot, but she just dropped off the *Jessie Sells!* key chain, turned on her Prada heels, and left. Now I was driving home through an early evening drizzle with the key chain turned away from me so I wouldn't have to look at Jessie's smug face. I wondered how and when this "favor" would bite me in the ass.

Outside, the air smelled like sweet herbs and gasoline. I played with the window button—up, down, up, down. Stone Blossom was already shuttered when I sped by it, head down to avoid any accidental interaction with Max. I was being good. I had promised Jamie I would go straight home. No stopping for chicken wings. No window shopping. No side forays to—

The Ref's Whistle plaza rose up on my left, red-and-white neon blurry in the wet air. Before I could look away I had scanned the parking lot. There it was, a flash of white in the dark lot: BEAST 25.

I stared at the black truck. Traffic slowed down but did not stop, and the truck, cocooned in its parking space, drifted past, light flashing off its mirrored surface. My foot danced over the pedals.

But, but, but . . . A pitter-patter of voices piped up in my head. *Jamie said to avoid Max. He didn't say anything about Nico.* This was toddler logic, and I knew it. *No cookies? Can I have candy instead?* The point was to stay safe. Jamie was right; I needed to back off and let him handle this. I stepped on the gas. The plaza disappeared in the rearview mirror.

When I pulled into the Shady Grove parking lot, a squad car was idling in the space next to mine. A skinny cop sat in the front seat, staring at his phone. I pulled in and stared at my building through drizzle, lit up white by the lampposts. *Up, down, up, down* went the window. *There's something I can do here that no one else can,* I had told my family this morning, their faces cycling through confusion, fear, derision, and doubt. I gripped the steering wheel tight. Somewhere, a car horn blared like a trumpet flourish and I saw the Knight of Swords on his racing stallion, rushing, slashing his way into battle, sword raised, face contorted with urgency. Except the face was Aunt Rosie's.

Let's go, kiddo, she said, *let's see some action,* the way she did when she was trying to get my ass in gear so we could get to the track before post time.

I smacked the window button closed, put the car in reverse, and peeled back out of the lot. The cop never looked up from his phone.

By the time I pulled into the Ref's Whistle lot, the rain had stopped but everything was still slick and shiny. I crouched next to my car in the aisle across from Nico's truck, waiting for him and another dude to finish vacuuming the store and close up. They came out trading shouted goodbyes, and I watched Nico shuffle toward me, digging keys out of his pocket. I slipped Marley's necklace off my neck and tossed it back into my car. I figured wearing Nico's dead girlfriend's necklace would not support my case that I just wanted to have a friendly chat.

Nico was in front of me now, fumbling with his keys.

"Hey, Nico." I stepped out into the aisle.

He spun and leaped backward like one of those cats some idiot menaces with a cucumber for YouTube laughs. Then he scrabbled in his pocket and yanked out a small round white object. It was a fucking head of garlic.

"You've got to be kidding me." Two accusations of being a vampire in one day were too many. "Did you just have that with you, or . . . ?"

"What the hell do you want?" Nico wheezed. He dropped the garlic and it rolled away. I bent down and picked it up.

"I just want to ask you some questions." I handed him the garlic. "About Marley."

"What are you, a cop or something?" He snatched at the garlic and stuffed it in his pocket. "I already talked to that guy cop. I told him I don't know what happened to her, okay?"

"I'm not a cop," I said. "I'm just, Marley and I were friends, and I want to know what happened to her. Same as you." I lowered my voice. "I'm not going to bite you."

He stared at me, clutching his gut, but it looked like his breathing was slowing. "You and Marley were friends?" He couldn't get his head around him and me having something in common.

"Yeah, that's right." I smiled a little. "We met at the mall and got to know each other."

"She ever talk about me?"

"Oh yeah, all the time." *Just not to me*, I added silently.

Two cars got in a honk battle on Lake Street and Nico turned to look. When he turned back to me his face looked rumpled. "Do you . . ." He scratched the back of his head. "You got those cards with you?"

I rolled my eyes. "Yes, but they're just cards, man, they're not . . ." I looked at him. "Wait, do you want me to read them for you again?"

He shrugged and tugged at the medal around his neck. "I've got some questions, too."

"Then maybe we can help each other," I said.

He closed his eyes and grabbed his gut again. "I need some ice cream. Right now."

Nico had two giant scoops of mint chocolate in a paper cup. I had a scoop of rocky road. He stopped shoveling ice cream into his mouth to glance at me. "Settles my stomach," he mumbled.

"There's not much ice cream doesn't help with," I said. We sat across from each other in a curvy orange booth at the Dairy Dee-lite a few doors down from the Ref's Whistle, like we were on a mildly disappointing blind date. The place was empty except for the teenage girl at the counter and her friend, parked on a chrome barstool with a soda and a trigonometry textbook in front of her. They were solving problems out loud. An oldies playlist was blasting and the walls were covered with 1950s nostalgia porn: Elvis clocks, pink Cadillacs, Marilyn Monroe serving a tray of fat burgers and fries to James Dean.

I watched Nico suck down his ice cream. This was not the same Nico who had stumbled into Firebird Imports a few days ago. This new Nico hadn't slept since then, or shaved, or had anything to eat. There were dark circles under his eyes, and his face was ashy and pitted. He looked ten years older.

"You look like you're having a rough time, Nico." I eyed his wrinkled Ref's Whistle shirt and stubble.

Nico glanced up and went back to his ice cream. "My stomach's a mess," he said. "I haven't even been to the gym since last week." Rough times indeed.

I swiped a napkin across my hands and the table and took out the cards. Nico sat up like the teacher had just called on him and he hadn't done the homework. I split the deck into three parts and swirled them facedown in a shell game pattern, tracing infinity on the table.

"So," I said. "What can the cards do for you today?" If I could get him talking, he would think I was answering his questions when he was really answering mine. Chief among them: who killed Marley?

Nico glanced at the girls and leaned in. "I need the cards to help me find something." He spooned up the last of the ice cream and pushed the cup away. "Something I'm missing."

My swoops got tangled in each other and I knocked the cards over. The gym bag. That's what all this was about. I wasn't sure what I was expecting—*I'm sad my girlfriend was shot in the head,* maybe, or *My brother Joey is a total dick*—but being treated like a psychic vending machine that dispensed treasure maps was not it.

"Look, I don't believe in this crap, okay?" He started talking fast like I was the Wizard of Oz and he had to get his pitch out before I blasted him with green lightning. "But I'm out of options here, and you . . . *know* stuff." He twisted his hands together, hard, and started popping each finger in its socket. "How else would you know that Marley was dead?"

I shuffled, savoring the electric tingle of the cards against my fingers. Part of me wanted to laugh, and part of me wanted to shut up and enjoy feeling talented and extraordinary, even if I didn't deserve it. "I'll see what I can do," I said. Why not? The gym bag was the perfect way in. "Focus on what you lost."

Nico scrunched his eyes shut like a kid trying not to think of an elephant. I pushed the deck toward him. He opened an eye, cut the cards, screwed his eye shut again. *Don't believe in this crap*, my ass. It occurred to me with a silvery thrill that this reading was both real and not real. Sure, I knew things he didn't know I knew, but was that so different from reading for a stranger? I always knew more than they thought I did, from my first look at them. What I didn't know, not now and not ever, was exactly what I was going to say next. For that I needed a spark of randomness, like a match tossed onto a waiting pile of kindling. I needed the cards.

"Five of Pentacles." I tossed it on the table between us. "Lost wealth. Bad fortune." I grinned at him. "Nice focusing, Nico."

Nico flung his eyes open. He stared at the miserable couple waddling through the snow with their rags and crutches past a window lit with five shiny pentacles. I traced one with my fingertip. "Pentacles are also called coins. This lost thing is very valuable, isn't it?" I cocked my head. "How valuable is it?"

Nico's eyes flickered but he didn't say anything. I shrugged like it didn't matter. "The more specific you can be, the better the read. Up to you."

Nico picked up his plastic spoon and swirled it around his empty cup. "It was two hundred grand. In cash."

I willed my eyes not to pop out of my head. There was no purpose for a wad of cash that big except to get stolen. I drew another card. "Seven of Swords," I said. A smug trickster, sneaking swords from under his enemies' noses. I racked my brain for what I knew about Marley and Nico's fateful Thursday night date. Someone got shafted, but who? "I'm seeing trickery here," I said neutrally. "Deceit. Betrayal."

Nico crumpled his napkin. His mouth parted and shut, like the words were too big to squeeze out. We were getting down to it. He just needed a nudge. I scanned the cards for something useful.

"This card here." I pointed to the Five of Pentacles. "It's a Five." I flicked my eyebrows at him. "I don't believe in coincidences. I'm seeing . . ." I double-checked my math. "The fifth day of last week." Under the table, I squeezed my knees together at the audacity of this crap logic, hoping Nico was too emotional to pay much attention. "Last Thursday."

Nico's eyes widened, then narrowed. "Isn't *Friday* the fifth day of the week?"

"Not if you start from Sunday. That's what they did in olden times. When the cards were created." I had no idea if this was true.

Nico looked like he was listening to an argument between a

tiny person perched on each shoulder. I swooped in before he could start thinking. "The cards don't lie. This loss, this betrayal, happened last Thursday night." *Crap*. I wasn't supposed to know it was nighttime. No amount of dipshit numerology was going to cover that gaffe.

But Nico wasn't listening. The antsiness on his face blossomed into pain. "She ripped us off," he whispered. "Me and my uncles. She cleaned out the safe at our warehouse."

Marley? I almost burst out. Jamie had said days ago that Marley was the thief in this scenario, and I hadn't believed him. "Marley," I said calmly, even though the skin on the back of my neck was crawling in all directions. "How did she break into your warehouse?"

"She didn't break in; she had keys." He gave me a suspicious glance. "She worked for us. Whenever we needed an extra pair of hands to haul stuff."

"Yes," I said quickly. "I knew that." I tried to distract him from the patchiness of what I did and did not know. "Man, she was really built. You two met at the gym, right?"

"That's right." Nico smiled. Talking about Marley always took the edge off. "About six months ago." Six months ago, I remembered, was when Marley had started working at Stone Blossom. "She said that little freak at the mall wasn't paying her dick. Treated her like shit, ordered her around. She needed a little extra scratch, so I helped her out, introduced her to my uncles."

I lifted an internal eyebrow. Max? The same Max who had organized a GoFundMe for a part-time stock boy with a diabetic cat? On the other hand, Jamie's security video flashed through my mind: Max may have had a few secrets of his own. Somebody was bending the truth here, and bending the truth was not Nico's strong suit. I did a jerky shuffle, my thoughts spinning in place. What next? I drew a card.

"Ten of Cups. Family." I pointed to the mom, dad, and kids frolicking under a cup rainbow. Joey's stony face swam up in front of me. "I can see your family was very upset by all this."

"Oh, they were fucking livid," Nico said. The words were flowing easier now and he was staring into space like he had forgotten all about me. We had reached that magical tipping point where they bought in and pretty much started doing their own reading. I just had to stay out of the way. "We were heading home from a scrap metal job, and we stopped by the warehouse 'cause my uncle Vito forgot his asthma inhaler. He went in, and there was Marley elbow deep in the safe! She pulled a gun on him, took the money, and left." Nico laughed like he was confused about who he was supposed to root for. "Do you fucking believe that?"

"I . . ." My tongue dried up in my throat. The room went dark around me.

"She had it all planned out." Nico's voice went quiet. "She knew we weren't supposed to be there that night. If we hadn't gone back for the inhaler, she would've gotten away clean."

I felt like I'd been edging through a darkened hallway, feeling bumps and bits of molding and cracks in the walls, and now the lights had snapped on and I was in an enormous room I could see all at once, all its doorways and corners and bends. Marley had been playing Nico and his family all along, playing a long, long game. It all snapped together, all the pieces that were askew from the start—that Marley was with a guy like Nico at all, that she lived in a house that was so clearly temporary, that she lied about the way Max treated her. *Ace of Swords: deadly cold control.*

Marley was the puppet master here. She was not some piece of flotsam sucked into the Battaglias' criminal wake. She was the fucking ocean. The block of ice sitting in my chest since Nico's interview Monday night began to shift and crack, needled by new tendrils of heat. No wonder Marley didn't tell me what she was up to. I wouldn't have told me either.

"Did you call the police?" I filled my voice with boneheaded concern and pretended it was totally normal for a small family-run business to have two hundred grand in cash lying around.

Nico twisted his napkin into a corkscrew. "Nah, it was, you know, pretty late. We didn't want to be tied up all night." He shrugged. "Anyway, my uncles like to handle things their own way."

No shit. *Hello, 911? Someone just stole two hundred grand of our drug money.* Nico was watching me now, like a rabbit that just heard a heavy crunch in the bushes. I was dying to ask him what the money was for, but it was time to back off. I drew another card.

"The Lovers." Nico's face melted. Marley again to the rescue. The front door jingled and a couple with matching salt-and-pepper hair walked in, hands linked. The Turtles' "Happy Together" spun into the air.

"She broke your heart," I said.

Nico was quiet for so long I thought he hadn't heard me. When he turned to me his face was hard but his eyes were shiny. "That cop thought I killed her, did you know that?" His eyes were little diamonds. A lot was riding on what I would say next.

"That cop thought all kinds of things," I said. "He brought me in, too. He thought you and I were working together to break into Marley's house and steal stuff." Nico scoffed.

"Listen." I leaned in and dropped my voice. "They're not

investigating this as a murder. That cop told me so himself." I laced my hands together in front of me. "I know you didn't kill her. So if you know anything about who did, it stays with me. The cops are done with this." I shrugged. "So I'm done with the cops." My eyes fell on the Lovers. The woman, facing the sky, the serpent spiraling up the tree behind her.

The Elvis clock swung its hips, *ticktock, ticktock*. Nico turned the balled-up ice cream cup over in his hands. "My uncles were, you know, pretty mad." I strained to hear him over the music. "They told me, they said: *You get that money back however you can.*" He raised his eyes to me. "*And then you make sure she disappears.*"

"Disappears," I said in a small voice. "You mean, like, goes to the Bahamas?"

Nico looked at me and I knew I was barking up the wrong coconut palm. "Here's the thing, though." A dopey grin brightened his face. "I told them I would do the job, but I wasn't going to. I was gonna take her away with me instead. Take the money and go somewhere warm, where my uncles or nobody could ever find us. I musta left a hundred messages on her phone. I went to her house Sunday, but she wasn't there, so I tried the mall." He sniffed. "I knew she still loved me, I just knew it. She just grabbed her shot to make bank. Who wouldn't?"

A sad little sliver of pain circled my heart. There was no limit to the number of boldfaced facts you could ignore when you wanted something to be true. Nobody knew that better than me. I looked away from Nico's blotchy, hurting face back to the Lovers. Someone had killed the buck naked woman on the card. If it wasn't her equally stitchless lover, who was it? I drew another card to see if I could rule out anyone else.

"Two of Swords." A blindfolded figure balanced a pair of

swords on its shoulders, against a mysterious ocean. I searched the scene for a hook. There it was.

"Two," I told Nico. "Doubles. Two men who look alike but are opposite. They want the same thing, but they go after it differently." I wasn't ready to reveal my encounter with Joey, so I waited for Nico to catch on. He stared at me, twisting the chain around his neck.

I tried again. "There's a man who looks just like you. In your family." I glanced at the blindfold. "His vision is bad."

A dim smile and a head scratch from Nico. Good, gracious Lord. "Nico, do you have a brother or a cousin or somebody, who wears glasses?"

"You mean my cousin Joey?" Nico spat. "What do you mean, looks like me? That ugly motherfucker. These cards are fucked in the head."

"I see that Joey has something to do with this," I said. "Is that possible?"

"He's got something to do with everything." Nico snorted. "That fucking guy. Vito's kid. Walks around like he owns the place. Always trying to prove he's smarter than everybody." He crushed the ice cream cup in his fist. "He's got a bug up his ass because he used to draw these little pictures, when he was a kid? Like, little comics. And my uncles used to rib him about it. He used to get *so mad*." Nico chuckled. "I mean, jeez, take a joke."

And I thought I had a toxic family. Joey's drawing of the kids on their way to school flashed in front of me. "Do you think Joey killed her?" I hoped Nico was far enough around the curve of the reading not to notice that we had transitioned from his questions to my questions.

"I thought of that, too," Nico said. "But it don't add up. See, the way I found out was someone texted me a picture." He swallowed hard. "Of her body." Marley's pale, wounded face shimmered in front of me, and the glob of ice cream turned in my gut. "But it wasn't from Joey. It was some hidden number. If Joey did it, he'd be rubbing it in my face that he'd popped my girlfriend. He was jealous, see? Because for once a girl chose me over him and his goddamn car and his suits." Triumph lit his face. "Marley didn't care about any of that crap."

Oh, boy. It was heartbreakingly clear why Marley chose Nico as her in to the Battaglias—and it wasn't because she was above lowly material things.

"Besides," Nico said. "He wouldn't've killed her before he got the money. And I know he don't have the money because they're all on my ass about it 24/7. Nico, you got the money? When you gonna drop by with the money? I can't keep saying I forgot it."

"Wait a minute," I said. "Why do they think you have the money?"

"Because I kind of told them I did the job on Marley." He cringed. "And showed them the picture, to prove it." He put his face in his hands. "I didn't know what else to do!"

Wow. That was actually kind of smart. I couldn't believe I was rooting for him. That's how low a bar the rest of his shit-show family set. "Did they believe you?"

"Yeah, they said, 'Great job, Nico, you popped your cherry.' Took me out to the strip clubs."

"You don't think Joey got the money and kept it so he wouldn't have to share?"

"A measly two hundred grand?" He scoffed. "Joey's got his sights set a lot higher. Wants to run the company someday. Shit, he's halfway there. He ain't gonna kill the golden cow over some chump change." Aside from the golden cow, that actually made sense.

The seniors were on their way out, each holding a cone. Nico stared at them like they were wandering off with his money. He snapped back toward me and his eyes flashed. "The fuck are we talking about Joey for? This ain't about him." He started to get out of his chair. "I haven't heard thing one about where that money is." The girls at the counter looked up. "Who's asking the questions here?"

I raised a hand at the girls to say Nico and I weren't about to kill each other on their watch. "We both have questions," I said to Nico, "and we're helping each other answer them." I motioned him back down and drew another card. "Two of Cups." A man and a woman, hands linked. A lion's head hovered above them, blessing their partnership. "Look." I tapped the card. "Look at these two. They're working together. You and I are on the same side here, okay? The more we both know, the better."

Nico dropped back into the chair, fuming. "All I know is, today is Wednesday, and if I don't come up with two hundred grand in cash by Monday, my uncles are gonna string me up by my nutsack." He rubbed his face like it was a bad drawing he wanted to erase. "I went back to Marley's house. I went through every hiding place I could think of. I got nothing. I'm hosed."

The spring was winding down on this reading. "Here's what I think," I said. "Whoever sent you that picture probably also killed Marley. *And* has your money. If it's not your family, who else could it be? Think, Nico." Nico shrugged miserably. "And what does the picture mean? Is it a threat? Do you have any—" I was about to say "rival gangs" but remembered we were still pretending the Battaglias were running a totally legitimate business operation. "Do you have any competitors? For your— For your business?"

Nico played with the balled-up ice cream cup. "I don't know, maybe. My uncles don't tell me that kind of stuff." He made a face. "That's Joey's thing."

I stared at the checkerboard floor, the tiles mingling into a black-and-white blur. Nico was a pawn. Whatever was going on here was above his pay grade. I drummed my fingernails on the speckled Formica tabletop. The girls were low-key singing along to Del Shannon's "Runaway." When the music abruptly cut off, they both belted *"Why-why-why-why-why"* into the sudden silence, then collapsed in a fit of giggles. The heist scene looped in my mind: Marley squaring off, fortune in one hand, gun in the other, with Nico's wheezing uncle. I didn't care that she was a criminal; she wasn't exactly stealing from an orphanage. Something else needled me about the scene, like an insistent stone in my shoe. *I can look the other way on a lot of shit*, Marley had said, her face calcified with old rage. *But stealing? Fuck that.*

And now she was a thief?

Nico slumped in his chair. "What am I supposed to do now?" His fingers crept up to his tiny gold monk chain again. *Saint Anthony, please come around, something is lost and can't be found.*

I shuffled the deck and offered it to Nico. He picked a card and flipped it faceup. "Eight of Cups," I said. "See this guy? He lost all these cups and he's bummed, but the only thing to do now is walk away." I tapped the card. "The money's gone, Nico. And you know it. You can't get it back without putting yourself and your family in danger. Tell your uncles things didn't go as planned." I couldn't believe I was actually helping him. I figured it was an investment in putting a lid on this thing so nobody else got killed. "Would they . . ." I glanced at the girls and lowered my voice. "You don't think your uncles would . . ."

"What, pop me?" Nico looked offended. "I'm family, for fuck's sake."

"Well, then what's the worst they can do?"

He sighed and buried his head in his hands. "They're never gonna trust me again. I'm gonna be fifty years old and still doing errand boy shit. Hauling couches that smell like farts and old people." He gave a grim laugh. "And I'll probably be working for Joey."

"They can't stay mad forever." I packed up the cards and put them in my back pocket. "Let it go, Nico. It'll all work out. Just keep doing what you're doing and you'll be fine."

He grinned. "Marley said that all the time. Man, when she saw something, she went for it." He gathered his trash. "We were at Mundelein Days a few months ago, playing those little carnival games? She saw this little trinket she liked. You had to knock down the bottles to get it." He got up and went to the garbage can in the corner. I followed him with my own garbage. "I shit you not, we were there for an hour. Spent fifty dollars. And you better believe she walked away with that goddamn necklace." He stared into space, caressing the trash like a treasure.

"You mean the black necklace? With the ace of spades charm?" Something eased in my chest. Maybe the necklace was just a necklace after all, and not the centerpiece in some criminal conspiracy. "Funny you should mention it . . ."

Nico was still daydreaming. "She loved that cheap locket like it was the crown jewels."

I went still. "What did you say?"

"I said she loved it." He tossed his trash and swiped his hands on his pants. "It was her favorite. I tried to buy her something better, but she—"

I cut him off. "Did you say it was a locket?"

"Yeah." He pushed open the door and the bell went *ding!* "You open up the spade, you can put stuff inside. A picture or a lock of hair." He grinned. "You remember it? She wore it all the time."

I froze, staring at him. "I do remember it." My mouth was dry. "No wonder it was special to her."

After I watched the black truck drive away I dove into my car and dug the necklace out of my backpack. In the moonlight spilling through the windshield, the black stones looked like spider eyes.

I ran my finger along the bottom edge of the spade and found the groove there. Why hadn't I noticed it before? When I pried the spade open, something popped out and I caught it in my palm. It was a tiny black square, thin as a blade, with white techy markings on one side and a row of gold electrical contacts on the other. A memory card.

I turned it over in my fingers. I knew whatever was on it led to Nico's bag of money. And whoever broke into my apartment knew it, too.

I snapped the card back into the necklace. Then I wound the necklace around my neck.

Keep doing what you're doing.

I fucking intended to.

19

By the time I pulled back into the Shady Pines parking lot, the cop was gone. Apparently, it was past break-in hours and the criminals had knocked off for the night.

When I burst into my apartment, Owen was there, perched cross-legged on the armrest of the couch with his headphones on, slurping at an unearthly green bubble tea.

"Oh good, you're here." I dropped my backpack in the middle of the floor. "I need you to look at something."

"Let me finish up," he said. I plopped down next to him on the couch and peeked at his screen. He was playing some kind of sim game. The little round-faced character on the screen had red hair and glasses and was drinking something green.

"Is this you?" I said.

"Yes." He took a slurp. Owen had a bubble tea addiction. He said he enjoyed the logistical puzzle of having to both eat and drink in the same mouthful. "I'm a student at Northwestern," he said, pointing to the screen. "I have two sisters and a terrarium of anoles."

"That's . . . your real life, Owen."

"This life's more fun," he said. He clicked away from the little Owen on the screen. "Speaking of which, I need to check on you. I think you were about to fall off a building. Want to see?"

"Maybe later," I said. Even in Owen's make-believe life, I was falling off of things. "Take a look at this." I opened the necklace and showed him what was inside.

He peered at it up close. "A microSD card." He looked up at me. "What's on it?"

I paced the room, filling him in on my ice cream date with Nico. "You were right," I told him. "Marley did steal a big bag of cash from the Battaglias." I pointed to the memory card. "And I think whatever's on there leads to it." I rounded the room again. "What do you even stick it into?"

"You need an adapter." He quit out of his game and upended his laptop case. A waterfall of tech gear spilled out, including memory cards of all shapes and sizes. He picked through them until he found what he needed. I had never been as grateful as I was at that moment for Owen being Owen.

"I knew it was all about money." He snapped the little card into a bigger card, and slotted the whole thing into his PC. "It's always about money."

I straightened *The Song of the Lark* on the wall. Owen must have used the patio door again. "How'd you get past the cop?"

"What cop? I didn't see any cop."

"Wonderful." I pointed to the PC. "Somebody broke in here yesterday looking for that memory card. Jamie sent a cop to make sure no one else sneaked in, and as you can see, they did a bang-up job."

Owen moused and clicked around the screen. A basic-looking password window popped up, and underneath it, in blocky white numerals, a countdown: 30 . . . :29 . . . :28. Owen yanked the memory card out. "It's encrypted."

"Ugh." I started pacing again. "Can you decrypt it?"

He scratched his head. "I bet Dylan can." Owen's roommate Dylan was a recreational hacker who had once defrauded Hershey's online ordering system out of a lifetime supply of fun-size Krackel bars.

"It's got to lead to the money, right?" I put the necklace back on and sat down. "Like, maybe it's a map? Or directions? Or a safe combination?" Owen zipped the memory card into the pocket of his laptop case and booted up his sim game again. Bright animated intro screens full of squishy balloon people and houses popped up, to jaunty background music.

I watched the screen, mesmerized. "Hey, Owen," I said. "What would you do with two hundred thousand dollars?"

Owen clicked through a bunch of selection menus. The little people blinked and waved at us. "I don't know. I could have bubble tea every day."

"You already have bubble tea every day."

"I'd get extra so you could have some, too," he said. "And Jamie. What would you do?"

I watched as the scene changed. Now we were looking at a city skyline, sun flashing off bright digital skyscrapers. "I guess I could start buying my own phones and laptops."

"And your own streaming subscriptions."

I could finally open that tarot shop, I thought, and a wave of terror washed over me. Now the truth came out. It wasn't money that kept me from cornering the North Shore psychic market. It wasn't time, poor market conditions, or any of the other bullshit I'd fed anyone who bothered to ask. I didn't open a shop because it would be hard and scary and a ton of work, and there was a pretty good chance it would fail.

"I probably wouldn't do anything," I said, watching the screen zoom in on the roof of a skyscraper. "Not with stolen money, anyway. I'd probably just present it to the cops with my sincerest middle fingers upraised and a hearty 'I told you so.'"

"Check it out," Owen said. There was a tiny figure on the crown of a skyscraper, a squishy, round-faced girl with dark hair, wearing skintight black superhero gear and big bug-eyed spy glasses. She was holding a grappling hook, swinging it in tight whooshing circles.

"Is that me?" I said. The girl waved to us.

"It's you," Owen said. The girl bounced in place, ready to leap. Spears of light flashed off her hook. "You're about to do something awesome."

"I did it," I told Jamie. I had my phone on speaker on the picnic table next to the thieving trucker report, which was now covered with loopy notes and multicolored markings. "I went through the whole thing."

"You did?" Jamie said through the phone. "When?"

"Last night." I sipped from my Styrofoam cup of hot tea and swirled my plastic fork through my food court fried rice. I had been too wired to sleep last night after Owen left with the memory card, so I fished the report out of my backpack, thunked it on the kitchen table, and assembled an army of pencils, highlighters, and notecards with the Ukrainian Village zip codes scrawled on them, so I wouldn't have to keep flipping to the front page. Eventually, I ditched the cards because the zip codes had branded themselves on my brain. I fell into an automatic dance, flipping faster through the pages, judging more quickly whether a place named Orchid Logistics would be a trucking company or a florist. At two in the morning, I turned the last page, tossed my pencil on the table, fell into bed, and snored through the night.

"I've got about a dozen truckers here who stole from their company," I told Jamie, paging through the report. I wasn't sure exactly what I was going to do with them.

"Well, you're way ahead of me," Jamie said. "I've left messages with Max but I don't think he answers his phone much. I've been in meetings all day, so I haven't had a chance to pop over there yet."

I groaned. "Ugh, Jamie!"

"Look, you know I can't spend any official time on this. I have to keep it on the back burner."

"I know, I get that, but the point is, I could have talked to Max like eight times by now. He's right here. Can't we just toss that over into my column of stuff to do?" My column seemed to be the only column with anything in it right now, but I wasn't about to make things more tense by pointing this out.

A sigh from the other end. "Katie, we've talked about this, it's not safe for you to—"

"You know what?" I took a savage gulp of tea and burned my tongue. "I am not some helpless little moron." I thought of Owen's little superhero me. At least *somebody* believed in me. "If something looks wrong, I know enough to run the other way. I can read people. I can read situations. It's what I do." I'd been putting off telling him about last night's date with Nico, but it bubbled out of me now. "You know what else I did last night? I went back to the Ref's Whistle and talked to Nico."

The phone was silent. There was a long angry honk from the

direction of the highway. "When were you going to tell me this?" Jamie said.

I filled him in on Nico and Marley's romantic drama, Marley's standoff with Nico's uncle, and the mysterious memory card hidden in Marley's necklace. When I imitated Nico's limp explanation of why his uncles didn't report the theft to the police, Jamie actually laughed out loud. I had never heard him laugh before. It made me want to find the nearest banana peel and slip on it over and over.

"Yeah, no shit they didn't call the cops," he said. "You're telling me he wanted you to use your psychic powers to help him find two hundred thousand dollars of stolen cash?"

"Like a psychic GPS." I switched into a robot voice. *"There are . . . four . . . stashes of stolen loot . . . in your area."*

"I can't believe you got all that out of him." He gave a final surprised laugh. "I might have to requisition tarot cards for all our investigations guys. If I had any doubt the Battaglias were dirty, this pretty much blows it away. I can't wait to see what Owen gets off that memory card."

"I thought you'd be mad," I mumbled.

"I am furious." He sounded like he was still smiling. "Mostly because he didn't tell *me* any of this."

"Because you're a cop, Jamie. Nobody likes cops."

Jamie scoffed. "None taken."

"You know what I mean. People who have stuff to hide don't like cops. I'm just some loser nobody expects anything from, and for once that's actually a good thing." I shielded my eyes from the sun. "Can we agree that there are some situations I might be better qualified than you to stick my nose into?"

There was a long pause. "Give me to the end of the day, okay? I'll try to get over to Max after this funding committee meeting in a few minutes. And then the squad car redesign meeting." He sighed. "And the birthday party."

I upended the carton of fried rice into my mouth. "Does any actual police work get done over there?"

"I did solve the dog shit case," Jamie said. "It was the ex-boyfriend." He sounded tired. "It's always the ex-boyfriend."

We hung up and I tossed my trash and got ready to go back inside for the afternoon. It was sunny but not boiling, and I wished I could stay out all day, staring at the highway. I hadn't been in the courtyard since Marley died; it seemed wrong, some-how, to be there without her. I ran my finger down the first page of the report. But she was here now, somewhere close by—or at least that's how it felt. Like she was watching me with that off-center smile, waiting to see what I would do next.

Across the court, the bald guy who ran the vitamin store chatted up a leggy girl in a Fighting Illini sweatshirt. She was trying to get him to shut it and ring up her protein powder. A security guard wandered by staring at his phone. He looked like he was in high school. Anyone younger than me looked like they were in high school. My age radar had been hinky ever since I'd left the stage of life where every year had some fake milestone to get excited about. First date, prom, graduation, college, first job. One year looked a whole hell of a lot like the next these days.

I shuffled the cards absently and stared at the report spread out in front of me on the counter in the empty store. I hadn't asked Jamie how I was supposed to narrow down the names I had found, and now he was busy eating cake or some shit. I would have to improvise. I flipped to the first highlighted name, picked up the phone, and dialed the first number on the list.

It was no picnic trying to come up with a convincing reason
for a beleaguered receptionist to plumb long-forgotten company
records about some piddly crime that happened years ago. I
impersonated family members, doctors, lawyers (lesson learned:
people don't like talking to lawyers), and, eventually, cops. That
cut through a lot of red tape, and I was able to cross a bunch of
names off the list by using the same formula: *Hi, I'm a cop, I'm
working a case related to X, can you tell me what he stole and what
it was worth?* I couldn't believe how easy it was to gain people's
trust when you put a little authority in your voice. *And lied like a
rug*, I thought. If anyone checked into any of my fake cop names,
I was screwed.

Thomas Brown of Roadways Transport gave me a bit of a snag.
"I'm sorry," a woman told me in a voice that made it clear she was
not in the least bit sorry. "We don't discuss personnel records over
the phone." A weird stillness echoed around her, like she was sitting alone under a glass dome. "You can submit a request in writing on your department letterhead to our Loss Prevention
address. Do you have a pen and paper?" She knew this speech by
heart, probably heard it in her dreams. "You can expect a response
in six to eight weeks."

"I'm afraid this case is rather time sensitive." I was amazed I
hadn't hit this kind of red tape sooner. *Thomas Brown, Thomas
Brown, Thomas Brown*, a tune started up in my head. My feet
scrabbled over the carpet in a spastic tap dance. "I don't have six
to eight weeks." I cleared my throat authoritatively. "There are
lives at stake here."

"I'm sorry." Her voice stuck to its oscilloscope flatness. "It's
company policy."

I flipped through the report, scrambling for some secret set of
instructions I had missed for getting people to do what you

wanted them to. My hands slipped and knocked the deck off the counter, scattering cards in a bright flood.

Shit! I dropped to the floor, reaching for the nearest card. Eight of Swords: a woman, blindfolded and bound, trapped, immobile, in a field of menacing swords.

"I can't help you," the woman on the phone said. She was tired, so tired of doing a job she knew helped no one, did no one any good.

I squeezed the phone. "I haven't been honest with you," I said. "I'm not a police officer. I . . . I'm nobody." I slipped to the floor, into the pile of cards, running my hands through them in circles. The woman, lost in the forest of swords. "I had a friend. A good friend. She was murdered, and the police can't help me. No one can. No one cares about her except me." My throat went dry. "No one thinks I can do this. But I have to. There's no one else. Just me."

A wispy sigh rose from the phone, high and soft.

"Please," I said. "I'm sorry I lied. But I need to know if Thomas Brown was my friend's father. I need to know what he stole, and how much it was worth. Please help."

I thought the woman had hung up, but then her voice came through the silence like a breeze in a desert. "Hold on just a moment."

The echoing stillness went dead; I was on hold. I crouched on my knees, eyes closed, among the scattered cards.

An eternity later, she was back. "I'm not supposed to do this," she said. "I could get in trouble, you know. I don't want to get in trouble."

"You have my word," I said. "Whatever you tell me, I didn't hear it from you."

"Thomas Brown, Thomas Brown . . ." she muttered. "Here he

is. It looks like he drove off with one of our refrigerated trucks. It was full of . . . raw fish, it says. Raw salmon. Estimated value, five thousand dollars."

Lights sparkled in the dark in front of me.

"Does that help?" the woman said. Bright threads in her voice, of something like hope.

"It does. Oh my God, yes, it does." I swallowed a lump in my throat. "I can't thank you enough."

"Well, you're welcome." A slight pause. "I hope you find what you're looking for."

"You, too," I started to say, but she had already hung up.

Thomas *Brown*. I ended the call and fired up a search engine. There were 261 Tom Browns in Illinois alone. Not much of a starting point, but it would have to do. I put the phone down and picked up a pen, circling Marley's last name over and over.

Brown, Brown, Brown. I see you. I'm going to find you.

20

Traffic was snarled up on 176 after work, so I looped around to the library through the north end of town. I had already filled Jamie in on my phone calls to the trucking companies, conveniently omitting the part where I impersonated a Chicago police officer. Later, a nice lady from LTHS told me over the phone that I could access the digital yearbook archive via the alumni portal on the internet. The dashboard clock read nearly seven. The library closed at nine, so I had plenty of time to get over there and find Marley, or whoever she was, even after I'd stopped for a burger and a Coke. The light turned green at Maplewood Lane and I hit the gas. The last time I was here, I had ended up at the police station. As the empty intersection slid past I looked down Maplewood for Marley's house. There it was, halfway down the block, the light blue house—

With its lights on.

I stomped the brakes and my Coke went down, splattering the pristine passenger seat and footwell. I groaned, swatting at the mess with my hoodie. This would not go over well when I returned the Camry of Death, but I would worry about that later. Maplewood Lane was dark except for Marley's windows, like blank eyes. My hands turned the wheel, and the car glided around the corner instead of going straight. The library slipped out of my mind for good.

I pulled up next to the fire hydrant in front of the house. Lights were on all across the first floor. A shadow moved behind the curtains, now dark and close, now melting away into the light. It was just the owner, I thought, the landlord. Some guy with a long last name — isn't that what Bailey had said? A guy who had known Marley, who maybe knew who she was and where she came from.

I shouldered my backpack, got out of the car, and walked up the front. *Hi, you don't know me,* I practiced silently. And *I know it's late, but . . .* I was halfway up the porch steps when a breeze blew the curtains open and I caught a glimpse of the living room. I stopped midstep, one foot on the porch.

The room was a wreck. The floor and the stuffy furniture were covered with mountains of clothing and assorted junk. I recognized the wispy black clothes from the entry closet where I'd hidden from Nico. Garbage bags sat open all over the floor, half full, like black tree stumps.

I crept to the window and peeked through the curtain slit. There was no one in the room. The hamster that had ratted me out to Jamie lay on its side on a pile of faded T-shirts. Boards creaked in the house as someone came down the hallway singing to himself in a high rock 'n' roll screech.

"*I'm a WRATHCHILD! Coming to get you! Oooh yeah yeah!*" He drummed on the wall as he sang the guitar lick.

I clapped myself to the side of the window, out of sight, heart whomping. Max. Again. I peeked back in. Today he was wearing a black Pegboy T-shirt choked with silver chains under a black hoodie. I couldn't tell if it was the same hoodie in the video from Chicago Asian Foods. He put his hands on his hips, surveyed the scene, and resumed stuffing the leftovers of Marley's life into the garbage, singing all the while.

Sharp little stones hammered my ribs from the inside. I pulled out my phone, eyes on Max, and texted Jamie: **Max is at Marley's!!**

Too late, I realized I had forgotten to silence my phone. The typing sound rose into the air, jackhammer-loud. I froze. Max, crouched on the floor with his back to me, stopped screeching and sat up. He turned toward the window just as I ducked under the sill.

Footsteps creaked out of the bedroom, heading for the front door. I scanned the yard wildly. Nowhere to hide. Too far to make a break for the car, standing cockeyed in the fire zone. And still running. That wouldn't look suspicious to him at all.

The front door light snapped on. I took a leap sideways off the porch, landing crooked on my ankle. Shock waves pounded through my leg. I took off limping along the side of the house and stumbled into a small weedy backyard. A large wooden shed took up most of it, backed by a patchy flower bed under a chipped wooden fence. There was a tangle of thick bushes on the other side. They were very tall and looked very prickly. So much for my plan of vaulting the fence and doubling back later.

My phone buzzed.

Jamie: **Go home. I'll see if we have a car in the area.**

It occurred to me that all this cloak-and-dagger crap might be unnecessary. Max could still be the wrong guy, as Jamie kept reminding me.

But . . . Max was *here*. Clearing away Marley's things. What possible reason would he have to do that unless he was covering his tracks? *The simplest explanation is usually the best,* Owen said in a rare appearance in my head. He was dressed as the Page of Swords, except instead of a sword he carried an old-fashioned barbershop razor.

The back door of the house screeched open behind me. No time to mess with the fence. I yanked open the shed doors and dove into blackness that smelled like wet wood and paint thinner, my backpack smacking me in the shoulders.

I turned back to the door and listened. The silence was really loud. Crickets chirped and a bird whoo-whooed in the distance, all of it screeching and howling over a low electric hum that may have been blood rushing through my ears. I tried to pick footsteps or a squeaking door out of the bedlam. Had Max come out into the yard? Was he creeping up to the shed right now?

I backed up. Something cold and sharp poked me in the ribs and clanged on the floor. I wheeled around, eyes bulging in the dim light, and came face to face with a gaunt man with fiery eyes.

I stifled a screech, then looked closer. The fiery-eyed man was Nick Cave, staring at me from an easel. Someone had painted him slouched, hand on hip, wild black hair flying, in front of an old-fashioned silver microphone. He was shirtless. There was some serious thirst in this painting. I grinned, despite myself. *Marley.*

My eyes settled in and I made out other paintings on easels and shoved in corners. Metal shelves lined the walls, stuffed with paint cans, brushes, rollers, palettes, and scrunched-up colored tubes. Scattered in between the shelves were gardening tools, bags of soil, and spray bottles of weed killer. The place couldn't decide if it was a gardening shed or an art studio. There wasn't enough room for both, and they held a sort of uneasy peace that threatened to collapse at any moment.

Lights snapped on in the backyard. The textured glass window in the side of the shed glowed.

"Uh, excuse me," Max shouted from the back porch. "I've called the police?"

"*You* called the police?" I stepped over the long metal thing I had knocked over. It was a garden tool with a flat edge that I knew was not a rake but I couldn't remember the name and my addled brain kept yelling *rake!* at me. I peered through the window but the glass was too curvy to see through. "*I* called the police."

There was a pause. "Katie? Is that you?" The steps creaked. "Oh, man, you scared me." A shadow darkened the window and the doors of the shed rattled.

"Uh-uh! Don't move!" I picked up the not-rake and tried to bar the doors with it but then I realized the doors opened outward, so I gripped the thing like a weapon and backed away. "I've got a— I'm holding a— Look, just get away from the door, all right?"

"Okay, man, whatever." The door went still. "What are you doing here?"

"What am *I* doing here?" I shifted my weight off my sore ankle. "What are *you* doing? Why are you trashing all of Marley's stuff?"

"I'm just putting it away. It's not like she's going to need it." Joking about it now, the cold son of a bitch. Now he was trying to peek in through the gap around the door latch. "Are you spying on me?"

"*Me* spying on *you*?" I white-knuckled the tool handle. "You broke into my house!"

Long pause. "I did what now?"

"I saw you at Chicago Asian Foods on Tuesday." In the dark, I fumbled with my phone and dialed up the video of Max in the store parking lot. "Here." I cracked the doors and thrust the phone at him. "Are you going to tell me this isn't you?"

A long-fingered hand wearing a skull ring took my phone. "Did you say Tuesday?" He went quiet, watching the video. "Hell yeah, this is me. Tuesday is half off vegan poke bowls." He eased my phone back through the slot.

"Oh, really? And did you get *everything you needed*? Or was anything *missing*?" I yanked my phone back, swiped to the pics from my patio, and jammed it back out.

Silence from the yard. Then: "This one is most definitely *not* me. Who wears shoes like that anymore? They're a crime against humanity." The phone came back. I grabbed it and squinted at the patio guy. He was wearing dirty sneakers that in better days had been white. They did seem distinctly un-Max-like. How did I not catch that before?

"You know what? You seem like you're kind of in a dark place right now." Max's voice dropped. "Have you been drinking? Because I've been there, you know? You're not alone."

There was a commotion in the yard. Footsteps, crunching sticks, and chattering radios. Flashlights played over the shed. The little window lit up and a sliver of light pierced the gap in the door latch.

"Oh yeah, hi, officers, thanks for coming," Max said. "I just heard some noises out here and we've had some break-ins recently, so I . . ."

"Hey. Hey." I leaped up to the door. "Don't talk to them. They're here about *you*."

Max's voice dropped to a whisper and I could only catch every few words. ". . . know her . . . usually pretty chill . . . drinking a little? Maybe?"

"I am not drunk and I am not crazy," I said in my sanest voice. "Officers, aren't you here because of a prowler?"

"Mr. Karakostas did call in a possible intruder at this address," a male voice said.

"Karakostas. You mean the owner? Did you talk to him already?"

"*I'm* the owner, Katie," Max said. "This is my house."

"Your house?" I was hearing words but they weren't fitting into the little meaning-cubbies in my brain. "But your name is . . ."

"Max Indigo is my stage name, man. If you were a club owner, would you hire Theodosius freakin' Karakostas?"

My head reeled. Owen and his razor hadn't said anything about getting all the facts before you jumped to a conclusion. "So . . . you live here?"

"Nah, this is my folks' old place. I just come here to paint." His voice got shy and proud. "Did you see my Nick Cave in there?"

I looked at Nick Cave. *Nice going, dumbass,* his eyes said. "I thought Marley painted this."

"No, Marley was just crashing here for a few months. Probably hiding from her boyfriend." Max grunted. "That guy was baaad news. You know he broke in here the other day? Trashed the place?"

"You're kidding."

"Yeah, I just found out this morning when I checked messages. I hadn't been here in weeks," Max said. "Marley was cool, though. I just wish she'd cleaned out her stuff before she split for the Bahamas."

She's not in the Bahamas, I wanted to say. *She's dead.* But my voice had fried to a crisp in my throat. *Isn't she?* I sat down heavily on the ground and dropped the fake rake. I felt like I was walking into a lake and the floor had dropped off, leaving me thrashing in a dark void.

The man cop spoke again. "How about you guys catch up out here, huh?" Lights flashed through the door slit again. "Miss, I'm going to open these doors. And I'm going to need you to come out real slow, all right?"

"Yeah, come on out of there, Katie," Max added. "Hey, I got cocoa inside. You want some cocoa?"

I did want some cocoa. My body felt heavy and I wondered what would happen if I just lay down on the floor and took a quick nap. Okay, so it was a stretch to think Max and his cocoa killed anyone or broke into my house. But if not Max, then who? And how about the picture of Marley's body? Someone had sent it to Nico. Someone who knew about the money. I wasn't crazy— there was something here.

But I wasn't going to figure it out sitting in Max's shed with a creepy painting and a nameless gardening tool.

I got up and pushed open the creaky double doors. The flashlight swept my face and I edged out with my hands up and my eyes squished shut. When I opened them, I saw Max standing next to two cops, a short guy with a mustache and . . . oh, shit.

"Well, well." Nicole Barton squeezed her thin lips together. "I should have known."

"You two know each other?" Max looked between the two of us. "Cool."

"Oh yeah, we're best buds," Nicole said. "Just saw each other a few days ago. She had a *break-in*." She didn't actually make air quotes, but they hung in the air anyway.

Max held his hands up. "Wasn't me, scout's honor." I decided anyone who used the expression *scout's honor* did not know how to crime.

"Don't worry, we've got suspects," Nicole told Max. "The Tooth Fairy. The Easter Bunny. Hope it's not the Easter Bunny. That sucker's fast." I had forgotten what a sarcastic grump Nicole could be.

"That break-in was real, all right?" I said. "We've got video."

"Oh yeah?" Nicole said. "Of what? You making a mess and having everyone else come clean it up?"

"At least I'm *trying*," I shot back. Something snapped in me; I heard an actual snapping sound. Black clouds seeped through my vision, like ink slipping through a glass of water. "A woman is dead. *My friend* is dead, people are breaking into my house and threatening me, and I'm the only one who gives a rat's ass."

Nicole and Mustache exchanged a look, but I couldn't stop. "All you people ever do is sit around on your phones and go to meetings about . . . about . . . repainting your cars and . . . and . . ." I struggled to remember the list of bureaucratic nonsense Jamie had rattled off on the phone earlier this afternoon. "And . . . eating cake."

"How about you just take it down a notch," Nicole said in a low voice.

"No, *you* take it down a notch." I stepped back instinctively, but I had forgotten about the gardening tool on the floor of the shed behind me. I stepped on its face and its handle swung up and beaned me in the back of the head like I was in a Three Stooges movie. I pitched forward, lost my balance, and careened straight into Nicole.

Nicole's self-defense impulses, honed by years of simmering rage, flipped into overdrive. She whirled me around and hooked me from behind, twisting my arm up between us. Fireworks exploded in my shoulder.

"Now, guys," I heard Max say. "Let's not go there."

I staggered forward with Nicole still glued to me and we danced into the shed. She smashed me face-first into a shelf of paintbrushes and my nose, which was always a wind-blow away from a nosebleed anyway, exploded into a gusher, spraying drops of blood into my eyes. I tossed my head and sent a trowel sailing into a crate of paint tubes. It was like someone had thrown the first punch in the simmering détente between the garden tools and the paint supplies because the shelves started to creak, and then they were shaking, and one went down, twisting crosswise with a sad moan, crashing into another one that also went down, and then they were all coming down in a thundering multi-colored trail of destruction. Colorful paint bombs exploded everywhere.

Nicole produced a wet gurgle and let me go. I collapsed on the floor in a blue puddle next to an empty can. When I sat up and looked around, Nicole was gone. In her place was a yeti, blue from head to toe with white blinking eyes. A hellscape of paint-splashed metal and plastic surrounded us, topped by wooden signs with cheerful gardening slogans. GARDENING IS FOR PANSIES, one of them announced.

There was a strangled cry. Outside, in the yard, Max clutched his mouth, eyes wide with horror. I twisted around to see what he was looking at. There, askew against the remains of a defunct shelf, was Max's masterpiece, splashed all over with cheerful pastel strokes. Nick Cave looked like an extra in an unusually grim 1980s breakdancing epic.

Max's face quivered. Mustache stepped toward him, but Max

waved him away. He turned toward me and his eyes grew dark. "Officers," he said, looking at me. "Would you mind getting this woman the fuck off my property?"

Nicole snapped to life. She grabbed a fistful of my shirt and yanked me up off the floor like a naughty kitten.

By the time she had frog-marched me, handcuffed, out to Max's front yard, the tow truck was already halfway down the block with the Camry of Death.

"Uh-oh." Nicole's blue death mask of a face brightened. She broke into a syrupy baby voice. "Looks like Daddy's car got taken away."

21

"Wait here." Nicole shoved me into the chair. She had wiped the paint from around her eyes and looked like a magical blue raccoon.

"Am I under arrest?" Nobody had taken my stuff or told me I had the right to remain silent, plus if I were under arrest, Nicole would be rubbing my nose in it. But she ignored me and turned to leave.

"Are these really necessary?" I called after her, rattling my cuffs.

She paused with her hand on the doorknob. "No," she said, and left, shutting the door.

I looked around. The meeting room was a lot like the one where I had first talked to Jamie, sort of cheery and institutional with cheap blond wood furniture and beige carpeting. There was a plastic crate of toys in the corner and one of those electronic noise boxes for babies with stuff that twirled and honked and lit up. At least the chair was solid this time—a spinny, rolly one with a bendy back that allowed me to fidget as much as I wanted to.

My brain, too busy of late to pay much attention to my body, was catching up on recent events. Aches and pains were settling in one by one, like a guided tour of the evening's calamities. The side of my face burned where Nicole had slammed me into the shelves, and there was a throbbing gash on my forearm from the sandpapery shed floor. I had a rash on the back of my leg from some noxious weed, and my ankle was still complaining about my escape off the porch. To top it off, my nose had started to bleed again, and I couldn't do a damn thing about it except sniffle the mess back up into my head. Which hurt from being smacked by a hoe. At least I had solved that mystery.

I slumped in the bendy chair and waited. My phone stuck partway out of my pocket and if I twisted my head upside down I could see part of a text message hanging on the screen. Jamie. I wondered if he had sent it before or after Nicole had used me as a weapon of mass destruction.

. . . turns out Max is the landlord. You're . . .

The *you're* hung in the air, mysterious and blank. I tried to guess what came next.

You're . . .

. . . trespassing on private property?

. . . twisting the facts to fit your imagination?

. . . pissing off everyone who's ever been nice to you?

I put my head down on the table, falling into a trance in which everyone I had pissed off paraded in front of me in a drunken conga line. Max. I had never heard him swear at anyone. What gnawed at me most was not that I had ruined his painting and destroyed his shed, but that I had accused him of horrible things despite glaring evidence to the contrary. It had seemed perfectly plausible to me that he broke into someone's house, turned on all the lights full blast, and spring-cleaned the place while screeching at the top of his lungs. I needed a murderer, and he was convenient.

I'd known I would piss off Jessie somehow, although I had wildly underestimated the level of my probable offenses against the White Camry of Death. And then there was, of course, Jamie, who had been patient with me long after I had stopped deserving it. I told myself that by the time he'd told me to leave Max's it was already too late, but that was just another excuse in a long line of them—the last domino in a trail I had set up and pushed off a cliff. I shouldn't have gone to Max's house at all. I should have driven straight to the library like I'd meant to. Before that, I should have left the mall parking lot and let Nico go his way instead of following him and landing on Joey's radar. And earliest and worst of all, I should have read Nico's cards straight up instead of cheating him and finding that terrible picture of Marley. I had caused all this because I wanted to feel good about myself. Because I was tired of feeling like a loser. Because I just wanted—

". . . vegan poke?" a loud voice said close by, rhyming *poke* with *joke*. "What the hell's that?"

My head jerked up. I had been asleep on the table in the police station conference room in a pool of bloody snot.

"It's a Hawaiian dish." Jamie's voice didn't correct the older man's pronunciation. "Made with raw fish. But in this case, with no raw fish. Or fish of any kind." The voices had been winding through my dream for some time. "The time on the receipt matches the video. He was in the area getting lunch. It was just a misunderstanding."

The muffled voices were coming from next door. I danced my rolling chair up to the wall and leaned my ear against it. A vent in the floor carried the sound, and also blasted cold air up my tortured nose. On the upside, I could now hear every knock, squeak, and rustle.

"So, we have two . . . no, three home invasions where nothing significant was stolen or damaged"—stiff paper was folded over—"and a woman who may or may not be missing or dead?"

"Yes, sir." A chair squeaked. "It's not enough to run with, and too much to drop."

"Uh-huh."

"Strictly back burner for now. I'm keeping up with my caseload."

"Jamie. Relax. You see these?"

"Your stars?"

"That's right. You know what they mean? They mean I don't give a shit how you work your cases. That's not the chief's job." The other voice was gruff but not unfriendly, like a foulmouthed Santa Claus.

"Yes, sir."

"What I want to know is"—the chief took a gulp of something. A clonk of ceramic on wood—"why this girl—this Katherine True—pops up in every single one of these." I flinched away from the wall as if the chief could see me.

"Katie? She's not mixed up in this, if that's what you mean," Jamie said. "I thought the same thing myself at first."

"Uh-huh. What was she doing at this guy's house tonight?"

Jamie hesitated. "She's . . . curious. The missing woman was her friend. I guess you could say Katie feels some ownership." I let out a quiet breath. He could have said a lot worse.

"Ownership, huh?" A piece of paper was crumpled and tossed into a metal garbage can.

"It's funny, some of the earlier leads actually came from her. She's very . . ." Jamie broke off.

There was a long silence. "Why didn't you just come out and say you were sleeping with her?"

"I'm not—"

"Jamie. Jamie. Listen. Sleep with her, don't sleep with her, I don't care. Again, not my job. But what you *don't* get to do is treat her like your partner. Does she work here? I don't remember signing her paycheck."

"I did share some information with her as a courtesy," Jamie said evenly. "It's possible I may have shared too much."

"You think? Because now she and her sense of 'ownership' are running around sticking their nose in things that don't concern them and getting their ass beat by Barton. What if this was an actual murder case? What if you spent weeks building something rock-solid and it all got tossed on some bullshit technicality? Because of your *improper relationship* with a witness?"

"Like I said, there's no relationship."

"Come on, Jamie, you know how this works. It doesn't have to *be* wrong, it just has to *look* wrong."

"So, that's what this is about? You're afraid to look bad?"

"You're damn right I'm afraid to look bad. That, by the way, *is* my job. You work the cases, I make sure you look pretty doing it. Do what you need to do with this girl, but keep it out of here. Are we clear?"

My neck was cramping from being zigzagged up against the wall. I shifted in the chair and it scooted out from under me. I dragged myself back to the wall with a grunt.

"Yes, sir. From now on I'll only share things with Miss True that concern her directly." He was calling me Katie before.

"You won't be sharing anything with her at all, because I'm turning her break-in over to Paulson."

"Oh. All right, I understand." There was a pause. "Paulson,

though, he's . . . I wonder if these cases require someone a little . . ."

"A little less of a drag-ass? That's why he's perfect. You said it yourself, there's hardly anything here. Any other staffing decisions you'd like to weigh in on?"

"No, sir."

"Good. Because I'm also putting you on patrol."

"*What?*" For the first time, Jamie's voice bristled with annoyance. "Sir, is that really necessary?"

"Listen, Malibu Barbie. This ain't LA. We are a *service department*. Everybody does their patrol rotation and they do it with a smile on their face or they find another job. Is that going to be a problem?"

"No, sir."

"Good." Chair springs began to squeak. Jamie was leaving. "Wait a second. Sit down." The chair squeaked again. A sigh and a very long pause. "Let me ask you something, Jamie. Why are you here?"

"I . . . what? Sir, I don't . . ."

"Right now, why are you here? Your shift ended hours ago."

"I'm catching up on a few things."

"Why are you hooked up?"

"They're short a few guys on the road tonight. I'm just listening in."

The chief fell silent. Then: "I'm about to say something I've never said in the thirty-three years I've been doing this. And if you tell any of these other knuckleheads I said it, I will kill you and make it look like an accident."

I pressed my ear to the wall.

"You work too much." The chief enunciated every word. "And when you start your patrol rotation, you will have a regular shift, with a beginning and an end. When your shift ends, you will go home. Is that clear?"

Jamie didn't answer right away. "Yes, sir."

"I know what happened in LA," the chief said in a low voice. "You know that, right? I read your psych profile." A chill skittered down my spine.

"I figured it was part of the hiring process." Jamie's voice was calm and even, but it had taken on an odd clipped quality, like he was measuring his words out beforehand. I tried to imagine his face and couldn't. I leaned my forehead against the wall and closed my eyes. Suddenly, I was exhausted.

When the chief spoke again, he was almost whispering. "Jamie, it was an accident. It wasn't your fault. You can't control everything. Shit, sometimes you can't control anything."

Something dripped on my arm and I realized my nose was bleeding again. I hadn't even noticed.

"I know what you must be feeling. But you're not going to make it go away by working all the time," the chief said. "Call Employee Assistance. Trust me, you ignore this stuff, it gets worse."

I was scared of what was going to come out of Jamie's mouth next. When it did, it wasn't what I expected. "Does this count as my first session?" he said.

The chief gave a startled laugh. "Well, you can do a hell of a lot better than me." Relieved to be in joke territory again. "Why don't you get out a little? Socialize." He snapped his fingers. "Hey! I'm doing my fishing trip up in Door County next weekend."

"I've heard." Jamie's voice was weird and cheery.

"You should come, huh? The guys will shit themselves if I say you're coming. What do you say?"

"I will definitely consider it. Thank you, sir. For everything." The hair on my arms stood up. I remembered where I had met this icky teacher's-pet Jamie before. A variation of him had bonded with Nico over their (fake) shared workout history. The real Jamie had no intention of going fishing with the chief.

"Great, Jamie, that's great." The chief was pleased with himself for *getting through*. I was embarrassed for him.

My face was still glued to the wall when the door to my room started opening. I shoved off and paddled frantically across the floor. Not until I was docked at the table did I see the bloody nose stain I had left on the wall. It sat there like a threatening message someone had started to leave at a murder scene before they got distracted and went for pizza.

Jamie was still wearing the same jeans and blazer from this morning but they seemed looser on him, like he had somehow shrunk over the course of the day. He was wearing an earpiece with a curly cord. I searched his face. He didn't look like a guy who'd just been chewed out by his boss. For a dizzy second I wondered if I had dreamed their conversation, too.

My eyes flicked to the stain on the wall. Nope. All real.

Jamie looked at my handcuffs. "Oh, geez," he said. "Sorry about that. Here, let me get that for you." I went stiff. The real Jamie would have just given me a look that I'd still be thinking about hours later. *It's me,* I wanted to yell at him. *You don't have to talk to me like that.*

He fished a set of keys out of his pocket and circled behind me to unlock the cuffs. "You're free to go." He made no move to sit in the other chair. "Max has decided not to press charges."

"He did?" I rubbed my scratched-up wrists. "I am?"

"He changed his mind pretty much immediately. Followed you to the station." Jamie was already walking to the door. "He said he wanted to make sure we weren't too rough on you." I watched him for sarcasm, but it wasn't there. There was nothing there except syrupy customer service friendliness.

"He said that?" I sank into the chair. Max's forgiveness was even worse than his anger. At least I had deserved the anger.

Jamie opened the door. "Oh, and by the way, if anything new comes in about your break-in, you'll hear from Detective Paulson. He's handling your case now." He caught sight of the stain on the wall, then glanced at me and the old Jamie flickered through his eyes. "But I'm guessing you knew that already."

I drooped even lower. "Jamie, I'm so sorry." My voice came out small and furry. "If I had left things alone like you told me to, none of this would have happened."

"Don't be sorry." Jamie hesitated with his hand on the doorknob. "I'm the one who should be apologizing to you." He examined my face. "You've got a . . ." He pointed to his own nose. "A thing. Right there."

Shit. I searched through my pockets for something to wipe my nose with and came up with the list of clues I had scribbled about Marley. I shoved it back in my pocket.

Jamie sighed, closed the door, and walked over to me. He produced a snowy white handkerchief from his jacket pocket—of course he had a snowy white handkerchief in his jacket pocket— and handed it to me.

"Yeah, okay, thanks." I took the hankie from him and got busy wiping my face so I wouldn't start crying like an asshole. "It's not as bad as it looks." I started jabbering to distract both of us. "It's just a thing my nose does. When I, like, get my face smashed against something, or really for no reason at all sometimes. They called me Red Tide in high school."

Jamie sat down. We sat across from each other for a long time without saying anything. I hated that he was watching me but I also didn't want him to leave.

"I should have cut this thing off right away," he said. "But I didn't. I encouraged you. Gave you reports to work on. Bounced my theories off you." He leaned down to meet my eyes. "I made you feel like you belonged in the middle of all this. No wonder you started imagining things."

"Come on, Jamie, give me a little credit, will you?" I smiled around the crusty blood under my nose. I'm sure it looked fantastic. "You're not responsible for my shitty decisions. I can fuck things up perfectly fine on my own."

He sat up and his face went still. He folded his hands together on the table. "Tell me something, Katie," he said. The breezy formality was gone and something low and cruel crept into his voice. "Have you ever had to take care of someone?"

I looked down at the crumpled handkerchief in my hands, red on white. The stain was larger than it looked.

"Have you ever had to teach someone? Discipline someone?" His voice was getting quieter. It was less sound now than a low vibration boring through me. "Has anyone ever died because of your 'shitty decisions'?" He was waiting for an answer. I shook my head.

"No?" He leaned toward me across the table. "Then don't talk to me about responsibility. Because what responsibility *doesn't* mean is doing whatever you want, whenever you want, no matter how it affects other people." Owen's superhero-Katie avatar popped into my mind, round and simple, like a child's idea of someone who does everything right. A fantasy, a game.

"Maybe you haven't learned that yet, but I have," Jamie was saying, "which is why I have no excuse for putting you in danger just because I like you and I want you around." He said it with no emotion at all.

I looked up at him. He really wasn't angry at me. This wasn't an *it's not you, it's me* thing that really meant *it's you*. No, he was genuinely disgusted with himself, but it didn't have anything to do with me. It had to do with his dead friend. Tyler Frank.

"Jamie—" I started to answer him, but he turned away and touched his earpiece, listening. He motioned for me to wait.

His face changed and he looked at me. "There's been a break-in at the old mall," he said. "Firebird Imports. Someone didn't arm the back door when they closed up."

A chill spread through my chest. I willed myself to remember arming the system, pressing the code into the little beige numbered rectangles, feeling their flexible nubs under my fingers. I couldn't remember it. All I remembered was rushing out to go to the library, to get to the next step in my great adventure. For whose sake? For Marley's? *The closer you get to someone,* Jamie had told me, *the less clearly you see them. You just see yourself.*

Hot, shameful tears sprang into my eyes. My phone rang and I looked down before Jamie could see me. It was Larissa.

"I'll let you get that." Jamie got up and walked to the door. "You can leave the door open on your way out, okay? Thanks so much."

22

"No work today?" Bear bellowed at me from the half-assembled back door.

I slumped in Jessie's wicker patio chair and struggled not to clap my hands over my ears. Bear couldn't even be bothered to check messages most of the time but today, the one day I had intended to sleep through in its entirety, he had banged on my door at eight in the goddamn morning. I knew if I told him to go away he'd never come back, so I waved him in and followed him and his old-fashioned flip-top toolbox out to the patio, grabbing a misshapen cereal bar along the way.

"Nope, no work today," I told Bear. "Lost my job." Larissa had yelled at me for a solid ten minutes over the phone last night, calling me a "goat," a "peasant," and a "tomcat." She couldn't believe I was careless and stupid enough to leave the back door unarmed and therefore concluded that I was acting at the behest of my gang of criminal goats. She commanded me to report to the store as soon as possible to collect my final paycheck, and then to proceed directly to the Devil.

"Oh, shit." Bear gave me a sympathetic look. He had a moony face that was too large for his birdlike body, with big round eyes and thinning hair that sprang up from his head like a scraggle of weeds. He was the least bearlike man I had ever seen, but at that moment I was uninterested in his origin story. "Skimming off the top?"

"If I wanted to do that, I'd pick a place where the top and bottom are further apart," I said. "No, I left the back door open and the place got robbed."

Bear made a disgusted noise that meant either *I'm sorry* or *what a dipshit*. "Well," he said, digging a screwdriver into the door lock. "They'd better give you the biggest cut, that's all I'm saying."

"Who? Of what?"

"Your crew." He leveled a knowing look at me. "They need to treat you right. You're the one that took the fall for them."

I stared at him. "There's no crew. I'm not taking any 'fall.' I forgot to lock the damn door."

"Oh, I gotcha." Bear chuckled and gave me a sly cuff on the shoulder. He looked around and lowered his voice. "Anyone comes asking, I got your back, sis."

Jessie had picked me up last night wordlessly, her lips a white line. She had laid a towel down on the passenger seat of the Porsche to ward off the noxious cocktail of blood and paint drifting off my person. Her car smelled so nice I wanted to cry. I'd had the Camry of Death for less than a day and it had already begun to develop an unmistakable funk of Me.

We stopped for the light at Lake and 60, half a mile from home. "Do you, uh, need the number of the tow lot?" I said.

"We got it," she snapped. "Mike's heading over there now." I cringed. Jessie's husband, Mike, was a nice guy who had played football in college and liked to barbecue. He didn't know me well enough to expect his kindness to be repaid with disaster. "And then he's taking it to the cleaners to get the stains out, thank you very much for that."

"I'm sorry. I—"

"No. Nope." Jessie stared straight ahead. The red light fell on her face, making her look slightly deranged. "Just. Don't."

"Okay." She was still going to yell at me, she just wanted to control exactly when and how. I sank into my seat and waited.

The light turned. Jessie gunned the motor and darted around the corner. "I don't understand it," she said. I hunched down farther. "I just don't understand why you want to *give up* like this." She turned to me. "Don't you want something better for yourself?"

"I do," I said. "I do want something better. But . . ." I made my voice as gentle as possible. "Maybe my better isn't your better."

"Okay, I don't even have any idea what that means," Jessie said. "Do you? Do you have any idea what you want? Enlighten me, O Great Enlightened One, what your 'better' is."

Good question. I didn't say anything. Chicago Asian Foods drifted past, all white stone and red neon.

"I give you furniture," Jessie went on. "I give you healthy recipes. Beauty products. I invite you over for dinner although of course you never come. I lend you a car. . . ."

"Wow. Yep. There it is." I sat up and pulled my backpack onto my knees. I needed to get out of this car. "The guilt trip took way too long to come out tonight. I'd like to speak to the manager." I faced her. "I specifically told you I did not need the car. I was fine without it."

"Well, then, why did you take it?" An angry squeak crept into her voice. "You could have said no."

"Oh, sure. If I wanted to watch you sulk and play the victim and whine about how nobody appreciates you. Like you're doing right now. You want to know why I never come over? This is it."

"All I do," Jessie said, her voice falling back down to a tense whisper, "all I've *ever* tried to do, is help you. I've been offering you a job—a good job—for years, yet you *choose* to work one crappy job after another instead of aiming higher." She clasped her hands over her heart and her voice wavered. "Do you know how that makes me feel?" She twisted the wheel and we shot into the Shady Grove lot.

"Look, I don't want to sell fucking real estate, all right?" I shouted. "Which you would know if you ever listened to anyone except yourself."

Jessie turned to me and the look on her face made my insides go soft. We were still staring at each other when the fire hydrant jumped out of the dark in front of us like a short, angry scarecrow.

Jessie gasped and yanked at the wheel. The car whined, and for a few agonizing seconds we skidded and rolled, coming to a stop inches from Bear's Camaro.

Jessie stared straight ahead, breathing hard. "Get out," she whispered. "Get out of my car."

I scrambled out, dragging my backpack after me. The Porsche roared through a three-point turn and sped out of the parking lot. I watched its red taillights fade along 60 and disappear around the corner.

Now, sitting on my patio, watching a bright orange truck back into a loading bay yards from me, I could still see the look on Jessie's face in the car last night. She looked like a kid, like the time she had spent all day learning how to use a Rainbow Loom so she could make a bracelet for Kaylee Kim and when she gave it to her, Kaylee didn't want it. I closed my eyes but Jessie's face was still there.

"It was only a matter of time," I said out loud.

"Before what?"

I had forgotten that Bear was still in the doorway, listening to me talk to myself. "Before I screwed everything up," I said.

"Aw, shit, you can always get another job," he said. "My cousin's looking for a driver. You just need your own car." He scratched his nose with the screwdriver. "And be able to drive good at night. Like, really fast. Want me to put in a word for you?"

"Thanks, Bear." I was astonished to find myself considering it. "I think I'm good for now."

After Bear left I stayed on the patio even though the cereal bar was a distant memory and I didn't own a coffee maker. The longer I sat in the chair watching truckers offload pallets into the market and smelling diesel fumes (which I kind of liked) and garbage (which I didn't), the longer I could put off doing anything else. I needed groceries. I needed to clean my apartment. I needed to call Jessie and apologize.

The last truck backed up with a mournful beeping, maneuvered slowly out of the loading bay, and rumbled off in a gray cloud. I got up and tested the patio door lock. It worked, yay. I walked into the bedroom. Marley's necklace hung on my dresser mirror. Yes, the video showed a guy breaking in. But there was zero proof he was after the necklace. There wasn't even any real proof that Marley was dead, as Jamie tried to tell me a hundred years ago at the police station with his hands in his pockets and those clear, intense eyes fixed on me. I fished my phone out of my shorts and reread the text he had sent me last night:

Checked with Bailey and it turns out Max is the landlord. You're probably home by now, I hope. I'll talk to you tomorrow.

Not likely. I shoved my phone back into my pocket. It beeped and I snatched it up again, heart pounding. The goddamn LTHS alumni association was cordially inviting me to my ten-year high school reunion. I hurled my phone across the room. Then I took a breath and pushed Jamie out of my mind, clear eyes and all. He was just another piece of the fantasy I'd created around Marley. He'd fade away with the rest.

I realized, standing in my shorts and T-shirt in the wreck of my bedroom, scratching the rash on my leg, that I was done chasing Marley. I was a reader. It was what I did: I read signs and made stories out of them. But I had done it all wrong this time, done it backward. I had forced the signs to fit a story I'd already written—a story in which Marley and I were friends. I was desperate to see myself as she saw me, as more than just a square peg in the round hole of my life. After she died, I'd latched on even harder. Cracking her murder was going to define me, sharpen me up, save me from becoming one of those slapdash weirdos who lived alone in permanently temporary digs surrounded by napkin blueprints, novel excerpts in drawers, half-finished repairs, dropped hobbies, lapsed friendships, and lost jobs.

I was using her—first alive, then dead.

I moved to the couch and flicked the TV on, but the illegal cable connection was out. I picked up the velvet bag containing my cards and ran my fingers over the blind, smiling sun in the soft material.

I took out the deck, shuffled, and drew a card. It was a picture. Just a picture, figures on a bright background. I stared at it but there was a white fog in my mind where the cards used to be. I saw the card but I couldn't remember—couldn't feel—what it meant. I drew another, then another, tossing them onto the couch, onto the floor all around me, but they were all the same, mute paper and ink, no stories.

I closed my eyes and squeezed the balls of my hands into them until the burning went away and my breath stopped hitching. Everything was going to be fine.

23

Poof! Out of thin air an angel appeared, blowing its trumpet over an ocean of the dead: Judgment. The dead were rising, holding out their arms because like it or not, it was time to go, time to make a change. *Get up*, said the angel who was really Aunt Rosie. The trumpet was a huge bong. *You can't sit there forever.* Her voice was a scratchy whisper because she didn't want to blow out yet. She pounded the bong on the ground. *Knock, knock*, it went. *Knock, knock, knock.*

I jerked awake on the couch. Someone was knocking. For a second I thought I was stuck in a *Groundhog Day* loop and Bear was here to fix the patio door again. Then I remembered that that was two days ago. Or maybe three. Somewhere between then and now I had briefly moved from my own couch to the Ortizes' couch for my "babysitting" gig.

Outside, the sun sat high in the sky, red gold. It was afternoon. Owen's face was peeking through the patio door, glasses flashing.

I got up and let him in, stepping over tarot cards and crusted cereal bowls.

"Your door is locked." Owen's laptop bag was slung over his shoulder. "Why is your door locked?"

"Because that's how doors work." I slumped back down on the couch and wrapped myself in the smelly blanket from my bedroom. "Things are not supposed to be *broken* all the time." I smacked at the couch cushion I'd been using as a pillow and it toppled unwillingly off the armrest.

"That's very interesting," Owen said, which is what he said when things made no sense to him but he knew he had to provide an answer. "Anyway, I have Marley's memory card." He sat down on the floor and unzipped his laptop bag. "Dylan decrypted it."

I had forgotten about the memory card. I tried to click the TV on and was greeted with static. I tossed the remote onto the floor. "I don't want to see it."

Owen stopped taking out his laptop and looked at me. "Does that mean you do actually want to see it and I'm supposed to talk you into it, or do you really not want to see it?"

I shoved my fists into my eyes. "I do. Not. Want. To see it." When I took my fists away silver sparkles danced across the room.

Owen scratched the back of his head, started putting away his laptop, then stopped. "You, um . . ." he said. "You seem . . . upset?"

Something sharp came to my lips but I bit it back. None of this was Owen's fault. "I am," I said. "I am upset, Owen. Something is wrong with me. With"—I gestured to the mess I had made of my life in the past few days—"with all of this. And I don't know how to fix it." My throat felt scratchy and I sipped at a glass of musty day-old water. "At least when Marley was around, it felt like maybe I wasn't a complete loser, but she's gone, so . . ."

I shook my head and got up, scaring the thought of Marley away. "But it's okay. It's fine. Because I'm going to clean up." I picked up a pair of shorts, my phone, and a dirty fork. "And then I'm going to shower and change. And I'm going to call . . ." The breath whooshed out of me when I remembered the call I still hadn't made to Jessie.

I swayed on my feet and threw the stuff I had picked up back down. Then I lay down, wrapped myself up in the blanket, and burrowed back into the couch. This sequence of events had occurred at least five times over the past few days. I had lost count. I breathed in the earthy food smell of the couch, but this time it made me feel worse, like I didn't have anything of my own. Everything good in my life came from other people's generosity. Had I done anything to deserve it? Maybe I really was a vampire.

The room went quiet. Then Owen cleared his throat. "There's a guy. He's got a star on his head. And he's stepping on some stars. One, two, three, four stars."

"What the hell are you talking about?" I twisted around to look at him. He was sitting cross-legged on the floor across the milk crates from me, holding a card. He turned it to face me. The Four of Pentacles.

"What . . . is this . . . ? What are you doing?"

"You said this helps people." He grinned at me and shook the card.

A dorky guffaw burst out of me. Four of Pentacles. A dude locking himself away, blocking off the world because things have gotten too tough. "Not bad," I said. "What else you got?"

Owen smiled and for a second it got lighter in the room, just a shade. He picked another card at random off the floor. "A guy with a bunch of sticks?" He showed me the Nine of Wands. "His head is broken."

"Yeah, it is," I said. "He's still got a stick, though. He's not totally boned." I motioned for him to keep going.

"This one looks pretty good," Owen said. It was the Six of Cups, a pair of children in the walled-off garden I had always thought was magic, like the old woman's garden in *The Snow Queen*. The little boy was giving the little girl a cup full of flowers. The card shimmered and glowed in front of me. I had always found it puzzling, the figures slightly off, the warm glow around them soothing and sweet but also sad, like it was in the past, or the future, or maybe just a dream. I looked at Owen, his open, curious face. If someone was willing to help me—really help me, even if they didn't always understand what I was doing—maybe I wasn't a complete loser after all.

"Hey." I stood up and stretched. "Help me pick these up. And then let's look at that memory card."

"You ready?" Owen said. He typed in a long password one-handed off a piece of paper and hit Enter. His other hand was holding a slice of pizza.

The scary password window resolved into a folder with a single video file. Owen opened it and hit Play.

The video opened on a dark screen: a close-up of a small notebook bound in old-fashioned red leather. A hand reached into the frame and opened it to a set of pages covered in neat, cramped handwriting.

I took a breath and my heart started pounding. The fingernails on the hand were painted black. Marley.

The lens zoomed in and the hand began to flip pages, stopping for a clear shot of each one. It was a list: names, dates, locations, and times. Addresses in Waukegan, Grayslake, Gurnee. Dollar amounts. Other amounts.

"I know only one thing that's measured in kilos," I said.

Offscreen, Marley's unmistakable low, raspy chuckle. "I've got you, you sons of bitches," she muttered.

On the screen, the hand closed the ledger. There was a hacking noise off camera. The video went dark but the counter kept moving. "What in the blue hell are you doing?" said the thickest Chicago accent I had ever heard.

"Uncle Vito." I scooted close. "This is Thursday before last. At the Battaglia warehouse." I peered at the screen, trying to make out anything at all, but it was a wash of darkness. Marley must have stuffed her phone into her pocket.

There was a heavy swish, a scrabbling noise, and some gasping. "You got two choices, old man," Marley's voice said close by. Flat, deadly. "Either I take this money, or I blow your fucking head off and *then* I take this money. You decide."

A long, sick silence, a few indistinct wheezes and gasps from far offscreen. "That's right," Marley said. "I didn't think so."

More noise, heavy steps. The screen was flooded with light and there she was, a flash of red hair and dark eyes, her mouth a steely half smile.

The video went dead. There was no more. The only sound in the room was Owen chewing on his slice of anchovy-and-mushroom.

"She didn't just want the money," I said. "She wanted . . ."

More was the word that sprang to mind, but what *more* could be, I couldn't see. It was too big, too far away, like a dark ship hovering below the horizon, only its mast visible.

I played the video again and slid the counter to the end, to the split-second glimpse of Marley's face. Her eyes were black coals, the smile on her face mean and hard and relentless.

Who are you?

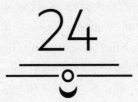

24

'd missed a spot: a glob of cheese on the milk crates.

I hopped up, grabbed a wipe from the depleted container in the kitchen, and wiped the glob away. Then I sat back down, picked up my chipped mug of Lipton, and stared at the thieving trucker report with *Thomas Brown* written all over it like a high school math notebook full of lovesick doodling. My cards were stacked next to it on the milk crates, in the eye of a whirling tornado of nervous energy that had left me showered and dressed and sitting in an uncharacteristically spotless apartment.

I slurped my tea and flicked the spade on Marley's necklace, with the tiny memory card nestled inside again. Ace of Spades, Ace of Swords. An abyss had opened up and swallowed everything I thought I knew about Marley—except that she was a bad boss bitch—but instead of feeling adrift, I felt free. I still didn't know who she was, but I was starting to understand why she did what she did, and why she lied to me about it. She was protecting me, keeping me from wading into the same dark undertow that had pulled her under.

Too late now. I owed her, and I knew what I had to do. I had to find out what happened, and who was responsible. It was just me now. Me and Marley—same as it ever was.

I drained my tea and actually got up to put the cup in the sink instead of leaving it lying around. Then I grabbed my backpack and packed my cards, a hoodie, a bottle of water, my phone charger, and a jar of peanuts that I had spilled all over my kitchen floor and stuffed back into the jar. I had no car to take me to the library, but the bus would do.

I was holding the doorknob when a small sheet of paper slipped under the door. I bent down to pick it up.

It was a cartoon. On white paper, black ink splashed across the page in familiar strokes of a heavy gold pen.

My heart skipped and whirred, like a machine someone had slammed with a baseball bat. The edges of the sheet were ragged where they had been torn off the pad. In the drawing, a man and a woman sat at a round table: Nico and me. We were digging at a single bowl of ice cream, giving each other scheming googly eyes. Nico looked like a moron again. I looked like a moron who thought she was smart.

Shadows choked off the light under the door. They swirled, then stopped—a heavy, immovable darkness. With a reptilian slowness, a second sheet slid under the door.

I picked it up and the room went dark around me.

Owen. He was drinking through a straw, hands wrapped around the cup, eyes closed in obvious pleasure. Tiny round beads floated in the cup, each with that luminous little window I was starting to recognize from all of Joey's drawings, the mote of joy that made the pictures sing.

The floor dropped away beneath my feet and I stumbled. The pictures burned in my fist. I backed up, tripping over the milk crates and dumping the report on the floor. Pages flew everywhere. I turned and plowed through them like a bear in a snowstorm. Clutching the pictures and my backpack, I shot through the patio door and slid it shut, locking it from the outside with my key. Sweat-blind, I ran for the chain-link fence that separated Shady Pines from the industrial park.

"Where you goin', gal?"

I shrieked and spun around. Bear sat on the patio of 1A, in a pile of mechanical parts that had known better days as an AC window unit.

"Bear." I didn't stop to celebrate, but took a running leap at the fence, ignoring the twinge in my still-sore ankle.

"Are you . . . ?" Bear stood up, watching me scratch my way up the links. "What are you doing?"

"There's a guy outside my door," I wheezed. "He's been watching me. I need to lose him, fast."

Bear's eyes widened in delight. "What's he look like?"

"Kind of a big guy. Good clothes." An educated guess. I hadn't dared to look through the peephole.

Bear scratched his pale gut. "The Ray Liotta–looking motherfucker in the Lexus?"

"You've seen him?" I paused, straddling the top of the fence.

"Oh yeah." He pointed toward the front lot. "He's been hanging out in his car all day."

"Shit." I hurled my backpack into the bramble of evergreen

bushes on the other side. It landed with a thunk and rolled into a patch of dirt. "Did you talk to him?"

"No." Bear narrowed his eyes and smacked a fist into his palm. "Want me to tell him to leave you the fuck alone, if he knows what's good for him?"

"No! Don't talk to him unless he talks to you first." I started down the other side. "Actually, if he asks about me, tell him I went to work."

"But I thought you got fired."

"I did." I scoped out a landing spot and jumped, favoring my good ankle. "But *he* doesn't know that." I got up and picked a dead bug out of my hair.

"Oh, man." A slow smile spread over Bear's face. "That's what I'm talking about!" He flipped me a jaunty salute. "Go, baby. You got this!"

I dusted myself off, straightened Marley's necklace, and wriggled into my backpack. "Thanks, Bear!" I shouted behind me, and took off into the industrial park. Just before I lost sight of Shady Pines I glanced back. Bear was crouched again in the middle of his work. He looked like he might be singing to himself.

For once, he had been right where I needed him to be.

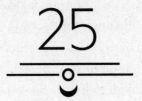

25

The Lake Terrace Public Library was five miles away by bus, but closer on foot if you didn't mind taking a few dangerous and only mildly illegal shortcuts through the industrial park. Joey's visit had caused me to reconsider my transportation strategy.

I stumbled through a sunlit maze of huge, flat gray-and-white buildings, yawning loading docks, and signs reading SHIPPING AND RECEIVING and DELIVERIES IN BACK. There were a few POSITIONS AVAILABLE signs, but a lot more that read FOR LEASE, standing cockeyed in empty parking lots with weeds breaking through cracks in the concrete. The highway hummed nearby, a low drone I could feel rather than hear. Mr. Ortiz used to work around here at a silicone plant before it burned down. I would see him walking to work along Route 60, a little hunched figure in a ball cap. Sometimes I would give him a ride.

When I couldn't ignore the stitch in my side anymore, I plunked down on a garbage-strewn patch of grass between the

Metra tracks and Lake Ruby and texted Owen. He had suppos-
edly gone home last night but I couldn't risk him showing up
again. **Joey's hanging around my place so stay away from there.
NO BUBBLE TEA!!!**

My fingers strayed to my pocket, where I'd stuffed Joey's crumpled drawings. I snatched my fingers out like they'd been burned.
Across Lake Ruby, the tiny white block of the police station sat
on the far shore. I'd have to start from scratch with the cops. Reel
out the whole story again to some pencil pusher waiting for me
to leave so he could go to lunch. But what choice did I have?
This was getting too dangerous to handle by myself.

Really? Jamie said, in my head. *If only someone had warned
you.*

You know what, I'm ignoring you, I said.

Mental Jamie gave me a sour look and disappeared. I had
come across his ruined handkerchief in my hoodie pocket this
morning during my cleaning frenzy. The blood had dried to a
dark crusty mess. I had stared at the hankie, then tossed it in the
trash. Owen would say I was in the grip of prehistoric brain pro-
gramming that triggered fluttering hearts for any dude who
offered to fight off the sabertooth tigers. He was probably right.
Heck, he was right about Marley stealing from the Battaglias.

I caught my breath, creaked to my feet, and crossed the tracks
into a grassy plain split by power lines. Beyond a chain-link fence,
a boy and a girl were building a skyscraper out of sticks and mud
on a patio littered with empty flowerpots. They stared at me as I
vaulted the fence, then kept building. This was Silvergrove's
older edge: dilapidated townhouses with brown siding, white balconies, and peeling paint. After a few minutes' walk, the townhouses turned into modest single-families with flowered walkways
and little plastic windmills and then, after a creek crossing and

an uphill climb into a hidden cul-de-sac, into a treeless expanse of rambling three-story new constructions. My parents' turf.

People with less money want more money, Owen said in my mind as I crept between two emerald green lawns that were no doubt trimmed and tweezed and pruned every week by a team of landscape architects. This time Owen was the Hierophant, complete with robe and headdress, but wielding his logic razor instead of a staff. *Marley was poor. She wanted to be rich. It's simple.*

How about me? I asked him. *I don't want to be rich.*

That's because you grew up with money, he said.

Tap, tap, tap. "Excuse me." I lifted my face off the keyboard to see who was tapping on my shoulder. A somber little boy in a Han Solo T-shirt stood next to me. "Nope, she's not dead," he shouted at a woman eyeing us from across the room. She gave me a sickly smile and waved her son back over to her.

I turned back to the screen, fighting the urge to put my head back down on the keyboard. I had pulled up every yearbook that spanned Ms. McAllister and Mr. Frakes's love story, since Marley had mentioned knowing about it. Scoured every back-of-the-book index for anyone named Brown. Pored over every group shot of every year's drama club for someone with Marley's sharp, eagle-eyed face . . . and found nothing. The closest was a girl named Tina Brown who did the spring musical her freshman year and thereafter disappeared into dance-team world. But all her photos showed a short Latina with a soft round face that did not match Marley's from any angle.

No Marley. Anywhere.

I stood up and looked around, blinking, rubbing my legs awake. An old man in a jaunty fedora was packing up. A pair of moms in immaculate sweats sat down at neighboring stations and dialed up some cat videos. The meditation class must have let out downstairs.

I went to the vending alcove, filled my water bottle, and went out into the courtyard. There was a small botanical garden of native prairie plants with bronze signs explaining the provenance of each one. An older librarian was out there eating a sandwich from a neat lunchbox with blue flowers and drinking from a matching thermos bottle. She was reading a book whose cover showed a shirtless dude holding a woman with long swishy hair. They looked a lot like Nico and Marley.

I ate my peanuts, blinking in the sunlight like a deepwater fish. Sure, Brown was a common last name, but between that and my small portfolio of other clues, I had expected nothing longer than a half hour of cursory digital flipping followed by Marley's face and real first name popping onscreen with a flourish of celestial trumpets. *Always have a plan B,* my mom nagged in my head. *Did you have a plan B?*

"No, I did not have a plan B!" I exploded aloud.

The librarian gave me a dull glance and went back to her book.

I emptied the jar of peanuts into my mouth and got up to toss it in the trash. On my way back to the computer lab my phone beeped with a text from Owen: **U find Merle yet**

I sat down at a workstation next to a twitchy guy in a suit and palmed the computer's mouse, making the little white arrow dance on the screen. I could leave. Make the sweaty trek home, where Joey was probably still lurking in his car. I could go to the police station and watch Detective Paulson yawn through my story. Or I could go to my parents' house, where I already suspected I would end up tonight. Admit to them that I didn't find what I was looking for, that I had no plan B, that I had nothing, not even Jamie. Watch my mom's face tighten up when she realized I was once again giving up, moving on to the next shiny thing down the line.

I gritted my teeth. No. Not this time. Not yet.

I logged back in to the LTHS alumni portal, dialed up the earliest yearbook that could possibly have featured Marley, and flipped to the A section in the pages of tiny, dense black-and-white student photos.

Almost there, I texted back to Owen.

The late afternoon passed much like the early afternoon, except that I was a lot more jittery and less optimistic. I was running out of yearbook, and hurtling with every digital page flip toward a dimly seen but very solid reckoning point. The Fuck-It point.

She was lying to you, the Owen-Hierophant whispered. *She probably didn't even go to LTHS.*

I shook my head and growled. A morose redhead in a T-shirt reading FLAWLESS started to sit next to me, then backed away and chose a workstation across the room. *She knew about the teachers,* I told the Hierophant. *How could Marley know about Mr. Frakes and Ms. McAllister and her questionable eye makeup choices if she didn't go to LTHS?*

Time blurred past. I dragged Marley's face from the depths of my memory and tried to paste it onto the body of a teenager. Marley trudging to school in an army jacket, head shaved, sucking on a cigarette she stole from her dad. Marley wearing a long velvety dress and playing the oboe in the holiday concert. Marley in a ratty Nirvana T-shirt and combat boots. Marley in a rhinestone-studded Nirvana tank top and low-rise jeans with her thong hanging out.

She was a shape-shifter, moving from one life to another like ink in water. I couldn't even remember her face anymore, just a vague person shape with removable identities like the magnetic overlays in the dress-up doll kits I played with as a kid. When we met, she was an aging scenester plugging away at a dead-end mall job. Then she was a muscle queen picking up guys at the gym. Then she was a badass with a gun in her hand and a bag of dark cash in the other, knowing that whatever came next, she would survive.

Until she didn't.

The faces on the screen swirled past me. If I was close to panic before, I had pretty much arrived. I'd been looking at the girls, but what if she had started out as a boy? I started looking at the boys. I started to slip up, missing photos and pages, having to retrace my steps because I had spaced out through whole sections.

Somewhere at the back of my hearing, a loudspeaker announced that the library was closing. I had one more yearbook to finish up. Page flip, page flip, nothing. My right eye was twitching and I had a weird taste in my mouth like a cross between rotten blackberries and Elmer's glue.

A librarian peeked into the lab. She looked like Queen Elizabeth in pink stretch pants. "Fifteen minutes, everyone." Staring right at me. I glanced around to see I was the only person in the room. Out in the main library, a few stragglers were packing up and moving out. The security guard, a skinny kid who looked like he was in high school, hovered in the corner.

A counter popped up on my screen: 5:00, 4:59, 4:48. I swept it aside and clicked through the last pages, pounding on the mouse so hard I knocked it off the table with a plastic clang.

"Five minutes." The librarian was at the door, glaring at me.

"Yeah, got it!" I said, more loudly than I meant to. "I mean, yes, thank you. I'm almost finished."

She didn't move. *It's over,* a voice in my head said. *Marley's gone.* The voice sounded like Jessie. I ignored it. I just needed to be sure, and I knew I could finish the last few pages if people would *stop interrupting me.*

"Miss," the librarian said, "the library is closed. We open again tomorrow at nine." She didn't sound sure she wanted to see me again, but courtesy demanded she extend the invitation anyway.

"I can't come back tomorrow," I said through gritted teeth, turning to her. Tomorrow I would wake up and see this thing for the absurdity it was. Tomorrow I would be a different person, and I needed to finish this while I was still me. *This* me. "I just need another few minutes and I'll be out of here." The librarian's face changed. She took a step back and looked outside toward the security guard. Great. Now I was the crazy person who wouldn't leave the library.

The security kid came in and stood next to me. "Ma'am," he said in a high voice, "we're going to need you to turn off the computer now."

"Yep! I am totally going to do that." I fixed my eyes on the screen and flipped as fast as I could. "I am finishing up right now."

Now they were both standing over me. There was a long pause. The guard reached for the mouse.

I don't remember exactly in what order things happened next. I was on my feet and the laptop was in my hands. I must have yanked it out of its docking station. The security guard stood there with his arms outstretched. The librarian took a step back and made a squeaky noise. Something fell. The printer turned on with its jet engine roar. The guard grabbed at me and I danced away from him, hugging the computer like a child I was carrying out of a burning building. I ducked under the librarian's arm and out the door of the computer lab, racing through the main library space. A large fern in a bright ceramic pot got in my way. I hopped over it but didn't quite clear the top. The pot fell over, scattering earth on the bright patterned carpet.

"Mommy, where's that lady going?" a toddler shrilled. I sprinted into the ladies' room and slammed the door just in time to hear him say "She must need to make a really big poop!"

I clacked the lock on the outer door and holed myself up in the farthest stall, sitting on the toilet with the laptop on my lap. Two more pages. Someone banged on the outer door and there were snatches of echoey conversation about who was going to go in after me. A set of keys jingled.

I got to the bottom of a page and hit the scroll arrow. Nothing happened. There were no more pages. I had gone through all the yearbooks. No Marley.

I clicked the arrow again stupidly. Outside the bathroom, things had gotten quiet.

I closed my eyes and tried to put my head down on the keyboard but there was no way to do that because I was sitting on a toilet. How was this possible? I had done everything right. Except for all the stuff that could have gone wrong that I hadn't thought about.

I came out of the stall and put the laptop next to me at the sink. In the mirror, a head smeared with sweat and eyeliner stared back at me, bits of fern in its disheveled hair. And Marley's necklace. I looked like a disgraced aristocrat rooting in the garbage for food. Oddly, the thought made me hungry. I splashed my face with some water and read the sign on the wall: YOU HAVE GREAT IDEAS! Sure. Unless your idea was to hijack a computer into a library toilet because you couldn't give up the stupid idea you had earlier.

There was a banging on the door. "Lake Terrace Police. Open the door, please."

Holy hell, that was fast. Did they have some kind of Bat-Signal for computer lab overstays? That was all I needed now, another encounter with Lake Terrace's finest. I unlocked the door and edged it open. The security guard, the angry librarian, the ladies at the front desk, and the mom with the curious toddler were huddled in front of the bathroom, peering in at me. In front of them, standing at the door with his fist raised, ready to bang again, stood Lake Terrace's own Officer Friendly. His round face was covered in ugly red scratches.

"Officer Bailey," I said. "What happened to your face?"

"My son's ferret scratched the shit out of it," Bailey said. The toddler's mom glared at Bailey and tugged her son toward the door, but he wasn't missing this for all the fruit gummies in the world.

"I was giving the little son of a bitch a bath," Bailey said.

"Ferrets get baths? I thought they just kind of licked themselves."

"Not the ferret. My son," Bailey said. "I was giving my son a bath and the ferret must've thought I was trying to drown him or some shit. Clamped on my face like a fucking toilet plunger. Had to blast myself with a bottle of hairspray to get him off."

He glanced at the small crowd behind him. "So." He looked back at me with an amiable curiosity. "What'd you lock yourself in the crapper for?"

26

"Thanks for not arresting me, Officer Bailey." We were in the library parking lot, with its old-new cobblestone walks and black gas-lantern-style lights. Across Magnolia Drive, lights were on in the giant houses, lighting up the forest behind them. Bailey's squad car idled at the curb. "I guess I kind of lost track of time."

"Ah, don't worry about it. That librarian's a mite jittery, you know what I mean? She's called us out here for a lot less." The librarian was displeased with Bailey's lenience and banned me from the computer lab for a year. I was surprised she didn't ban me from the bathroom, too.

Bailey got in his car, slammed the door shut, and poked his head out the window. "Hey, you need a ride home or anything?"

"Would you be able to drop me at my parents' house?" I wrestled my backpack onto my shoulders. "It's not far."

"Sure, I can set you up." He turned to his dash monitor and

started punching buttons. "I'd take you myself, but we got two guys out sick, and I'm ass-deep in calls." He thumbed his radio just as a car pulled into the emptying lot. My face got hot. The car was a familiar crappy beige Ford.

"Hey, you're in luck," Bailey said, squinting at the headlights. "Hang on a sec." The Ford pulled up alongside Bailey's while I looked for a hole in the ground I could jump into.

Bailey leaned out his passenger window to talk to the other driver, then leaned back toward me. "Got your ride all squared away, my lady. Now if you'll excuse me, I have *real* bad guys to catch. Stay safe, okay?" He threw the car into gear and took off, rounding the planter island and moving out onto Magnolia Drive.

Jamie put the car in park, got out, and folded his arms on the roof. In the amber light he looked like a moving shadow.

"What are you doing here?" I said. I wanted to look anywhere except at him.

"I was on my way home."

I crunched a discarded plastic bottle under my foot. "That doesn't sound like you."

A car drove by, showering us with light. "I heard the call over the radio," he said. "Something about a young woman locking herself in the bathroom to look at yearbooks."

I twisted my hands in my backpack straps and stared at the ground.

"Bailey said you needed a ride," Jamie said. The radio was on in his car and its chattering blended with the sound of crickets and faraway cars.

"I don't need a ride." I scanned the parking lot and walked over to a gray Toyota. "I have my parents' car." I started hunting through my backpack for some imaginary keys, turning my back to him. I was not in the mood for a sequel to our last conversation.

The security guard came out of the library and headed straight for me, fishing a set of keys out of his pocket. He clicked open the car I was pretending to get into, gave me an odd look, got in, and drove away.

"Stop. Thief," I said to nobody.

"How did you get here?" Jamie's voice, behind me, was mild and sad.

I hooked my thumbs in the straps of my backpack and stared down at the pavement. "I walked."

"You walked from your apartment? That's five miles."

"There's a shortcut. Through Silvergrove and the industrial park." I shrugged. "It's only three miles that way."

"You've been here all day, looking for Marley?"

I looked up, daring him to laugh, but he wasn't laughing, or smiling, or even giving me his usual blink. "Did you find anything?" he said.

"Nothing." I kicked a rock.

Jamie put his hands in his pockets. "I'm sorry about the other night," he said. "What I said was condescending." He looked up at the sky like he was reading cue cards. "I want you to know that I fully support and believe in your ability to make shitty decisions."

"Thanks, Jamie." I sighed. "I'm glad someone does, because I've been making a lot of them lately."

"I'm guessing you lost your job?"

I nodded and turned away from him. Focusing on Marley had allowed me to stuff the wreckage of my current life into a corner closet, and now that I was exhausted, hungry, and disappointed, the mess was threatening to come bursting out all over me.

Lights went off in the library. The parking lot grew darker.

"So," Jamie said. "Since I've been told to work less and socialize more, how would you feel about picking up some food and joining me for dinner?" He rubbed the back of his head. "But just for a few hours, because I brought some work home."

I raised an eyebrow at him.

"I'll give you a ride home afterward," he added quickly.

I felt something small move inside me. Marley was gone. Her trail was cold. I was alone. Jamie turned to watch a car sweep by. He looked like he did days ago, staring out his car window at the mall like he was seeing not the empty weed-strewn parking lot but his own past and all the mistakes he had made. He was alone, too.

Maybe we could be alone together for a while.

"Orders are orders." I shifted my backpack from shoulder to shoulder and moved toward his car. "Are you sure it's okay for you to socialize with me in particular?"

Jamie shrugged. "I'm not working your cases anymore. I can do whatever I want with you." He closed his eyes and shook his head. "That sounded creepy."

I laughed. "Socializing is hard." He opened the passenger side door for me and I got in. "You'll get there."

"I'm sorry I got you demoted," I said to Jamie.

We were sitting side by side on cracked vinyl chairs at a late-night carryout place on Butterfield. It was just a counter with a cash register and a window into a bright, noisy kitchen where two cooks shouted at each other in Thai. On the opposite wall there was a painting of a peacock climbing a branch full of blue and purple blooms. Loud music played, something with a lot of strings that sounded like background for a World War II soldier and his pregnant wife running into each other's arms.

Jamie didn't answer me. I got ready to eat serious crow, but when I turned to him, he wasn't pissed. He was asleep.

I touched his arm and he jerked awake. He stared at me, then closed his eyes and dropped his head back against the wall with a thunk.

"Are you okay?" I said.

"I keep having this dream," he said. "I'm putting together all these little plastic people out of a million parts on this giant table. Arms, legs, heads. I have to do it fast, before the glue dries. But I keep screwing it up. There's glue everywhere. And then they're trying to walk away, but they have legs where their arms should be. Or heads glued to their asses." Jamie yawned and ran his hands through his hair, disturbing the last vestiges of gel. "I have that dream probably once a week. Wouldn't you think I'd recognize it by now?" He shook his head. "I fall for it every time."

"That is some straight-up Freddy Krueger shit," I said. "You need some decent sleep."

Jamie crossed his arms. He looked shivery and pale, like he had just come out of a warm house into the cold.

"You know," I said carefully, "your chief seems like he wants to help you. Maybe you should go on that fishing trip."

"So I can watch rainbow trout suffocate to death?" He gave me a wry glance. "The point is to *stop* having nightmares."

"How about his other idea?" I said. "About seeing someone?"

Jamie grinned. "You mean like a psychic?"

I gave him a prim look. "My mom says using humor to avoid a

problem is juvenile and cowardly." I folded my feet under my butt on the chair. The seat made a satisfying squeak. "I saw tons of therapists when I was growing up."

"You did?" He turned to me. "For what?"

"When Owen was a kid, my parents sent him to all these behavior therapists. Sometimes they would send me along so he could have someone to practice on. Mostly we'd just sit there and play. Take turns putting pieces into a puzzle, or get on a big swing together so he could get used to having someone in his space."

Jamie smiled. "You did a good job with him."

"He does okay. His social skills are still what they call *emerging*." A wind rose outside and the power lines made small sad moans under the flowery kitchen music. "And when I was older we all went to family therapy because my sister had some pretty extreme anxiety that was kind of hard on everyone." I shuddered. "The therapist was nice but she was a little aromatherapy-happy. To this day, lavender actually makes me *more* stressed out."

There was a bright metallic clang in the kitchen, followed by a lusty laugh. A grim version of "Oops! I Did It Again" began playing.

"Any therapy of your own?" Jamie said.

"Nah." I traced a crack in the chair that looked like a face wearing dark glasses. "It turns out being lazy and spacey are not actual disorders listed in the DSM."

"You walked three miles so you could spend all day sifting through a mountain of yearbooks." Jamie gave me his best slow blink. "And you still think you're lazy and spacey?"

"I do. But then I get tired and bored and think about something else."

Jamie laughed and I felt a sudden disorienting hunger, like

someone had stabbed me in the gut and hit me on the head at the same time.

"I've seen therapists, you know," he said. "I saw every staff shrink at the LAPD." Outside, a power line moaned and he turned toward the window like someone had spoken. "I was actually part of a study. Psychological responses to death and loss in law enforcement settings."

My fingers hit a sharp edge in the chair crack. "What did the study find?"

"The study found that it sucks." He stared at the peacock, his eyes tracing a path through its jungle of feathers and foliage. "Am I using too much medical jargon? It apparently 'sucks' to watch your best friend ripped apart by bullets. You can read all about it in the New England Journal of the Fucking Obvious."

The weepy song ended. I swallowed. "Tell me about him."

Immediately, I was sorry I asked. But when Jamie turned to me, he didn't look angry or defensive. He just looked blank and lost, like he had misplaced something and looked for it everywhere but now had to admit it was gone forever.

"He was a pain in my ass," Jamie said. "Our first day at the academy, we were at lunch. Everyone had moved off into their little groups, and I was by myself. Tyler came and sat down next to me and started jabbering. Didn't care if I was listening or not." He was smiling a little now. "People like that usually drive me nuts, but it must have been just what I needed. He was like my daily push toward the rest of the world." He turned his hands palms up and examined them. "Until I killed him."

A shiver wound down my neck. "I thought it was an accident."

"It wasn't an accident. He wasn't supposed to be there that day." His face was strained, like he was working out a difficult calculation. "I was putting together a team to hit this crew of arms dealers. Tyler was perfect for it. Tactical stuff was his thing." Jamie shook his head. "But I didn't ask him. Didn't want him stepping on my big moment." He closed his eyes and took a deep breath. "We were always neck and neck. Tyler versus Jamie. Like a college basketball rivalry."

There was a flash outside and a tiny crystal pattering started on the roof.

"When we arrived he was there anyway, all suited up. He'd switched with one of my guys. Probably told him he'd take desk duty for a month or something. And he just looked at me with this huge smile and said, 'You weren't going to start the party without me, were you?'

"He only came because I'd tried to keep him away. If I'd just asked him, if I had been the bigger man, he would have said *Nah, go ahead, I'm swamped anyway*." His voice was a whisper, thick with rage and grief. "He would still be alive. He's dead because of me. Because I had to be the best."

Streaks of light wheeled in my eyes. I didn't know what Jamie's dad looked like but here he was in front of me, the Emperor on his gray throne, stiff and absolute: *You'd better be good at this.*

Minutes passed, or hours. The power lines went quiet. "Have you ever told anyone else the whole story?" I said. "The therapists in LA?"

"No one." He shook his head. "Lucky you."

"Either they were terrible therapists," I said, "or you're an even better liar than I thought."

"Haven't you heard?" He gave me a flinty look. "I'm the best." He shifted in the chair. "My first day back from admin leave, I went online and applied for the first job I saw. Didn't care where, as long as I didn't know anyone there. As long as I didn't have to prove myself all the time or one-up anyone, or listen to my parents say *I told you so.*" He shook his head. "I should have known you can't run away from yourself."

"That's true." I turned to him. "I read it in the New England Journal of the Fucking Obvious."

Jamie's face rippled with the barest hint of a smile.

"At least you picked a good place to run to." I elbowed him. "The very best."

27

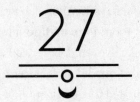

Jamie lived in an old farmhouse up in the northern reaches of town by Green Oaks, past the cemetery. You could see the house off the highway; I had passed it dozens of times but thought it was abandoned.

"I didn't think anyone lived here," I said as we turned off the frontage road onto a long gravel driveway.

"I'm renting it," Jamie said. "You wouldn't believe the deal I got on it."

"Looks like a real steal," I said, looking at a rickety barn and a cluster of sheds that hadn't been painted in years.

We left footprints in the dust on the large screened-in porch. A dilapidated swing hung cocked from one chain behind a dusty wicker table. No one had enjoyed a glass of lemonade here for some time.

Inside, the house was large and open, with tall windows covered in heavy, old-fashioned curtains. It smelled musty, like old fabric and ground-in dust, and made me think of terms like *parlor* and *sitting room*. A dark wooden staircase ran through the center of the house, with a banister perfect for sliding down in your pinafore dress.

Jamie walked through the house turning on chandeliers. I half expected him to light an oil lamp. "Make yourself at home," he called from the kitchen, somewhere far away.

I wandered from room to room through stately archways past empty knickknack shelves and bare walls. This wasn't what I expected, but it also made perfect sense. A heavy polished wooden table dominated the dining room. On it was a laptop and a mountain of papers. Behind it, a matching china hutch proudly displayed nothing. In the living room, a threadbare couch and striped armchair faced a cold fireplace with an empty mantel. A neat stack of taped-up boxes took up one corner of the living room. The house was huge, and its odd combination of stuff made it seem even bigger, like a cave some shy creature had taken over.

"I love what you've done to the place," I said, walking into the kitchen. It was papered in bright yellow and white flowers. Jamie had set the bags of food on a round table by a window that was painted shut. Through it I could see headlights sweeping by on Route 137.

"The decorator's on vacation," Jamie said. He was getting plates and silverware out of the cupboards. There was a lightness to him now, a spring I hadn't seen before. How long had it been since his last real conversation with someone?

"No, really, it's charming here," I said. "Do those stairs go any-where, or do they just drop off into a pool of boiling lava?"

Jamie put the plates and silverware on the table. "I don't spend a lot of time up there."

"That's right, I forgot. You prefer to sleep in takeout restaurants."

"The highway's too loud up there. It's incredible. You should go check it out." I tried not to feel any kind of way about him inviting me into his bedroom.

I looked into the living room. "What's in the boxes?"

He followed my gaze. "I don't remember. Nothing I need, apparently." He tore open one of the paper bags. "The place came furnished, which I think just means they left all the stuff they didn't want." He shrugged. "It's kind of nice. Every time I need something, it just pops up."

I cracked open the other bag and started taking out white cartons. "So, let me get this straight. You moved here over a year ago, but you haven't unpacked. You work all the time, you don't sleep, and you have no friends." I sat down. "Does that sound about right?"

His eyes sparkled. "Why do you think I have no friends?"

"You never go out with the guys at work and you keep turning down invitations to have dinner with the Baileys."

"What are you, spying on me?" He ladled noodles onto both our plates. "I have friends."

"Like who?"

"The lady who does my dry-cleaning is very friendly. She keeps trying to set me up with her daughter." He scooted a Styrofoam bowl of soup toward me. "I'm running out of excuses. I'm going to have to tell her I have an incurable disease."

"Oh God." I paused in the middle of tearing open a crinkly bag of spring rolls. "You don't have an incurable disease, do you?"

He stared at me. "Yes, I do. It kills slowly, with many questions." He got up and took two beers out of the fridge.

"You know, you're making this very difficult for me. I never have to work this hard to get all up in somebody's business."

He cracked open the beers and handed me one. "Is that right?"

"Most people are dying to talk about themselves. All I have to do is say *Really, that's interesting, tell me more,* and they spill their guts." I took a long swallow and motioned to him with my bottle. "And I somehow end up looking like the interesting one."

"You ought to teach a class."

"Nosiness is an art, really. I'm an artist." I opened my soup container and inhaled the fragrant steam.

Jamie picked up a jumble of noodles with his chopsticks. "I'm still amazed you got Nico to spill the beans the other night." He drummed his chopsticks on his plate, staring into space. "I would love to know what the Battaglias are bringing in."

I popped a tiny shrimp into my mouth and watched him. I'd never heard that kind of thirst in his voice before. He had taken off his jacket and loosened his shirt collar and he looked flushed and glowy. I liked this new semi-feral Jamie.

"I think I can answer that question." I put down my chopsticks, took off Marley's necklace, and snapped open the spade. The memory card dropped into my fingers and I held it up for Jamie. "Remember this? Owen decrypted it. It's a video."

Jamie looked at the memory card, then at me. "Show me."

We got up, still holding our food, and went to the dining room table. I gave Jamie the adapter Owen had left me, and he plugged the memory card into his laptop. We crowded in front of it like kindergarteners trading stickers. He watched the video twice while I stood behind him, sucking up noodles and shifting my weight from foot to foot.

Jamie removed the card, got up, and went back to the kitchen.

I followed him. When we sat down, he had that starving wolf look on his face again. "I was right about the drugs, but this is a lot bigger than I thought." He took the mini-card out of its adapter and gave it back to me. "That little home movie has all their connections, drop points, everything. It's like a blueprint for their whole operation." He squeezed a mustard packet in his fingers. "Marley wasn't some two-bit crook. She was the real deal. She scoped them out, worked her way in, figured out where they kept what she needed, and only then made her move. No amateur is that organized." He tossed the mustard packet back on the table. "She has to be high up in some other crew that's trying to move on the Battaglias' territory."

I snapped the card back into the spade and put the necklace back on. I felt like I'd just stepped, dripping and cold, out of a river I didn't know was infested with sharks.

"I'm going to have to turn this in," Jamie said. "I just need to be careful how I do it." He put his chopsticks down on the table. Then he set them parallel to each other. "We need Marley's real name, first and last. You didn't find her in the yearbooks?"

I shook my head. "There wasn't a single Brown who looked like Marley. Not in the drama club, and not anywhere in the student candids. I got desperate and checked every single picture."

"Did you check the staff pages?" he said.

"She didn't seem old enough to be a teacher. I just stuck to the places where she was most likely to be."

"You're probably right," he said. "But sometimes you don't know what you're looking for until you stumble across it."

"Ugh, don't tell me that." I rubbed my eyes. "I was starting to settle into the disappointment. Hope is a lot more work." I ate a spring roll in two bites. "Should we talk to Paulson, since it's probably related to the break-in?"

The expression on Jamie's face made me laugh out loud. "Wow. You look like I just ran over your puppy."

Jamie pulled his soup bowl closer. "I just want to make sure this gets handled in a way that . . ."

". . . lets you catch the big bad drug dealers yourself without having to share the credit with anyone?"

He blinked. "Am I that transparent?"

I fanned my face, my mouth burning from the soup. "It's kind of adorable."

Jamie got up and rummaged in the wreckage of the takeout bags on the counter. "The old man told me to stay out of this." He produced a small plastic cup of hot sauce and brought it back to the table.

"You call your chief 'the old man'?"

"Well, not to his face." He emptied the hot sauce into his bowl. "If he thinks I'm blowing him off, he can make my life very difficult." He stirred the soup, staring into it. "But if I bust up a drug pipeline in the process and possibly prevent a turf war, he's not going to split hairs." He picked up the soup and drank directly from it. I expected his face to explode, but he didn't show any signs of hot sauce distress. "I just need something a little more solid than Dominick's story."

I stirred my soup, drawing golden spirals in the broth. "What if I told you the CFO of Battaglia Bros. Moving and Hauling came to my house and threatened me?"

Jamie stopped chewing and went still. "Come again?"

I started to tell him what had happened but when I opened my mouth all the words dried up. I put down my chopsticks and fished the crumpled drawings out of my pocket.

Jamie moved his bowl and spread the little sheets of paper out in front of him, first one, then the other. When he saw the one of

Owen, his face tightened for a second, like he was fighting a spasm of pain.

I looked down at my soup. I didn't want to watch his face turn hard with blame, for either himself or me.

When I looked up, Jamie was watching me, chopsticks down, steam rising around his face. "Well, Katie," he said, "this is a problem."

"You're telling me," I mumbled. "I'm going to have to go stay with my parents again."

Jamie reached out, and for a second I thought he was about to take my hand. But then he hesitated and picked up a crumpled napkin. He squeezed it over and over again like he didn't know what it was for.

"You're safe here," he said. He tossed the napkin aside and clasped his hands in front of him. "I won't let your parents in."

The laugh that burst out of me was at least part tears. I could have hugged him, right there at the table, for making a stupid joke totally inappropriate for the gravity of the situation.

"Why don't you just stay here tonight?" he said. "I have two spare bedrooms upstairs." He paused, counting. "No, three." He shook his head. "You know what, I actually have no idea."

I nodded and slurped a spoonful of soup so I could pretend the spice was making my eyes water. Jamie pretended to look elsewhere.

He pointed to Marley's necklace. "Hang on to that for now." He picked up his soup and drained it. "And if Paulson happens to contact you, keep quiet about it."

I zipped my lips. "Keep quiet about what?"

The locket snapped open and the memory card tumbled out and landed on the table between us.

28

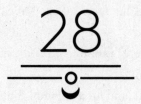

I n 2004, Ms. McAllister got an unfortunate perm. It didn't make it to 2005. I snickered, flipping through the faculty pages and sipping the remains of my beer.

I had helped Jamie clean up after we ate. Well, I tried. Mostly I followed him around the kitchen with empty containers until he told me to throw them away. Now we were sitting on opposite sides of the huge dining room table like a couple trapped in a dreary Scottish manor with a ghost staff. Jamie was working and I was using his laptop to revisit the yearbooks, lazy from food and beer, but also wired and twitchy. Jamie worked like no one I had ever seen, sitting perfectly still, every once in a while flipping a page or marking something down in heavy slashes of his pencil. I didn't even know it was possible to work without fidgeting or looking for a better chair or getting up to open the fridge for a soda that wasn't there five minutes ago when you had checked the last time.

So far, my plunge back into the yearbooks had yielded only

hair snark. I flipped through the faculty pages and on to the special events pages at the front, forcing myself through pictures of the Chess Club's annual pizza party, the Latin Club's trip to Italy, endless panoramas of football games, dance competitions, pep assemblies, and band concerts. Teenage faces moved backward through time, cycling through activities until they were replaced by new faces.

The 2003 yearbook devoted a full-color two-page spread to one Latisha Evans, who had won a coveted spot in the Lake County Players' production of *Grease*. Apparently, it was a big deal, some kind of super-choosy countywide theater group. Here was Latisha, representing LTHS with pride in a Pink Ladies jacket and cat's-eye shades, her name lit up under her photo in cheesy Broadway-style marquee lights.

I scanned the rest of the cast but Latisha was the only LTHS kid to make the cut that year, so I flipped the page and moved on.

Or I tried to. An afterimage hovered in the air, like a flashbulb had popped and left a ghostly row of bright letters in ball lights. Slowly, I turned back to the Lake County Players and went through the cast again, each member's smaller version of Latisha's marquee.

There it was, the word that had popped in front of my eyes before my brain could register it: *Brown*. A velvety haze passed over me, like a veil someone had dropped and pulled away. The girl in the picture was a tall brunette posed in a dramatic slouch, fist in her side, hip cocked. The look on her face, the crooked half smile . . .

Dazed, I read the caption underneath the photo: *Regina Brown*. And underneath: Lake Forest High School.

The mouthful of beer I'd just gulped went down my windpipe with a loud, gurgly snort. I coughed and spat out warm beer all over myself and Jamie's laptop. Jamie looked up. I jammed my finger at the screen. He got up and leaned over me to look.

"That's Marley," I wheezed.

"Are you sure?" He peered at the photo.

"It has to be. The way she's standing. That smile. That's her." My fingertips went numb, like I had dipped them in ice. "No wonder I didn't find her in the yearbooks." I felt better knowing I wasn't as spacey as I thought. "She didn't go to Lake Terrace. She could have gotten the stuff about the teachers from Latisha. Maybe they rehearsed at LTHS, who knows."

"See if they have a website," Jamie said. I liked that he asked me to do it instead of pushing me out of the way and doing it himself.

A quick browser search popped up a site with a garish green background and blocky banners. WELCOME TO THE WEBSITE OF THE LAKE COUNTY PLAYERS!!! Some barely readable text plagued by unnecessary exclamation points told us that LCP was an elite community theater group bringing together exceptional high school theater students from all over Lake County. There were pictures and bios of alumni who had gone on to join city improv groups and star in cat food commercials.

I scrolled over to the menu and found CAST PHOTOS. Jamie pulled up a chair.

A list of years appeared on the screen. I clicked on 2003 and the cast appeared, in full *Grease* finery, with the name and high school of each member listed underneath the photo. Marley towered over the other girls, hand on hip, holding the hem of a poufy fuchsia dress. A shark's grin was pasted on her face.

It was her. Between the website and the yearbook, there was no mistaking her. Her face was exactly the same.

I flipped between browser tabs, back and forth between the two Marleys until they made a crude sort of kinetoscope movie, a living, moving thing I had created myself. Whether she left the trail for me or not, I had followed it and come to the end. I had found her.

29

"You are not going to believe this," Jamie said, walking in through the front door the next morning. I had bugged him to go to the station last night and look up anything he could find on Regina Brown. He left this morning but was already back with a large cream-colored box, and hopefully some answers.

"Did you find her?" We were in Jamie's kitchen, where I had spent the last half hour searching for a coffee maker. Like most of my attempts to make myself useful, this one went nowhere.

Jamie set the box down and pushed it across the table toward me. Inside were twelve gorgeous donuts.

"I found a Regina Brown." Jamie opened the largest cabinet in the most obvious, central spot in the kitchen and took out a Mr. Coffee. "But her record is spotless."

"You're kidding." I selected a chocolate with sprinkles. "No theft? No fraud or anything?"

"Not even a parking ticket." Jamie scooped coffee into the basket and flicked the coffee maker on. "But that's not the weirdest part." He took two mismatched mugs out of a cabinet. "Not thirty seconds after I ran the search, my desk phone rang." He gave me a meaningful look. "FBI." He slipped into a stuffy voice. "'Regina Brown has been a figure of interest to our team for some time, and we feel involving another agency may jeopardize our operations.'" He picked up a long john and leaned against the counter. "He could have saved me ten minutes if he'd just said 'Butt out.'"

"Wow." I got up and circled the table, still holding my donut. The sugar felt tickly and sweet in my mouth. "She really is the real deal."

"She has to be," Jamie said. "Otherwise they wouldn't bother shooing the little suburban pissant cop away. They want a big fish like that all to themselves." The coffee maker gurgled. Jamie filled the cups and brought them to the table steaming.

"But we're still no closer to finding out who killed her." I sat back down and drummed my fingers on the table, scattering sprinkles. The whole point of nailing down Marley's identity was to follow her history to her killers. But she still had no history.

I stared at my own face floating in the coffee. I sure as hell wasn't giving up now. I was too close. "I think we should look at that video again," I said. "Maybe there's something useful in that little book."

Jamie produced a carton of cream from the fridge and sat down across from me with that smile he got around his eyes. "There's that laziness and spaciness I've heard so much about."

"Look, this is not normal for me," I said. "Normal is forgetting to set the alarm on the back door and causing a burglary."

Thursday night's litany of catastrophes sprang up in my mind like a grinning jack-in-the-box I had stuffed shut. "I think my brain might be broken."

"Your brain is not broken. It just works its own kind of way," Jamie said. "You have to figure out what that is and do what works for it."

"Marley told me something like that once." I took a tiny sip of coffee to keep from burning my tongue. "She said it's not enough to have something you're good at. You have to figure out how to do it your way." I finished my donut and eyed my next choice. "For a career criminal, she gave surprisingly good advice."

"Well, as soon as we finish up here we can get to work." Jamie popped the nub of his donut into his mouth. "You look very, um, that's a nice . . ." He pointed up and down at me.

"Oh. Thanks." I had showered and was now wearing an improbable coral dress I had found in a closet upstairs. It made me look like the wife in a 1950s period drama just before her husband beats her for making his martini too dry. I had finished off the outfit with Marley's necklace. Plot twist: now the wife has a secret night job waiting tables at the beatnik bar down the street. "It was either this or Dora the Explorer footie pajamas."

Jamie looked pretty good, too. He was wearing jeans and a gray T-shirt that clung to him nicely, but that wasn't why he looked different. He looked . . . rested. He glowed. I wrapped my hands around the hot mug and tried not to stare at him. A long, heavy silence unrolled with something very loud trying to burst through it.

"Can I ask you a question?" Jamie said.

"Sure." My heart started pounding.

"The woman at the trucking company. The one who gave you Marley's last name." He traced the rim of his mug. "How did you know to give her the real story? Why her and none of the others?"

RISE AND SHINE, his mug read. There was a sun wearing sunglasses on it. "How did you know it would work?"

"I didn't know it would work." I searched for what I saw in my mind when I was talking to the small-voiced woman alone in her office, but it was gone. Like it had happened to someone else. "If I could have done it differently, I would have." My face rippled in the coffee cup.

When I looked up, Jamie looked down quickly. His face had been raw with some emotion I couldn't name. My heart leaped with either joy or terror. Sometimes they felt to me like the same thing.

"That's amazing." He glanced at me. "I'm usually more careful."

"That's . . ." My mouth had gone dry and I had to swallow before I went on. "That's fine." I smiled. "Careful's good, too."

We sat there grinning like fools until it began to look like whatever agreement we'd just struck was about to be tossed out the window, but then my phone rang in the dining room. I sprang up to answer it.

When I came back into the kitchen Jamie was refilling his cup and everything was normal again.

"My car is ready." I sat back down at the table. "That was the repair place."

"I can drop you off there after we go through the video." Jamie brought the coffeepot to the table and refilled my cup.

"Great, thanks." I picked up my cup, relieved to be talking about something safe again, like murder. "It's weird, isn't it? That Marley's never been busted for anything? She's either very lucky or very good at what she does. Either that or . . ."

I put down my cup with a thunk and hot coffee scalded me. I didn't feel it. The room was turning around me, grinding slowly around some axis I didn't know was there, and now I was looking through the far side of a mirror, everything the same but backward. And much, much clearer.

I saw, from my new 180-degree vantage point, how sharp Marley was, how watchful. How much time she'd spent in places where laws were routinely and cheerfully broken, with no mention of joining in, and certainly none of getting caught. The way she sized people up, understood them. Became them when she needed to. *No amateur is that organized*, Jamie had said.

I sprang out of my chair and went to the window. The morning haze had burned off and a fiery sun streamed in over the low, frilly privacy curtain. "Hey, Jamie." I turned to him. "Is it possible that FBI dude was lying to you? Can they do that?"

"The federal government, lying?" Jamie clutched his palm to his chest. "I'm shocked you would even suggest such a thing." He picked a jelly donut out of the box. "What would he lie to me about?"

"What if her record was clean," I said, "because she wasn't actually a criminal?"

Astonishment spread over Jamie's face. Now we were both standing. Jamie put his cup in the sink. When he turned to me the starving wolf was back. "I need to make some calls."

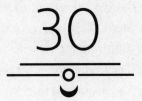

30

"Oh, good, you're here," Sam said when I walked into Firebird Imports. He was perched on the stool behind the cash register with a gargantuan frozen coffee in front of him. He looked up from his laptop and did an exaggerated double take. "Well, la-di-da!" I forgot I was still wearing the coral dress from Jamie's house. "You got a hot date or something?"

"Something like that." Jamie had dropped me off at the repair place, and I'd driven to the mall to pick up my last paycheck from Firebird Imports, having already spent it. "Where's Larissa?"

"She went away so she wouldn't be tempted to kill you."

"That's nice of her," I said. "I'm surprised she didn't have me arrested."

"I took care of it." Sam waved it off and slurped his coffee. "She tried to tell the cops you did it on purpose, but I told them you're an idiot who screws things up all the time." He winked and gave me a thumbs-up.

"Thanks, Sam," I said. "You're a pal."

The store was empty except for a skinny guy in sunglasses and a hoodie over a T-shirt celebrating STURGIS RALLY WEEK 1997. When I edged past him, a waft of Eau du Stone Blossom drifted past me. My heart skipped a beat before I realized he'd probably just been shopping there. I peered across the court. In the darkened storefront of Stone Blossom, a chick with pink Harley Quinn ponytails sat at the counter, staring at her phone.

"Have you seen Max around today?" I asked Sam. I'd walked by Max's car on the way in and felt like shit all over again. At the very least, I owed him an apology.

"The guy across the way? He's in and out." Sam stared at his laptop screen and broke into a flurry of typing. "You know somebody broke into his house a few days ago, too?"

"What an asshole."

Sam shook his head. "I don't know why anyone would choose to live up here." He launched into his usual diatribe against the mall, the suburbs in general, Lake Terrace in particular, and any place aside from the four-block area of River West where he lived. He might have actually used the phrase *hustle and bustle*.

"Thanks for being cool about this, Sam," I said. "Sorry I got your stuff stolen."

"What do I care?" He shrugged and suppressed a belch. "Larissa's insured up the wazoo." He tossed me an envelope that presumably contained the last money I would see for a while. "Here. I put a little something extra in there."

"Really?" I opened up the envelope. It was my last paycheck . . . and Sam's phone number. I guessed I should have been happy it wasn't a pile of dog shit from Larissa. "Great, thanks, Sam."

"Call me if you ever want to get out and see civilization," Sam said. He had taken the straw out of the coffee and was chewing on one end. "What are you going to do now? Got anything lined up?"

"I have a few leads," I lied, so as not to inspire any spontaneous career advice.

"Get into real estate," Sam said. "The market's booming around here, God knows why."

My stomach dropped into my toes. *Shit.* I'd forgotten to call Jessie. I fished my phone out of my backpack and saw with great pleasure and relief that it was about to die. I willed the battery meter to shrink so I could keep procrastinating. Instead, the phone rang. For a second I thought Jessie had figured out how to read my thoughts, but it turned out to be Jamie.

"You were right." He sounded flushed, excited. He was driving. "You nailed it."

"I was? I did?" I shouldered my backpack, waved goodbye to Sam, and swept out of Firebird Imports. "Tell me."

"I figured I'd start with the FBI, so I called a friend of mine at the Chicago field office who owes me a few favors."

I plunked down on the planter in the middle of the court. "And?"

"She wasn't a criminal. Not that we know of, anyway."

"Is that why her record is blank?"

"Her record is blank because the FBI doctored it. This way, anybody who searches for her will see only what the Feds want them to see. It's to protect her cover. Throw off anyone who gets too nosy."

"So she . . ." I looked around even though the mall was empty as usual. "She was an FBI agent?"

"Not an agent. A contractor. A professional informant." Electronic dinging from the other end and a car door slam. Jamie's

voice got clearer. "Sounds like she did have some law enforcement experience, but at the moment she was a hired gun. They
called her in when they didn't want to get their hands dirty." Keys
jingled. "Apparently dirty hands were her specialty."

He paused for dramatic effect and I wanted to kill him. "What
the hell does that mean? Spit it out, Jamie."

"Sounds like she was something of a legend around the office.
Total genius with cover, but kind of unstable. Took all the assignments no one else would touch." Jamie took a bite of something.
Probably raiding the donut box again. "She spent three months
getting initiated into some women's gang out in McHenry, and I
now wish I could unhear some of the things she had to do. They
called her Firebird because years ago she did an assignment pos-
ing as a gambler. She got her guy, but she also burned down the
casino."

My vision went black. Sparkles of light danced in the dark in
front of me. I craned my neck up, up at the skylights, blue light
filtering through a grid of luminous squares, and let my eyes slide
out of focus the way I did when I was a kid, staring through a patterned school window or a chain-link fence until it deepened
into a new dimension, a secret reality only I could see. Marley,
guzzling a 40 in the tattoo artist's chair while a gang of drunk FBI
suits cheered her on. The firebird, emerging from her body living and whole.

"My friend also said she was a pain in the ass." Tissue paper
rustled. "But she got results, so she kept working."

I rubbed my eyes, stinging from staring into other worlds. The
wandering, the blanks, the encyclopedic knowledge of things she
had no business knowing. They were assignments, lives and
worlds she had dropped into, becoming part of their scenery. *It's*

not enough to have a thing, she had said. *You've got to figure out how to do that thing your way.*

"She'd been off the radar for months," Jamie went on. "Some kind of DEA assist. My friend said all the files were locked, need-to-know only."

"DEA is what, drugs?"

"Right. She was using Dominick to get into the Battaglias' operation."

Nico. I knew she was playing him, but I didn't know how hard. He hadn't stood a chance against her. "Does the FBI know Marley's dead?" I couldn't stop thinking of her as Marley.

"They've got to by now, and if I know the Feds, they will be *pissed.*" He sounded gleeful. "The Battaglias have no idea what's coming for them."

"You sound like you're going to enjoy it immensely." I watched the shopping biker wander out of Firebird Imports and move down the court.

"I'd enjoy it a lot more if I could help, but I'm okay with watching from the sidelines." A smile crept into his voice. "You did it, Katie. You found her. I knew you would."

I grinned, still shaky, thoughts tumbling. "You did, huh?"

"Call it a hunch."

"I suppose you helped a little."

"A good boss knows how to delegate."

"Hey, what about the memory card?" I fingered the necklace. The card was safely nestled back in it. "What should I do with it?"

"Keep it safe. If anyone needs it, they can ask," Jamie said breezily. "My only concern right now is Joey. Where are you?"

"Mall. Just picked up my last paycheck."

"I want you to come straight back to my place and stay with me for a few days."

"I don't have any of my stuff," I said. This was not necessarily my most pressing concern, but it was all I could think to blurt out while my brain turned over this fascinating new development. "Can your house conjure me up my toothbrush and PJs?"

"We'll deal with that later. Just come over. You need to lay low while the Feds catch up to these guys. Don't stop anywhere." I couldn't tell if he was more concerned about me or about doing his job. I suspected that for him, the two were all twisted up in each other.

We hung up and I sat on the planter like my butt was glued to it. *At least she was one of the good guys,* I thought weakly, but it didn't alleviate my disorientation. When I'd first found out Marley was a criminal she dropped automatically into a category of people fundamentally different from me, like people who jump out of airplanes on purpose or play ten musical instruments. But one thing had stayed the same throughout the story, between all the variations of Marley I had met: that she was at heart an overgrown child just like me, a wayward ball bouncing through the world looking for its slot, looking for home.

But she had not been looking for home. She had been home all along. And with that tiny but insurmountable difference—more final than her death—she had left me behind for good.

I headed toward the escalator and wandered past Stone Blossom. Inside, Harley Quinn had her phone sideways, bobbing her head at a video.

I still needed to apologize to Max.

But I'd told Jamie I would come straight to him, no stopping.

I scratched the back of my leg with my other foot like a stork. I was already here. I knew I would never make a special trip back to the mall for this. I would mean to, and I would want to, and I would feel really bad that I wasn't doing it, and then months would pass and then years, and the whole thing would dwindle to another embarrassing flicker in the rearview mirror of my lurch through life.

I set my jaw. No. I was not a child anymore, who ran off and left toys scattered all over the floor when she found something more fun to do. It would only take a minute to say *I'm sorry*.

I marched into the store. "Hi," I said to Harley Quinn. "Is Max around today?" The incense smell hit me like a brick wall.

Harley was watching a Korean period drama with loud, swelling music. She jerked her head up a few times, then gave up, like she was stuck in a tractor beam. "Yeah, I don't know," she said. "He might be in the back. You can go look if you want."

I pushed through a set of purple velvet drapes into a small storeroom that smelled like wet cardboard. Rows of messy ceiling-high shelves were packed together with narrow aisles between them. A ceiling lamp with a curved metal shade cast a dim yellow light.

"Max?" I called. No answer, except the buzz of a low-voiced conversation, almost a whisper. I followed it to the back of the storeroom. The voice was coming from outside the back door, from the service hallway.

". . . before you decide everything is fucked? Take a breath, guy." I leaned in. "Yeah, I went to her apartment, but it wasn't there," a muted, husky voice said. It wasn't Max. Max was a shouter even when he thought he was being quiet. I turned to go.

"Nah, she got fired from the Russian place, but she's here now. I'm just waiting for her to come out."

A cold spike slashed through me, freezing me to the spot. A pause, then: "Oh yeah, I'm sure." I was hearing one end of a phone conversation. I spun through my mental catalog of voices: Nico? Joey? The flat, predatory voice on the other side of the door was not one I had heard before. "I was just in there and got lucky. She was picking up a check or something."

Pressure rose in my chest. It was the biker from Firebird Imports. I shoved my ear to the door.

"Because I had it under control." He sounded tired. "I'm not going to call you with every cough and sneeze. That's not what you guys pay me the big bucks for."

The door grew hot against me. Who was paying him the big bucks? And for what? Was he a rep from the Battaglias' source, tired of waiting for his money? A corner guy from a rival gang? Another goon Nico's uncles had hired to get their money back? I imagined on the other end of the phone a fireplug of a guy in an expensive suit sitting at a card table in a warehouse full of brown paper bricks, surrounded by bruisers with guns.

"For sure." A yawn. "I mean, she knew about everything else, right? She knew I got rid of Marley." He snorted. "No idea how she figured that out."

My stomach roiled and I tasted metal and salt. Marley's killer was feet away from me with nothing between us but a few inches of door. He had been watching me the whole time. He was the one who broke into my apartment to get the necklace. Frantically, I overlaid the guy from the store onto my memory of the figure on the security tape. The incense smell weaved past me again and I felt faint, like I'd been breathing paint fumes.

"Her pal at the PD is the one that really worries me, though." There was a metal scuffling, like he was trying the handle on the outside door. "She won't know what to do with it, but he will. And then we are truly fucked. Game over."

Jamie. They'd been watching him, too.

"Yeah, you're right." A deep sigh. "Okay. I'm going to grab her and finish this."

My throat squeezed shut. The man and his partner had been talking in circles around me, moving closer—and now they had homed in. *Finish this.*

I backed away from the door. If I had walked past the service hallway toward the escalator—if I hadn't stopped to apologize to Max—he would have seen me.

I turned and marched through the velvet curtain, past Harley Quinn, and out into the atrium. By the time I left the store I was running, flying past Firebird Imports and toward the side door that led past the picnic tables to the parking lot shortcut. I had a head start. He didn't know I'd seen him. I could still make it to my car and haul ass to Jamie and the police and the FBI and whoever else would take this cursed necklace off my hands. I never wanted to see it again.

I burst through the door to the courtyard into sticky air and glaring sunlight. The invisible highway roared like an angry ghost. I plunged through the bushes, branches whipping my face, and burst into the lot, lunging toward the railing by the old Sears, where my car—

Leaning against my car, arms folded, feet crossed, still as a lizard sunning itself on a rock, was Joey. He wore a suit of some light-colored summer fabric. Next to him, like a petulant gargoyle, Nico hunched in dark, washed-out sweats and dirty gym shoes. The two of them looked like warring pieces on a chessboard.

And between them, like a lost piece from a different game altogether, was Owen.

31

"There you are," Joey said, like I was a lost dog he'd scoured the whole neighborhood for. The silver Lexus loomed behind my car. "Right where your landlord said you'd be." He shrugged apologetically. "I kind of thought he was covering for you."

Bear. He pulled off his end of our little ruse perfectly, and I, the weak link as usual, had completely forgotten about it. I tried to step back, but I couldn't move. There was nowhere to go. Cars stood in clumps by the JCPenney door, but they were too far off. No one would hear me if I called. No one would help. My phone, buried in my backpack, had long since died.

"Owen," I said, "are you okay?" My brother looked pale and clammy, hair sticking out from his head in red-gold clumps, wearing pale jeans and a blue-gray shirt like a swath of blank sky between Nico and Joey's day and night. Rocking back and forth on his heels, humming what sounded like a medley of 1970s love songs, snatches of clear notes rising and falling into a tuneless wash. His eyes were fixed on something the rest of us couldn't see. I thought of his picture folded up in my backpack, the perfect circle of his face. My throat closed up and I blinked back fire. What did they say to him? What did they do to get him into the Lexus? I scanned him, but he didn't have a scratch on him. He was just fucking terrified.

"Hang on, Owen," I told him. "We'll figure this out." Owen's humming hitched and his eyes flicked toward me. I wheeled on Joey. "What is he doing here? This has nothing to do with him."

"We picked him up at that supermarket," Joey said. Afternoon sunlight flashed off his gold belt buckle. "By your apartment."

"Owen," I said, keeping my voice soft, "remember how we said you weren't going to go there anymore?"

Owen hummed louder, like someone had twisted a volume knob inside him. For a second, I thought he wasn't going to answer me. "You said no bubble tea." He stared at the ground. "I got a mango smoothie. No bubble tea." His voice cracked. "No bubble tea."

Joey didn't take his eyes off me. Next to him, Nico squirmed and fidgeted, running his hand over the back of his neck and twisting his medal on its chain. He looked like a child who had just been spanked.

"How about we step into my office?" Joey moved off my car and put his hands in his pockets.

"First, let my brother go," I said.

Before I could react, Joey snapped forward and grabbed my elbow. I flinched but he didn't clamp or twist, just nudged me toward the stairs. His dead-flower cologne flooded my nose and I gagged. He half-led, half-shoved me down the steps into the patch of scraggly concrete by the dumpster. Nico and Owen tripped along behind us. A swath of shadow cut the stairs in two, like we were sinking into a pool of dark water. The dumpster, the pipes, the garage doors. The place where Marley had died.

Joey let me go and I tripped down the last few steps, hurtling toward the brick wall. I caught myself on the hard, cool surface. Up close it was all craggy bumps and hollows like an alien landscape. Cards wheeled through my mind, stark blank sheets, figures with no faces, a tornado of bleeding, melting inhuman shapes.

Nico and Owen hunched at the bottom step. Joey, leaning on the rail, folded his arms. "Here's how this is going to go," he said. "You're going to tell us what Nico's *lady friend* did with our money."

Nico's head snapped up. He and Joey traded a glance, like Marley was a subject on which they had agreed to disagree. A card shone out of the murky foam in my mind: *Temperance*. An angel, both man and woman, on water and land: balance. Water suspended in air, flowing in both directions at once. *Wait*, the angel said in its brushed-silk whisper.

Nico's face was set in the grim pout I recognized from all the other times I had seen him get busted and refuse to own up. I tried to catch his eye, but he kept staring at the ground.

"Nico," I said, "what are you doing? I thought—"

"You thought wrong," Nico said, looking up at me. "You been messing with me all along."

I didn't say anything. What could I say? He was right.

Joey moved lazily back and forth on the railing like a lion scratching himself on a tree. "Our Nico is a little impressionable," he said.

"Yeah, well, that don't mean I'm stupid," Nico snapped. "Joey and I talked it out and I understand plenty good now." He let go of Owen and pointed at me. "You and Marley were tight. She told you something about that money. I know she had to."

"She didn't tell me anything." I licked my lips. They felt like a moonscape, cratered and dull. "There was a lot she didn't tell me. Honestly, I didn't know her at all." A sick little jolt in my heart at the truth.

"You're a fucking liar," Nico said. Joey's dark eyes flickered between us. "You're wearing her necklace, for Chrissakes," Nico went on. "You had it all along. You had it that night, and you didn't say nothing to me. You're a fucking *liar*." He roared the last word. Owen flinched and began humming again.

I drew back and grabbed the necklace. I couldn't help it. Joey's eyes clamped on me. He slid off the railing. "The necklace," he said, moving toward me. I pressed myself hard to the bricks. "She wore it all the time, didn't she?" Working it out in his head. Voice slow and soft, like a shadow creeping across a sunlit plain. "What is it? A key? A camera? Was she watching us?" He stopped inches from me, staring at the necklace. I could feel his breath moving the air between us.

"Oh, would you quit with the conspiracy bullshit!" Nico flared up behind him. "She wasn't some con artist. She wasn't *casing us*."

Joey's eyes went pitch-black. They'd had this discussion before. Something ratcheted up inside me, like the slow, painful grind to the top of a roller coaster. *Wait, wait, wait . . .*

"She just needed some extra dough, saw that her boyfriend had some, and took her shot." Nico ran his hands through his disheveled brush cut. "You look me in the eye and tell me you wouldn't have done the same thing."

Joey's face settled into an easy half smile, like the moment he'd been waiting for had finally arrived. "You were not her boy-friend," he said with a quiet satisfaction. "You were her *fucking mark*." He turned to Nico and I was glad not to have to look at him anymore. "She set us up," Joey went on in that gleeful, poisonous whisper. "When will you get that through your cinder-block of a head?"

Nico's lips disappeared in a white slash. He clutched Owen savagely and Owen squealed and began to rock, humming louder. My blood spiked in my body, rose in jagged peaks, trying to fight its way out.

Joey snapped his fingers. "Shut him up."

Nico turned to Owen. His hand curled into a slow fist and my senses shut down one by one, like someone throwing a bank of switches. In their place a cold peace welled up from some deep place inside me, the place where the cards lived. *Now*, the angel whispered, but it wasn't an angel anymore, it was Rosie, and the whisper was a roar, a rush of raging water. *Stomp those suckers!*

I pushed off from the wall, took a breath, clenched my fists, and sang in my shitty, off-key voice: *"I'm not in love . . ."*

Owen froze. His eyes locked on me. Without missing a beat, he picked up the tune.

". . . *so don't forget it . . . it's just a silly phase I'm going through . . .*"

Everything went still. Nico's crooked half fist froze in the air. The sun paused its race to the horizon. Somewhere, a lawn-mower was starting up in a fit of mechanical growls and coughs and the sound joined the angry chirping of sunset crickets and the bass tone of the highway, all melting into the background track of Nico and Marley's doomed love song: a lone, clear voice rising through the dead air, lying to itself over and over about being free.

Nico's eyes widened. He trembled and his hand hung limp. He stared at it like it wasn't attached to him. Emotions crossed his face: love, anger, loss. And then, like a push-puppet toy that collapses when you press it, he let go of Owen and dropped to his knees, sobbing.

"Owen," I shouted, "*run!*" I was terrified my brother's brain wouldn't allow him to stop mid-song, but when my words hit him, he shut up and bolted like an arrow up the steps.

"Goddamn it!" Joey screamed at Nico, who was huddled on the ground holding his knees, his face a mess of dirt and snot. "Go after him, you moron!"

Nico struggled to his feet and loped up the stairs, snuffling. Joey brushed himself off, straightened his cuffs, and turned to me. I pressed myself into the wall again, trying to disappear.

"He's already gone," I said. "He ran track in high school." This was not 100 percent true. My mom signed Owen up for track because he couldn't sit still and ran like a berserk wind-up toy exactly when she needed him not to, like the time he crossed the whole mall to get into the playland before she was even on the escalator. She was big into *channeling sensory dysregulation into purposeful activities*. Alas, Owen was not great about starting and stopping on cue, so organized sports were quickly scratched off the list of purposeful activities.

"A regular Forrest Gump," Joey said. He had a wad of spit at the corner of his mouth. It made him look like a wild animal trying to pass for human. "Well, that's okay." He wiped at his mouth but the spit stayed put. I couldn't stop staring at it. "Just you and me."

He shot toward me and grabbed my throat, smashing me against the wall before I could move or make a sound. Lights flashed in my eyes, then went dark.

"There's one thing I can't figure out." His face was inches

from mine. I could see the scar where he cut himself shaving, a birthmark on his upper lip. I closed my eyes but I could still see him, outlined in the dark against my eyelids. His breath fanned my face, coffee and spearmint gum and that nauseous cologne. I gasped for air but nothing came. I was drowning, going under.

"Marley was a little piece of trailer trash." He sounded private and cozy. "Put money in front of her, she was going to grab it. Nature of the beast." A spark of hope lit my dull brain. He didn't know Marley was working with the FBI. He was no Nico, and yet she had tricked him anyway. I imagined the two of them circling each other coolly, smashed together by a stretched-thin rubber band of circumstances—until the rubber band snapped.

"But you," Joey went on. "Little silver spoon baby." His other hand stole up my body, over my chest, toward the necklace. I thrashed but he held me still, solid. "Your family could whip up some bullshit overpaid desk job for you, just like *that*." He snapped his fingers in my face. "Keep you in Starbucks and Sephora the rest of your miserable, ordinary little life."

Don't you want something better for yourself? Of all the faces that could have swum out in my darkening sight, it was Jessie's that floated in front of me now. I would never get to apologize to her. For some reason this jolted me back into rage. I did want something better, goddamn it. I deserved it.

I scrabbled at Joey's fingers and caught the necklace by a tiny heart on a thread. My feet dangled off the dirty pavement, but I managed to brace one on the wall. The other, I spiked upward.

I was aiming for his nuts but got a knee instead. It was good enough. He gave a sharp canine howl and let me go. I crashed to the ground. The necklace, still tight in my fingers, tore off my neck. Black wires and stones flew everywhere, skittering across the pavement like spiders fleeing a sudden light.

I gasped and crouched on all fours, clutching my throat. Joey hunched over, lopsided, holding his knee. The spade of the necklace was still in his fist. As I watched, he crushed it like a walnut and the little black disk appeared in his hand. He stared at it, turning it over and over while I watched from the ground, torn and bleeding, my lungs screaming for air. A slow grin spread over his face and for a second I thought he was going to pop the memory card into his mouth.

Thud—an impact, dull and close. Joey staggered forward and clutched his back. A rock clattered away, a sharp hunk of concrete that looked like it'd been ripped off the side of the building. Joey looked around wildly and I followed his glance but saw nothing. The next rock hit him square in the back of the head. He reeled and fell to his knees. The card fell out of his hand, bouncing and rolling toward me. Joey, on one knee, clutched the back of his head and his fingers came away bloody. He stared at them, goggle-eyed.

I snatched up the card and scrambled to my feet. Joey, still off-kilter, blocked the stairs. I spun wildly. The garage door leading to the shuttered automotive center loomed in front of me—a wide wooden framework inlaid with glass panels. One panel was smashed, leaving an opening just large enough to squeeze through. I shot toward it.

Behind me, Joey staggered to his feet. His face was smeared with blood and sweat, a great swatch on his forehead like war paint. Blood had dripped on his cream-colored suit and I flashed back crazily to Nico bleeding all over himself, spinning through the door of Firebird Imports.

He bled on the suit after all, I thought woozily, and dove through the panel into the oily darkness.

32

hit the ground hard, tearing clothes and skin on the way in. Behind me, through the glass, Joey was on his feet, holding a thick wooden plank with a sharp edge.

The garage reeked of dust and old machinery, a cavern of oil-stained concrete stretching off into dark corners and empty repair bays. On one side, it flowed into the customer service area, a swath of dirty cinder block covered in bits of discarded metal shelving and carpeting shreds. Dusty light streamed from a skylight.

Behind me, glass shattered, spraying me with icy needles. I sprang to my feet. Joey slammed at the door again and again, smashing the remaining panels. Now he was hammering the wooden frame, tearing the rotten beams apart to make an opening he could fit through.

I took off for the service area. The counter curved under overhead shelves, empty now of the tires and shiny gadgets that had fascinated me as a kid. Thick swirls of dust hung in the air, twisting in the pale stripes of sunlight. My throat filled with an oily coating. I thundered over the bare concrete, every step shaking my bones. The banging went on behind me, like the slow stomping of a fairy-tale giant too big to hurry.

I shot into housewares, another desert of platforms that had once offered beds covered in flowers and stars. My footfalls rose into the air, probably telling Joey exactly where to find me. If the noise didn't do it, the footprints I had left in the inch-thick dust would. There was no hiding in this wide-open place.

An outside door loomed in front of me, and I banged into it, rattling the handles. Boarded up from the outside. I should have known. I *must* have known, when I plunged out of the sunlight into the dark garage, that there was no way out.

I slid down with my back against the door. The coral dress was dark now, torn and smudged with oil and dirt. My breath rattled in my chest like loose parts in a box. I was wet all over with sweat, blood, snot, tears. Someone threw that rock and saved my ass. Owen? Owen couldn't hit the broad side of a barn, as a disastrous round of high school baseball had shown. Nico, turning again on his cousin, catching me in the crossfire of their intrafamily war? I doubted that, too, and it kind of didn't matter anymore. Yes, I'd been given a second chance, but for what? So I could die alone, surrounded by rat turds?

I opened my fist. The gold teeth of the little black disk smiled up at me. I tried to remember what it meant, like a word repeated until it was just sound moving through air.

"What am I supposed to do with you?" I whispered. My voice was a tiny explosion in the silence. What would Marley do? I had no idea. All this time I thought we were the same, that she was another nobody, a loser trying to keep her head above water, and instead she was a superhero pretending to be a loser so she could manipulate the losers around her. It was too much, way too much, for me to stay on top of.

And yet, she was dead and I was alive, cleaning up her mess. *Well, who the hell asked you to?* the memory card said, and it hit me like a bolt out of the blue that I would have ended up here all along. I would have done nothing differently, given a do-over. I would have lied to Nico and sneaked after him into Marley's house, and again later on, when I thought Max had killed her. It's not that I wasn't sorry for some of these things, or didn't know how stupid and dangerous they were. It was just that I understood, sitting there in the mall at the end of the world, that I could have done only them, being who I was, and nothing else. A knot loosened in my chest. I closed my fingers on the memory card and got to my feet.

The faraway banging had died away—a bad sign. I looked around for another exit, but saw only the photo studio across the room—big glass doors overlaid with a ghostly photograph in aqua tones: a mom with perfect curls and shining teeth smiling at a baby reaching up to paw at her face. They looked like the survivors of an annihilating flood.

Behind me, footsteps. I ran at the woman and child, yanking at the doors. Miraculously, they swung open. I darted through and slammed them shut. More good luck—a lock no one had bothered to engage because there was nothing to steal. I snapped it into place.

The small waiting room had a curved service desk, the twin of the one in the garage. A hallway led to the studios. I had hated coming here as a kid, wrapped up in scratchy, uncomfortable clothing while smarmy photographers tried to make me smile.

Through the pearly marine haze of the reversed mother and child, Joey's pale form drifted in like the faraway outline of a monstrous deep-sea fish. He came closer and I saw he was covered in muck, his sand-colored suit jacket hanging in shreds. Face red and swollen, glasses cracked. His human suit was slipping off. He put his face against the glass and we stared at each other like high school enemies meeting at the DMV, realizing it was too late to pretend we didn't see each other.

He rattled the doors, then stepped back and put his hands on his hips. I pressed my face to the glass and watched him root through the junk that dotted the empty concrete cavern, picking up bits and pieces and tossing them away. A crooked metal rack with one of its four legs missing turned up. He tried to hoist it, but it wouldn't budge. Hiking up his pants as if they weren't already ruined, he sat on the floor, rubbed his hands together, then tested each bar. None of them budged. He chose one, put his hands around it, and started to twist and pull.

I watched him with a sick fascination. It would take forever to pull off that bar. I should have felt relief, but I felt only dread. Either he would pull the bar off, smash the door, and kill me, or we would end up skeletons buried in the mall for aliens to find millennia later, me still clutching the memory card and him with his finger bones wrapped around that goddamn bar.

I backed away and searched the room for a door, a weapon, anything. There was nothing. Nowhere to go. I wandered behind the counter like a sheep into its pen and watched Joey work away at my death. His face, already blue through the glass, was turning purple. A smile surfaced on it through the strain. "That redheaded skank didn't fool me for a second."

He looked up and the broken lens of his glasses flashed. I watched his hands work the bar, twisting back and forth in slow circles, and I couldn't help it, I started laughing. Great big gulping snorty laughter that made snot run from my nose.

Joey peered at me through the door. "Something funny?"

"Just thinking about what a liar Marley was." I wanted to tell him the whole truth, strip that self-satisfied smirk off his face, but I liked knowing something he didn't. Not much of an upper hand, given the circumstances. I wiped my nose on my dress. It was trashed anyway, as was any use for civilized behavior.

Joey cocked his head. "What story did she give you?"

"Oh, you know." I wiped my eyes. "That she was a drifter. Rolling stone. Might skip town at a moment's notice, definitely not for any crime-related reason at all." A final round of giggles bubbled out of me. There was an old black-and-white movie my dad loved, where this demented preacher hounds a couple of kids, for what reason I couldn't remember (probably money), and tracks them to the house of this nice old lady. The old lady sits on her porch with the gun locked and loaded all night long while the preacher lurks in the yard, waiting for her to nod off. And then, for no reason at all, they burst into fucking song, this beautiful old-timey hymn that the two of them, good and evil, sing in harmony.

"Huh," Joey said. "Makes sense now."

"What makes sense?"

"You do." He looked up at me. "You really don't care about the money, do you? You're after something else."

"Oh yeah? What am I after?"

"Just that," he said. "*Something else.*" He gave an ironic little shrug, like he knew it was idiotic, and it was clear which one of us was the idiot. "Something new and exciting. Maybe even dangerous."

"Are you charging me for this?" I said. "I'm not sure my health insurance covers therapy."

"You grow up getting everything you want . . ." He scrunched up his face and twisted. "Pretty soon you run out of things to want." He let go and shook out his hands. "And then along comes Marley, and she's such a bad girl! Doing bad stuff! Must have been like catnip to you." He shook his head. "I got to hand it to her, she knew how to get what she wanted from people."

I turned away. I didn't want to look at him anymore, but there was nothing else to look at. Just the dusty counter, same as the one I sat at day after day, wishing for something to happen, even something bad. Something to burn it all down so I could start over. My reflection loomed in the glass, pale and distorted like in a carnival mirror, but still me. I touched my clammy face. It felt like a stranger's. Was it me he was describing? This simple, lost, deluded person, just another one of Marley's pawns?

"What would she need from someone like me?" I said, mostly to myself.

"Who the hell knows," Joey said, already bored. "If she weren't dead, you could ask her."

Out of the corner of my eye—motion. Just a flicker. I pressed my face to the glass and squinted. Across the room behind Joey, out from behind a pillar, a face in dark glasses leaned out.

Marley's killer. He had followed us. A fresh wave of sweat rolled over me, followed by an odd thought: did he throw the rocks that let me get away? Joey was still at it, wrenching at the bar. Behind him, the killer watched. Slowly, he tapped a phantom wristwatch and rolled his hand. *Stall him.*

A tiny flame of hope sparked in my chest. He did throw the rocks. But why? Could I trust him? Did I have a choice? Joey was wiggling the leg back and forth in its socket, bracing his feet against the shelf. It was starting to move just the tiniest bit. The flame of hope was doused by a wave of terror.

I licked my lips, not looking at the pillar. "You were right," I said to Joey. "What you said. It was true. Some of it, anyway." I got up and pressed myself to the door, trying to keep his attention. "When I found out Marley was dead, I wanted to know why. What she did to get killed. I want to know why people do what they do." My heart was pounding so hard I was sure he could hear it. "Just like you."

Joey swatted sweat off his forehead without looking up. "I don't give a rat's ass why people do what they do."

"You sure? You just read me a dissertation on what I'm doing here," I said, watching his fingers. "It's also why you draw so well."

The fingers slacked around the bar, then tightened again. He wiped a trickle of blood off his forehead, squared up, and kept pulling silently.

"You're really good. You know that, right?" I steadied my voice, staring only at him. "Nico said you never studied art or anything. Just taught yourself."

This time he let go of the leg and looked at me. "*Nico said*," he mimicked. "Like I give a crap what that imbecile said."

"He says you've always been really good," I went on. "But your family wasn't supportive."

Joey took hold of the metal leg again but didn't pull on it, looking at me straight on now. "You sure Nico used a word with that many syllables?" He let go of the rack and pumped his hands like they were hurting him. Taking a break. I let him think. A quick glance at the pillar. The face in the sunglasses was nodding. I held still.

"I showed my dad this picture I drew one time when I was a kid." Joey sounded like he was talking to himself again. "Copied it out of a Spider-Man comic book." He let go of the bar, ripped off his beleaguered suit jacket, and used it to mop his face. "Know what he did? Tore it up. Went into my room and tore up all my comics and left me a bunch of titty mags instead. Signed me up for boxing the next day." He tossed the mess of a jacket away. "He said: *You can be a pussy if you want to, but you're not going to be anybody's bitch.*"

The bar was loosening, moving in its socket, making tiny metallic squeaks. I splayed my hands out on the countertop, moving them in fast, senseless circles.

Joey's lips tightened. "He did me a favor."

"By calling you a pussy for drawing Spider-Man?" I glanced at the pillar. The biker nodded. *Keep going.*

"Who gives a shit if they thought I was a pussy? Boo-fucking-hoo. You like something, you do it because it feels good, not because somebody's going to give you a cookie." It sounded like something Marley would have said.

"The part about not being anybody's bitch—that part was worth hearing." His eyes flashed. "But here's the thing. It doesn't mean what my dad or my uncle or Nico or any of those guys think. It doesn't mean pounding the shit out of anyone who looks at you wrong. What it means is pay attention. Follow the money. Know where it is, where it's coming from, where it's going." His face darkened, and he sat up and reached for the bar again.

A cold certainty settled over me. Joey wasn't working for his family, like Nico. He was working for himself and sooner or later his family would find themselves in his way. Reap, sow. Did the Battaglias create Joey? Or just set him loose? Either way, they would get what was coming to them.

Joey grabbed the bar again. The metal squeaks grew into painful shrieks. I stole a glance at the biker, watching from his hiding place, tight and poised. *Fine, I stalled him,* I shouted in my head. *For what? What are we waiting for?*

With a loud wrench, the bar came free. I stood up, backed away. In two quick steps, Joey was at the door, his face leaping at me in the glass.

He raised the bar on his shoulder like a baseball bat. I backed away and screwed my eyes shut. The last thing I saw through the faces of the mother and child was Marley's killer stepping out from behind the pillar.

"Excuse me!"

My eyes flipped open. The killer strolled toward Joey, hands up, a thin but solid guy in shabby, washed-out clothes. Loose, dirty jeans, a dark hoodie pulled up over a thin, pale face in dark glasses. His clothes were sloppy, but he wasn't. He moved like a coiled spring. *Potential energy*—the phrase popped up in my mind out of elementary school science class.

Joey spun, red-faced. The bar stayed in the air. "The fuck did you come from?"

The man smiled and kept walking. There was something off about the way he moved, like a snippet of film running backward. Owen told me once about the uncanny valley—when things that look almost-but-not-quite human are creepier than things that don't even come close.

"Can't help but notice your intentions toward this young lady seem less than honorable," the man said in a low, smoky voice. He had adopted some kind of down-home accent he didn't have when I overheard him on the phone. Something flickered through my memory and fluttered off.

"You just back up, slick," Joey said. "This doesn't concern you."

"Oh, but it does," the man said. "See, where I come from, we treat our ladies with a little respect." He stopped and squared off, hands on hips. "Why don't you just let her be, and go on about your business?"

Joey gripped the bar. He looked at me, then back at the man.

"That's right," the man said. "Why don't you put that down and step away from her, so we can settle this like men?" He leaned in. "Or are you a *little bitch*?"

Joey's lips went white. My eyes flickered back and forth between them. Cold spikes dug into my chest with every breath.

It happened too quickly to see. Joey feinted, then spun back toward the door. The bar arced in slow motion down, down, down, I dove behind the counter, and then the crash exploded in my ears, like the sky splitting open. A cascade of water-colored glass rained over me. If I screamed, I didn't hear it. I was locked behind a wall of ringing noise. Far away, a muffled howl, then nothing.

I peeked out from behind the counter. Joey was on the ground holding his side. A twisted red blotch was spreading over his shirt. The metal bar lay next to him, lost in a sea of blue glass.

Across the room, standing stock-still with his gun still trained on Joey, stood Jamie. His face was blank. He was not here. "Katie, are you okay?" he said flatly.

"I'm okay." I could barely hear my own voice. I staggered to my feet behind the mangled remains of the photo studio window. The mom's disembodied eye hung in the corner, watching.

Joey emitted a gruesome hiss, like a snake someone had stepped on. He lifted his head and let it fall with an audible crack. His eyes fluttered open and shut. Jamie, keeping the biker in sight, spoke into a radio clipped to his shirt, calling for an ambulance. When he saw Joey wasn't getting up, he trained his gun on the other man. "Put your hands on your head and face the wall, please," he said. Always polite.

The man had been standing nearby, hands on hips, watching Joey writhe on the ground like a bug on a pin. He gave Jamie a cool, appraising look. Deciding if this was someone he wanted to fuck with. He did not raise his hands.

"Don't want no trouble with the law," he finally said. "I just need something from my friend here first." He turned and stretched his hand out to me.

I stepped back and clutched the disk behind me, like I could make him forget it was there.

Jamie gave the man the slowest blink I had ever seen. "Put your hands on your head and face the wall," he said. "Or I will shoot you." No threat, just stone-cold facts.

The man looked at Jamie, down at Joey, then at me. "Katie," he said. "What do you say?" Something turned in my mind like a kaleidoscope toy, all the little colored pieces tumbling and mixing and fitting back together in a new pattern made of all the same pieces. Something in the way he said my name . . .

Joey groaned and stirred. His eyes flew open again. The man looked at him, then sighed and put his hands up. He caught my eye, nodded toward Joey, and shook his head firmly from side to side. Then he wiggled his hoodie off one shoulder. Underneath, on the man's biceps—dark shadows wreathed in fire.

I went dizzy. The ringing in my ears rose to a roar.

"Jamie," I said. "It's okay. Put the gun down. Trust me." Jamie looked at me, then lowered the gun. But even as I walked over and dropped the memory card into Marley's waiting hand, I wasn't sure.

The room faded away around me. All I could see was Marley, her face still hidden behind the hood and glasses but definitely her. I didn't know how I didn't see it before. It felt like when you sang the wrong lyrics in a song all your life, and after someone corrects you, you can't hear the wrong ones anymore.

I closed my eyes and sank to the cold concrete floor because I couldn't take any more. I couldn't take this final truth about her because I was afraid that, like all the others, it was only temporary.

33

"Mmm," Gina said. "It's nice to eat something besides applesauce packets in my car." She popped a stray piece of pepperoni into her mouth. She'd been trailing me for days, I remembered. I wondered what stupid shit she'd seen me do.

We had found a slightly rumpled Owen, hungry but no worse for wear, sitting in the passenger seat of Jamie's car with granola bar wrappers all around him. He nodded to us, got in his car, and left without a word. Now we were sitting at the picnic table, Jamie and I on the mall side and Marley—*Gina*, I kept reminding myself—across from us, with the fading sunlight flashing off the glass office buildings across the highway. The table strained under an obscene mall feast we'd scraped together from the ragtag collection of food court windows still open, dudes in white serving hats throwing us dirty looks as they slopped the day's leftovers onto our trays. We ended up with a mountain of soggy egg rolls, a carton of fried rice and limp steamed vegetables, a few greasy pizza slices, and a heap of glazed cinnamon rolls. I was ripping an egg roll into tiny bits to make it easier on my throat, still sore from where Joey had pawed at me.

After I had tossed Gina the disk, the room burst open, EMTs rushing in to ease the groaning, half-insensible Joey onto a gurney and wheel him away. I couldn't take my eyes off Gina. When she was sure Joey was gone, she took off her hood and glasses to reveal pitch-black hair hanging around her face in thick hanks that looked bathroom-cut. Her face was graveyard pale and there was a look on it that was regret-adjacent, but I couldn't be sure because she had rarely regretted anything in the Before Times. *I had to do it this way*, she said. She was still using the low, flat biker voice that I now understood was her real one. She hadn't even used her real voice with me.

Now I was picking at the Band-Aids covering my arms and legs and trying to overlay the raggedy, dead-serious person in front of me onto the one I had known. Every once in a while she would toss what was left of her hair or throw me a sardonic grin like she used to, and I could see Marley in this thin stranger in the faded black sweatshirt, reeking of Stone Blossom. Then the light would change, and like a kid's lenticular sticker she would turn back into Gina. Gina was smaller, but not in size. More like a shapeless hunk of hardwood whittled into a knife, all the extra layers gone, leaving only the sharp, clean deadly essence.

"How long have you been watching me?" I said. She'd been there all along, hanging over my shoulder like a ghost, watching me stumble around in the dark. And doing nothing to help.

"Since"—Gina scrunched up her face—"last Monday? Nico managed not to find the money I left for him in plain sight at the house, so I followed him to that shoe place he works at, and surprise, there you were." She motioned to my neck. "Wearing my necklace." She picked up her slice of pizza and took a bite. "It fell off while I was playing dead in the dumpster. When I came back for it, it was gone. We must have just missed each other."

Just missed each other, like it was a coffee date mishap instead of the start of a weeklong wild-goose chase that had nearly gotten me killed. I felt my face heating up. So much for any secret significance to the necklace being there. Sticking sensitive tech in a broken piece of carnival junk seemed like an engraved invitation to disaster, but I kept my mouth shut.

"Why did you leave the money for Nico?" Jamie said, holding a speared chunk of broccoli on a plastic fork. He was listening to Gina but watching me when he thought I wasn't paying attention, like he thought I might crumble to dust and blow away. After the EMTs had left, he'd gotten a first aid kit from his car and cleaned up the worst of my scratches with a blank, public-service efficiency. No part of him had looked like he'd just been ready to shoot someone. I wasn't sure I would ever get used to that. "Why steal it if you were just going to give it back?"

"You liked that?" Gina cackled and licked her thumb. "A little bit of improv on my part. If they'd seen me taking pictures of that ledger and figured out why I was really there, it was all over. Months of work down the drain. Even if I got away with the video." She shrugged. "So I let 'em think I was a thief." She reached for a hot sauce packet. "Good thing that money was there for a delivery later that day, otherwise I would have been fuuucked."

So it was true, what she had told me about her dad. There was a real person in there after all, underneath all the *improv.* "Wouldn't the video still be evidence?" I said.

Gina shook her head. "It was just a starting point for where to *look* for evidence. If they knew I'd gotten my hands on it, they'd go back and clean house. We'd have nothing." She took a giant bite of pizza. "It was critical these guys never figure out who I was." I did a quick mental count of all the times I had almost blown Gina's cover in the few hours I'd known about it.

Jamie said, "They seemed like such a rinky-dink operation."

"They started out that way. Doing the usual old-timey Italian shit. Basement gambling rooms, loan sharkery," Gina said. "But then Joey got them bringing in research chemicals from China."

Jamie caught my blank look. "Synthetic drugs that are just chemically different enough from illegal ones to get past the laws. Really tough to enforce." He turned back to Gina. "They must be moving quite a bit of product to even get noticed."

"They're the biggest supplier of synthetics in the whole Northwest region." Gina reached dreamily for a second packet of hot sauce, and then a third. "Or they *were*."

Jamie watched her drown the pizza in hot sauce. "I'm impressed," he said like he'd just been forced to admit he liked chopped liver.

Gina took a huge bite of pizza. "Where are those two dopes now, anyway?" She wiped a dribble of grease off her chin.

"Joey's at Condell Hospital and Nico is at the station. They're both looking at assault at the very minimum," Jamie said. "We picked up Nico over by Macy's. He was trying to flush Katie's brother out of a tree with a stick"—he gave me a questioning look—"and crying."

"Perfect," Gina said. "This way they stay out of our hair while we figure out what to do with them. So, you know, thanks for cleaning up your own mess." She slurped noisily at her drink. "That said, you breathe a word of this to either of them while you're processing them, I will personally wrap your face in a knot."

"Where's the money now?" Jamie asked.

"Back at Battaglia central, as of this morning." Marley grinned and mock dusted off her hands. "Beds are made, toys are put away, and no one is the wiser." She gave me a wink like everything was all good, totally back to normal. *Am I the one who's nuts?* I thought. *Or is she?*

"Did you really need to fake your own death?" I tried to sound curious and not at all resentful and crazy.

"Think about it." Gina tossed a piece of crust into her cardboard pizza triangle. "I was a loose end. They weren't going to rest until they saw me dead." She changed her mind, dug the crust out of the box, and took a crunchy bite. "So I let them see me dead."

"*You* texted Nico the picture?" I said. Gina flicked her eyebrows at me over her soda.

"What if he didn't buy it?" Jamie said.

"Have you *met* Nico?" Gina said. I winced. She loved to point out what a moron Nico was. Nico had hurt Owen and sold me out to his psychopath cousin, and I'd been guilty of a few jokes at his expense myself. I didn't have much reason to stick up for him. And yet her constant swipes at him grated on me. He had loved her, the fucking dope, and once she cleaned up and reset and moved on to her next assignment, she wouldn't give him a second thought. He would be a punch line, a footnote in a case report. Just like me.

"How about Joey?" Jamie pressed. "What if Joey didn't buy it?" He was asking all the questions I wasn't brave enough to ask.

"I'd have been fucked," she answered promptly.

"You keep saying that," Jamie said mildly. "It seems like a lot of things could've gone wrong."

She shrugged. "Shit goes wrong all the time. You deal with it. Improvise. Like, did I know I would lose the necklace?" She conveyor-belted the rest of the crust into her mouth. "Did I know Nico wouldn't be able to find his ass with both hands and a flashlight?" She reconsidered. "Okay, that I should have known." She brandished the pizza crust at me. "But I also didn't know the necklace would turn up again." She turned to Jamie. "See? Sometimes things go right." Jamie looked unconvinced.

The table swayed in front of me, like a ship deck I was trying to cross in a storm. She was talking about me like an object, a tool, a hinge the rest of her grand adventure turned on. The Seven of Swords I had shown Nico clicked through my mind again, the trickster and the fools he was playing. Except this time the fool was me.

"Can I ask you something?" I said. Jamie gave me an uneasy look. "Why didn't you just come to me?" My hands were clasped tight under the table. "You could have just asked me for the disk and avoided all . . . this." I waved my hands around.

"For one thing, I'd have scared the shit out of you." She grinned. "Being dead and all."

"I would have gotten over it," I said.

Her grin faded. "I wanted to tell you. I just figured the more people who knew, the higher the chance I would get made. And then it wouldn't matter if I got the disk back. It would be too late." She looked around for a napkin. "I stopped by your place to pick it up, but it wasn't there." She wiped her fingers one by one, the way she used to. "I wanted to keep you out of the whole shitty business. Keep you safe."

"Keep me *safe*?" I was shaking. Everything went white around me. "Well, thank you so very fucking much for your concern."

Gina stopped wiping her fingers and went still.

"I thought you were dead," I said in a voice I didn't recognize as my own. I was standing up. I didn't remember standing up. "I thought you'd been murdered. Of course I was going to get involved. Who wouldn't?"

Her eyes narrowed to slits. "Most people wouldn't," she said.

"Well, I'm not most people, and you should have known that."
I was shouting now. "Keep me *safe*? You put me in more danger
doing all this bullshit than if you had just come clean with me,
either before or after." My voice broke and I sat down. "Joey came
to my house, did you know that?" She blurred in front of me into
a black cloud. "He . . . my brother . . ." I closed my eyes and
shook my head. "I can't believe you."

Jamie stood up. "I need a . . ." He jiggled his soda. "I'm going
to get . . ." He nodded firmly. "Yes." He disappeared into the mall
and suddenly Gina and I were alone.

I was shivering, gripped by some kind of fever. I jerked and a
plastic fork skittered across the table and fell over the edge.
Everything was so loud suddenly, the highway, the clamor of
crickets coming out of the blue evening; everything was shouting
at me. Gina and I sat across from each other in the empty roaring
dark.

"Look," she finally said. "You have no idea how much I wanted
to clue you in that Thursday. Remember that day? When you
brought the donuts?"

"Croissants." The eggroll on my plate had spilled its guts. I
pushed it away.

"I almost told you everything," she said. "That's not a normal
impulse for me."

"Well, then why didn't you?"

"Because I can't do that." She ran her hands through her short,
floppy hair. "I can't get chummy with people when I'm working.
If I do, they tend to get arrested, or shot, or even killed. Trust me,
it doesn't turn out well for them." She was trying to stack her
trash in a pile but it kept falling over. "And if I'm being honest, it
doesn't turn out well for them even when I'm not working."

That look again, the one I would call regret if I saw it on

anyone else. "I *was* trying to keep you safe." She gave up and let the trash scatter over the table. "But not just from the Battaglias. From me. I'm just not a very good . . ." She smacked at a balled-up napkin and trailed off.

"Friend?" I said.

"Person." She turned to me and I finally recognized her. Not just her face but all of her, especially the lightning-quick anger that had flashed underneath her skip-through-life lightness. Anger aimed at least partially at herself. The card wheel clicked and clicked and settled with a rattle: Justice, red-robed protector of choices. *This is your past,* Justice said, sword raised. *What will you do with it?*

I started laughing.

She glared at me. "What the fuck is so funny?"

"Sorry, it's just, that might be the most personable thing I've ever heard you say."

Gina scoffed. "You know, most people are selfish and lazy and stupid." She squeezed her lips tight. "They lie. They beat the shit out of each other. They fuck each other over. You think I'm any different? I'm not." She tossed away a napkin and I saw a faded scar on the back of her hands, something old and deep that looked like it had hurt bad when it happened. I wondered if anyone had been there to help her bandage it up. "But you're not like that," she said. "I didn't want you to end up with a Gina-sized hole punched through your life."

"Well, I don't know." I dug around in the trash and found a couple of cinnamon rolls. I pushed one toward her. "Maybe I needed a hole punched in my life."

Gina said nothing, but she picked up the roll.

"Hey, you're not—" I took a gooey bite. "You're not lying to me right now, are you? This isn't, like, a bit? A piece of improv?"

Gina paused with the roll halfway to her mouth. "Fuck you."

"Okay, just checking."

We ate in silence. "There's just one thing I can't figure out." She put down the mangled remains of the roll and fished a lighter and a pack of cigarettes out of the sweatshirt. "How did you know I was dead? Nobody was supposed to know except Nico."

"He came into the store right after he saw your text. He was all messed up. He had smashed his head on a door or something." Gina snickered and took out a cigarette. "I offered to read his cards." I scratched the back of my head. "And then when he wasn't looking, I sort of snooped on his phone and pretended to have a psychic vision."

Gina blew her bangs out of her eyes. Then she burst into hacking laughter. "Way to read the room." She put the cigarette in her mouth and sparked up the lighter. It opened a bright hole in the evening. "So, then what?"

Bit by bit, I told her the rest of the story, from finding the necklace by the dumpster, to sneaking into Max's house, to the yearbook search at the library and everything that came after. And she sat and listened the way she used to, invisible on the other side of the table except when the fireball of her cigarette lit up the dark, outlining her in flame and shadow. By the time I finished it was night, the only light coming from a pale overhead bulb and the gray of the city in the southeastern sky.

"I owe Max a beer," Gina said. "He gave me an untraceable place to live, let me use his car, and lent me a sweatshirt, which I apparently forgot to give back. And he never suspected a thing." She looked like she was working out a math problem. "He might be the best person there is."

"See? That makes two of us who aren't garbage."

"I'm going to miss that necklace." She put her hand to her throat. "It went with everything."

"It kind of made me feel, when I was wearing it," I said, "like I was a different person."

"What would you want to be a different person for?" she said, and a disorienting ripple passed through me, as if this were just another end of another week at the mall, and Marley and I would be here forever until something better came along.

"Here." Gina dug in her pocket and handed me a business card printed on thick, creamy paper and embossed with a persnickety cursive.

"Chelsea Witherspoon," I read aloud. "Dealer, Exotic Birds." I imagined Gina in a sequined cocktail gown with a sculpted platinum coif, drinking a glass of something bubbly and golden. It looked totally natural on her. Anything would.

"It's left over from a job, but the number's still good." She fished her sunglasses out of the sweatshirt. "I probably won't answer it or anything. I'm bad about that." She thought about it. "I'm also moody. Stubborn. Total shit at compromising." She thought about it. "But that's because I'm usually right. I'm also a mean drunk but it kind of takes me a long time to get there, so that's not so bad. You know what, just give me that back." She tried to swipe for the card and I held it away from her.

"Are you finished?" I said. "I know all of this already."

Gina licked her thumb. "I just keep hoping you'll see reason."

"Reason and I are not great friends, as Jamie likes to keep pointing out."

"Yeah, about that." She stood and tossed her trash into the bin next to the table. "What's going on with you and that hot dork?"

I flushed. "Nothing."

Gina watched me. "*Nothing yet,* is what I'm hearing. Is he a good cop?"

"He's the best," I said.

She wrinkled her nose. "Too bad. He'll make a shitty boyfriend. Stay away from him. See? You can be reasonable." She put her sunglasses on top of her head like a headband. "Hey, I have to go, okay?" She pointed to the card in my hand. "Don't call me." She climbed up the path to the parking lot, rustled through the bushes, and disappeared.

I had been sitting in the dark for a long time when Jamie sat down next to me.

"Did she leave?" he said.

"She did." I traced a thin figure eight on top of the table. "I just have this weird feeling, like if I sit here long enough a butler will pull up in a limo and tell me she was actually my eccentric aunt Florence, and all of this was a test to see if I'm worthy of inheriting her fortune."

Jamie rooted around in the pile of crinkly tissue paper and unearthed a cinnamon roll. "Did you pass the test?"

"You know, I think I just might have." I found another roll and took a bite. The sweet dough melted in my mouth.

"She put you through some crap." Jamie put his roll on a clean paper plate. "I'd be ticked off, too."

I shrugged. "She was trying to run away from herself. Must have missed that issue of the New England Journal of the Fucking Obvious." I resisted the urge to lick my fingers. "We're good now."

I watched Jamie saw at his roll with a plastic knife and fork. "Thanks for babysitting Owen, by the way. Did he call you?"

"He did," Jamie said. "You need to explain to him that an

urgent call for help does not require one to recite all the lyrics to 'I'm Not in Love.'" The cinnamon roll was not responding to Jamie's utensil assault. He gave up and picked it up with his fingers. "I want to hear the whole story, but not right now. I'm not prepared for another heart attack."

I thought of his blank face, the robot efficiency of his motions. "You were scared?"

"Well, yeah." He said it like it was obvious and also totally beside the point. "It took me a whole year to make a friend. If something happens to you, I'll have to make another one."

We fell silent, finishing up the rolls. A flock of cranes burst into the sky, black against the white moon. Jamie watched them. "You want to come to dinner with me at the Baileys' this Saturday night?"

I cleaned myself with a sticky napkin. "You're working on another friend already?"

Jamie popped a stray piece of roll into his mouth. "It's just a work thing. He needs help planning the department picnic. I guess the clown he hired backed out at the last minute."

"Just one of the many reasons clowns suck."

Jaime stuffed a pile of napkins into a paper bag. "I told him I knew an experienced tarot card reader and psychic adviser who might be able to fill in."

I gaped at him. "Are you serious?"

He shrugged. "If you're free."

"Only for the next five years or so."

"Think of it as a job interview." He dumped the paper bag into the bin and dusted off his hands. "Also, we've got three families in the department that are either getting married or having babies in the next year. That's a lot of bachelorette parties and gender reveals. You might want to have business cards made up."

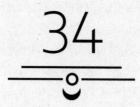

34

t was only one exit to home, but I took the highway because I felt like going fast. Flying down I-94 past the sleeping shadows of the industrial park, cards flew past me out of the dark, settling into patterns, blowing away, and starting over again. The World, a thousand tiny vines braiding to completion around me. But there was one more thing left to do, one thread to weave in: I had to call Jessie. I hit the gas, dizzy for a moment from the acceleration. The thought didn't fill me with dread anymore.

When I flicked the lights on in my apartment, one of the bulbs in the kitchen sparked and burned out. Everything looked yellowish and dim.

I collapsed on the couch, dumped my backpack, and plugged in my dead phone. The black screen turned white. Before I could dial Jessie, the voicemail icon flashed. I tried 1234 as my password, and it opened right up. Of course.

"Hi," a soft, hesitant female voice said. There was noise in the background, kids shouting, ferocious barking, and what sounded like a foghorn going off. "Um . . . I . . ." A sad little laugh. "I don't usually do this kind of stuff, but I saw your ad in the *Lake Terrace Observer*, and, well, I guess you could say I need help. And I can't afford a therapist, ha ha, so I guess a psychic will have to do. So, um, if you could call me back to schedule something, that would be great. My name's Linda." She left a number and hung up, leaving the dial tone ringing in my ears.

I stared at my phone, then dialed up the *Lake Terrace Observer* website. Did people even use the local classified ads anymore? Maybe people who needed a psychic did.

There it was, a neat square block under Services: *Got problems? Savvy, caring EXPERIENCED card reader and psychic adviser is ready to help. Call OUT OF THE BLUE Psychic Services.* The ad ended with my cell number. I scrolled up to the top of the screen. It was placed the Wednesday before last. The day before Marley died and Gina went underground.

If I could have clients just appear out of the blue, I had told her, *I could do it.*

So she did say goodbye. The only way she could.

I dug in my pocket for the cream-colored card. *Chelsea Witherspoon.* I tacked it up on my fridge under a Mars Cheese Castle magnet. Then I got my phone again.

"Hello?" Jessie answered in a cool voice that was supposed to make me forget she had caller ID. I supposed I was lucky she picked up at all, but then I remembered that Jessie wouldn't miss a groveling apology for anything.

"Hey, Jessie, don't hang up, okay?" She wasn't going to hang up. I just had to act like my whole existence hinged on her kindness and mercy. It was okay. I deserved this. "Listen, I'm really sorry about the other night. I'm sorry I was so rude and mean. I'm sorry about the whole argument, and, and . . ."

"The car."

"Yes, the car, and um, everything else," I said, before she found more things for me to be sorry about.

A pause. "I suppose we both let things get out of hand."

"I also wanted to talk to you about something else." I licked my lips. "You've been saying for a long time that we should work together."

Jessie gasped. "I knew you'd come around." She started jabbering like a blue jay. "You'll find there is a lot of room for creativity in real estate. It's a very—"

"Jessie. Hang on." I bit my lips and got ready. "I don't want to work in real estate."

A long silence. "I'm confused."

"Look, hear me out, okay?" I got up and paced around the kitchen table. "I appreciate what you're trying to do, but I just wouldn't be any good at selling real estate. No matter how much you helped me. I would mess it up. I would make you look bad. Not like, on purpose or anything, but I know myself. I'm no good at stuff that I, um . . ." *Have no fucking interest in?* Try again. ". . . when my heart isn't in it. You just have to trust me on this."

There was a long pause that shot past pregnant into emergency C-section territory. "I suppose that makes sense." I waited. "I'm just trying to help you, you know."

There it was, my in. "And you are *so* helpful, Jessie! That's another reason I called, because I need your help with something. Something I can't handle by myself."

"Go on."

I took a breath. "I'm starting a business." Apparently, I had already started one.

"Doing what?"

"Reading tarot cards." A disgusted sigh on the other end. "This

is not up for debate, Jessie. It's what I do. It's what I'm good at, okay?" I flicked a dead bug off *The Song of the Lark*. "I just need your help with all the other stuff. The selling, the organizing, the, you know, the *business*. I don't know crap about business."

"Well, I don't know, K," Jessie said slowly. "It's not really my area of expertise." I had her. We were at the fishing-for-compliments part of the conversation.

"Come *on*, Jess. You're, like, the most business-savvy person I know. You can sell anything, and if you don't know how, you'll figure it out, and you know why? Because you love it, that's why."

"I . . ." She sighed. "Well, I suppose I do."

"So help me do what *I* love, because it's what *you* love." I scratched my nose. "Especially because I can't, like, pay you or anything."

The rest of the conversation was all giggles and smiles, Jessie's hyperactive brain already racing ahead with ideas. We made a date for lunch the following week so she could help me write a business plan.

I went back to the couch, lay down, and closed my eyes. It felt like I came out to go to work last Sunday but got lost in the parking lot and accidentally boarded a rocket ship. Last stop: Parts Unknown. I had friends. I had a job to do. I had something to shoot for. I felt dizzy. It was a lot for me to screw up.

My hand fell on my backpack. I groped in it for the velvet bag of cards. Eyes closed, I shuffled and cut, but was too scared to look at what came up. I took the card to the patio door and slipped outside. The sky was clear and black, speckled with silver stars, and I thought if I went blank and listened hard enough I would hear the whole universe streaming toward me at a million miles an hour, bright voices and signals and snatches of music from light-years away.

The card was the Fool. "Great," I said. "This guy again."

ACKNOWLEDGMENTS

Thank you, first and foremost, to my family, my biggest fans and steadiest supporters. You understand not only that writing is its own reward for me, but that other rewards are tough to come by and that landing here was the wildest of long shots. Thank you to my husband, Brian, my best friend and the world's best listener, whose satellite dish is always turned outward. Leo, you inspire me every day with your quiet resilience, intelligence, and empathy; Tammy, with your oddball brilliance, creativity, and optimism. Thank you for believing in the brightest future. To my mom, dad, and sister, thank you for the base of love that everything else rests on. To my extended family, especially my in-law cheering section along the central Illinois / Iowa / Florida axis: thank you for always asking how my writing is going. It's going great! Thank you to our dog-like parakeet, Fluff, whose incessant hopping on my keyboard I've chosen to interpret as support.

Kristen Lepionka and Ernie Chiara, my Pitch Wars mentors: thank you for tossing me over the finish line to the starting line of something that once seemed out of reach. Joanna MacKenzie, my wonderful agent, thank you for zeroing in on the essence of my book and for never backing away from a challenge. Thank you to my editor, Jenny Chen, and her team for teaching me more about writing and storytelling in one short year than I knew all along.

To the Vernon Hills Police Department, particularly Commander Andy Jones (retired), thank you for a keyhole glimpse into the mechanics of a small suburban police department; any inaccuracies are mine and, I'm afraid, totally intentional. To the Cook Memorial Public Library and to all libraries everywhere, thank you for being the brightest, kindest, and most comforting place to stare out the window and work out a line of dialogue. An extra thank-you to the library's writing group and to anyone who has ever read and critiqued even a word of this book: every bit has made me a better writer.

And finally, a special duplicate thank-you to my hilarious, sci-fi-loving, knowledge-devouring, future-facing dad, who first taught me to read, wonder, and reach. He did not live to see my book on the shelf, but I know he will pick it up in the library of his rocket ship on his final exploratory voyage through deep space.

ABOUT THE AUTHOR

LINA CHERN has been published in *Mystery Weekly*, *The Marlboro Review*, the *Bellingham Review*, *RHINO*, *The Collagist*, *Black Fox Literary Magazine*, and *The Coil*. She lives in the Chicago area with her family. *Play the Fool* is her debut novel.

Twitter: @ChernLina
Instagram: @linachernwrites